THE
MAGE OF
TRELIAN

THE TRELIAN TRILOGY

The Dragon of Trelian
The Princess of Trelian
The Mage of Trelian

THE
MAGE OF
TRELIAN

MICHELLE KNUDSEN

CANDLEWICK PRESS

Copyright © 2016 by Michelle Knudsen

First paperback edition 2017

Library of Congress Catalog Card Number 2015954527
ISBN 978-0-7636-7436-6 (hardcover)
ISBN 978-0-7636-9456-2 (paperback)

17 18 19 20 21 22 BVG 10 9 8 7 6 5 4 3 2 1

Printed in Berryville, VA, U.S.A.

This book was typeset in Adobe Jenson Pro.

Candlewick Press
99 Dover Street
Somerville, Massachusetts 02144

visit us at www.candlewick.com

For my parents,
Flo Knudsen and Paul Knudsen,
who opened the door

CHAPTER ONE

"AGAIN."

Calen quickly closed his eyes, trying to refocus. He knew that closing his eyes made little sense, given the perfect darkness of the vast hall surrounding them, but it seemed to help. And he needed all the help he could get.

He pictured the hall in his mind as clearly as he could, imagining the long empty tables, the wooden benches, the huge windows like gaping open mouths filled with thick glass. He pictured the tattered banners hanging limply from the rafters and the cold stone floor and on every surface — tables, rafters, floor, window-sills, everything — hundreds and hundreds of candles. Maybe thousands of candles, certainly more than he was ever able to count. They sat in the ceiling fixtures hanging from heavy iron chains above him and blanketed the stones around him except for a narrow pathway leading to the hallway door.

He envisioned them all, tried to hold every last one firmly and completely in his mind. Then he took a breath, and on the exhale released a burst of magic energy, lighting every wick at once.

Or . . . almost at once. *No, curse you.* Calen opened his eyes just in time to catch the last few candles flickering into life at the far end of the hall. He'd felt them, at the last second, struggling to light. He tried to control his heartbeat, tried not to let his — concern — show as he looked at last to the older man sitting at the table beside him.

Mage Krelig smiled slightly in the glow of the candles around him, but that didn't mean anything. The man smiled when he was angry as often as when he was pleased. His face rarely gave clues to what he was thinking or feeling, and Calen had learned to just be wary at all times. Wary, but not afraid. Krelig had no patience for fear.

"That wasn't quite perfect, was it?" Krelig said.

Not afraid, Calen reminded himself. *You're not afraid.* He willed his breathing to be even and steady, willed his heart to slow down.

"No," Calen said. The mage's back had been to the straggler candles, but he still would have been able to feel their lateness to light. Bluffing was not even a remote possibility. "The last few were slow."

He waited to see what Krelig would do. He remembered how he used to be afraid of Serek. Afraid of being yelled at, or insulted, or given tedious tasks as punishment.

He could almost laugh.

The first time he'd failed one of Krelig's tests, the mage had struck him, hard, across the face. That had been a shock, but now Calen missed those first few days, when the back of Krelig's hand was all he had to worry about. The next time Krelig had been sufficiently disappointed in his new apprentice's progress, he'd set Calen's hand on fire. Just for a few seconds, and Krelig had healed him immediately afterward — but those few seconds had been agony. Since then, Krelig had demonstrated various ways he could inflict pain as a consequence for failure. Knowing that the mage would heal Calen afterward didn't matter when the pain was happening. It wasn't always fire; sometimes it was pinpricks, or knives, or cold. Cold was surprisingly painful. One time he'd sliced off the tip of Calen's ear. He'd put it back; you couldn't even see a scar. Since then, though, Calen had noticed that he'd developed a nervous habit of touching the top of his ear with his finger. Just to make sure it was still there.

It was an effective method of teaching. Calen had never worked this hard in his life.

"Once more," Krelig said finally. He blinked, and all the candles went out.

Okay, Calen thought, closing his eyes once again in the new darkness. *I can do this. I can.* He set about envisioning the hall again, every feature, every candle. He had to do it this time; Krelig's "once more" had suggested that one more attempt was all he would allow, and then there would have to be punishment. Calen really, really didn't want to be punished. He wanted to go back to his room, to lie down on his bed, and think about his plans. And then he wanted to go to sleep.

When he slept, he dreamed. And sometimes he dreamed about Meg.

About home.

But that was for later; first, he had to do this. He cleared his mind, thinking only of the candles, of the countless wicks waiting to burst into flame at his command. He imagined them wanting to please him, wanting to help him please Mage Krelig. *No stragglers,* he thought at them firmly. *All at once. Together.*

He took three breaths this time, in and out, and as he released the third breath he released the magic with it, pushing it outward to reach those farthest candles a few seconds sooner than before, willing all of the wicks to ignite as one. *Please,* he started to think, and then crushed that impulse. *You don't beg magic to work for you,* Krelig had told him that very first day. *You don't ask. You don't hope or plead or wish. You command. You direct the magic to do your will, and it obeys.*

Obey! Calen shouted in his mind as his energy reached the candles. *Light!*

They lit. All at once.

He felt it, felt the single great rush of his command received, his goal accomplished, and didn't need Krelig's satisfied grunt to know that he had done it perfectly this time. He opened his eyes again and took in the brilliant glow from the combined flames and smiled a little smile of his own. It felt good, being able to do it, to light so many at once. The candle-lighting spell was one of the first things every new apprentice was taught, but he'd never lit more than a handful of candles at a time before today. And he'd never even attempted lighting multiple candles at the exact same instant. He understood, of course, that it would probably never be necessary in a real-life situation to light a thousand candles exactly at once. It was impressive, sure, but not very practical.

But this wasn't about the candles; it was about learning control, about learning precision. And he was able to do something tonight that he hadn't been able to do this morning. Just like the night before, and the night before that. Whatever else Krelig was, and he was a lot of very, *very* terrible things, he was keeping his promise. He was teaching Calen more magic, more swiftly, than Serek had ever done. He had not yet told Calen that anything was beyond him, that there was anything he wasn't ready to learn. Quite the opposite, in fact.

There was a price, of course. And it was more than just the pain and punishment, more than being alone with a madman in some distant fortress, preparing to wage war against the Magistratum and anyone else who stood in their — in Krelig's — way. It was the memory of his friends' faces as he'd turned away from them and gone off with the enemy. It was the knowledge that his true master thought he was a traitor. It was having to be away from Meg, knowing she needed him and that he'd left her alone to face the insanity of everything that was going on without him. Not that Meg wasn't totally capable of doing anything she wanted with or without his help, of course. Meg was the most capable person he'd ever met. But he knew what it meant to have a true friend to count on when things were bad, and he knew he'd been that person for Meg just as she'd been that person for him. And now neither of them had the other to count on, and it was because of what he'd done. He'd done it for her, for all of them, to stop Mage Krelig from killing them all on the spot. But they didn't know that. And so they probably all hated him now. He wanted to believe that Meg, at least, wouldn't have given up on him, that she would know in her heart that he'd had a good reason for leaving. But she might still hate him for it. She might trust him and believe in him and hate him all at the same time. She wasn't exactly the most even-tempered person.

But he still believed that he could make it right. He would pay for his new knowledge, do whatever it took, suffer whatever he had to. And once he had what he needed, he would escape. He'd get back to Meg and Jakl and Serek and the others, return to Trelian and help them win the war and defeat Mage Krelig once and for all. He'd show them all that he was not a traitor, and more — that they had been wrong not to trust him in the first place.

But not yet. Not tonight, and not tomorrow, and probably not for weeks and weeks to come. But . . . soon. Eventually. As soon as he'd learned everything he needed to know.

"Pleased with yourself, are you?" Krelig asked, jarring Calen out of his own thoughts. He looked up, startled, but the mage's good humor seemed genuine.

"Yes, Master," Calen answered truthfully. "I like how it feels when I get something right."

The mage nodded. "As you should. There's no shame

in acknowledging your own accomplishments. Every mage should be proud of his talent. Proud and unafraid to use it. Our ability is what sets us apart, after all. It's the most important piece of who we are."

"Yes, Master," Calen said again. Krelig often waxed poetic about mages and their abilities, and how much better they were than everyone else. It was one of the reasons he hated the Magistratum so much, and the rules that other mages lived by. The idea of being marked or having to hold back from doing whatever magic he wished was offensive to him. Calen had heard plenty of rants on the subject at this point. He barely listened anymore.

"That's enough casting for tonight," Krelig said finally.

Calen nodded and started to rise. But before he was halfway out of his chair, Krelig spoke again. "I didn't say you could go."

Calen froze, then sat slowly and carefully back down. Krelig's face was expressionless.

"Master?"

"You didn't learn that quite as quickly as you should have."

You said once more, Calen protested silently. *You said once more, and then I did it!* But out loud he only said, "I learned it as quickly as I could. I thought you were pleased."

"But it *wasn't* as quickly as you could. You could have done it faster. You're still holding back."

"No, I —"

"*Don't you say no to me,*" Krelig snapped, anger suddenly pulsing in his voice. "I sense the power inside you, but you refuse to release it. You insist on reaching in bit by bit, accessing a little more, and then a little more — *I don't have time for this!*"

Calen swallowed, afraid that anything he said would be wrong. But Krelig hated when you didn't answer him. "I'm trying as hard as I can, Master."

"It's not enough. You must need some incentive."

No. No, no, no. It wasn't fair; he'd gotten it on the third try! "I —"

"When my visions during my exile showed me that you would be . . . important . . . to my success, I am quite certain they meant you at your full power. Not this partial strength you insist on clinging to." Krelig was studying him, eyes narrowed. "You must not truly want to unlock your full ability. How can I encourage you to want that, Calen?"

"I do; I do want that. I'll do better tomorrow, you'll see. I promise. You don't — you don't have to . . ."

Krelig shook his head, and Calen's stomach shriveled to a hard little knot inside him. "Apparently I do."

And then the pain started.

Calen desperately tried to block the spell before it hit, but Krelig batted his attempt away without any apparent effort at all. The first wave of red fiery energy tumbled Calen backward onto the floor. He didn't even have a chance to scream before the impact knocked the breath out of him. Krelig walked over and stood looking down at him.

"I know it's in there. I can almost *see* it — such power, the power I need to defeat my enemies — and you keep it safely . . . locked . . . away. . . ."

With each of the last three words, Krelig sent another beam of fire into Calen's chest, as though he were trying to burn a hole through him in order to let the magic out. It wasn't literal fire; even through the pain Calen could tell that he wasn't actually burning, but oh, gods, it felt like he was.

"Stop . . . please. . . . I'm sorry. . . ." He gasped out the words even though he knew they wouldn't do any good.

It seemed like a long time before Krelig felt he had been punished enough.

Calen lay there for a while after Krelig left. Eventually, once he stopped shaking and his heart felt closer to its normal rhythm again, he got up and picked his way along the candle-lined path. He took one of the candles near his feet and relit it, continuing down the hall toward the stairway that would take him to his room.

Most of the halls and corridors were kept dark, but Calen knew the way to his room, and to the kitchens, and to wherever else he needed to go. And if he needed to go somewhere he didn't already know the way to, he knew how to find out. That had been an early lesson, and he had learned it well. On their second night at the apparently long-abandoned castle that Krelig had claimed for his new home, the mage had deposited Calen in the dark in some random corner of the lower levels and told him he'd have to find his way to his room without light or help. And then left him there alone. And then set some sort of hungry, monstrous creature loose nearby, to give Calen a little extra motivation. Calen had never found out exactly what it was, that thing, but he could still recall its insistent, eager cries and the sound of its too-many legs scrabbling against the floor in the darkness just behind him. Calen had learned what he needed to very, very quickly.

He carried a little map in his head now, all the time. It was incredibly useful; he wished he'd known it was possible a long time ago. He could add to it whenever he wanted, and so could always find his way back from wherever he went. His room, the one he'd chosen from the entire wing that Krelig had given him for his own, was at the end of a long hallway on the uppermost floor of the castle. It wasn't the largest room of the lot, but it opened up onto a huge balcony that provided a breathtaking view of the surrounding countryside. Calen still wasn't sure what country or kingdom they were actually in, but whatever it was, it was beautiful. He spent as much time out there as he could, looking at the trees and the mountains and watching the birds during the day, and staring out at the stars or the moonlight glinting on the distant river at night. He tried repeatedly to figure out which direction Trelian might be, but there was no way to tell without knowing where they were now. He didn't dare ask Krelig. Krelig would answer questions about magic without hesitation — he *wanted* Calen to want to learn, and as long as the questions weren't stupid ones, he would answer willingly. He was less tolerant of other kinds of questions. Calen had learned that lesson early, too.

When he reached his room, he doused the candle and reset the wards in his doorway (he wasn't entirely sure that the too-many-legged creature wasn't still out there somewhere) and went outside to look out at the night.

He really wished he knew what Krelig was talking about.

How could he have some secret reservoir of power within himself and not be able to tell? Krelig thought that he just wasn't trying hard enough, but if that extra power was really in there somewhere, Calen couldn't find it. He had tried. From the very first time Krelig had mentioned it, he had tried. But how could he access something he didn't really believe was there?

As always, he automatically searched the sky for a dragon flying toward him from the distance. It was foolish, but he couldn't seem to help it. And as much as part of him wished to see Jakl — Jakl with Meg riding on his back, coming to save him, coming to yell at him and probably kick him but also to save him and take him home — he couldn't *really* hope for that, because it was too dangerous. Maybe Jakl's resistance to magic would be strong enough to protect him from Krelig, but maybe not. And the mage could still set one of his nasty flying slaarh at the dragon, or more than one. He didn't think Jakl would be able to fight, say, five of the disgusting things at one time.

And he could hurt Meg either way. Calen had no doubt that Krelig could rip her apart just as he'd threatened that first terrible day when he'd come through the

13

portal and everything had gone so very horribly wrong. The man had *stopped time*. Killing one girl would hardly cost him any effort at all.

No. Meg could never come here. *He* had to go to *her*. He just had to figure out how.

And when.

Because that was the other thing, of course. He couldn't leave until he'd learned what he needed to defeat Mage Krelig once and for all.

Calen washed and changed his clothes and got into his bed and lay there for a long time before he fell asleep.

In the morning, as always, there were more lessons.

Calen ate his breakfast alone in the dining hall, as usual. Krelig must have acquired a cook from somewhere, because there was always food waiting on the table at mealtimes, but Calen had never seen anyone working in the kitchens or delivering supplies or even cleaning up. Krelig had never explained, and Calen suspected that questions in this area would be the kind Krelig considered a waste of his time. So Calen just ate what he found waiting for him without thinking too much about how it got there and left his dishes on the counter when he was finished. Then he went to wherever Krelig was waiting for him for that day's learning.

Krelig never told him where that would be; Calen had to find him. Which wasn't hard once he figured out how — it only took a bit of white energy sent along the castle corridors to locate the mage.

Today Krelig was waiting up on the battlements that ran along the entire perimeter of the castle. Calen emerged into the windy morning, clutching his cloak around him as he approached the older man. Krelig had cut his shaggy hair and beard since his return, and now looked somewhat less like a madman to the casual eye. But Calen's eye was anything but casual, and he knew that Krelig was completely crazy. Not stupid, though. He was about as far from stupid as someone could be, in fact. It was hard not to respect that about him, even while hating the rest. He was evil and terrible and cruel and unpredictable, but he knew so much. And, like Calen himself, he always wanted to know more.

What Krelig most wanted to know about, other than why Calen "refused" to access his full power, was Calen's special ability to see the colors of the different types of magical energy involved when someone was casting a spell. But unlike Mage Brevera and his friends back at the Magistratum, Krelig seemed to understand that it wasn't something Calen could teach someone else how to do. He just wanted to understand what Calen could see and, Calen assumed, figure out how to use it in his war against the other mages. Calen just had to make sure he wasn't around to be used by Krelig when the time came.

He'd tried, early on, to lie about what he saw. But Krelig had known. He had known, and he had made it very clear to Calen that he should never attempt to lie about his ability again. Very, very clear. And so Calen always answered truthfully now, and held fast to his determination to get away. If Calen wasn't here, Krelig's knowledge about what he could see and do wouldn't make any difference.

Krelig was standing at the far edge of the battlement, looking out into the distance. He didn't turn or acknowledge Calen's presence at first, but as soon as Calen was close enough to hear him, Krelig said, "Stand there, and tell me what you see." Then he sent up a swirl of multi-colored energy into the air around him.

Calen stopped walking. "It's mostly blue and yellow and purple, but there's a lot of black and orange all along the outer edges of the other colors. As though all the colors have black and orange outlines, somehow." He squinted, interested despite himself, as was usually the case. Orange was nullifying or neutralizing, and black was for conceal-ment. "Are you trying to hide the colors themselves?"

Krelig let the magic dissipate and turned toward

Calen, a half smile on his face. All traces of yesterday's anger seemed to be gone. For now. "Trying and failing, it would seem." Without changing expression, he suddenly sent a bolt of red and black energy directly at Calen.

Calen immediately sent out blue and orange magic to meet it, and the spells smashed into each other in the space between them, canceling each other out. Calen wasn't sure what Krelig's spell had been, exactly — although red magic was rarely anything pleasant — but he didn't need to know in order to counter it. This was one of the aspects of his ability that Krelig seemed most interested in: that Calen could create counterspells and defenses based on the colors he was able to see.

And Calen was getting better at sorting out the colors all the time.

Krelig sent a few more easy-to-decipher spells at Calen, all of which Calen was able to block or neutralize without any trouble. They started coming faster, requiring more concentration, but Calen had gotten better at concentration, too. And at casting for longer periods of time without resting. After a few more increasingly speedy but not-too-difficult spells, Krelig turned away as if getting bored. Then he raised his head to look at a bird flying above them. It was one of the bright blue and yellow birds Calen sometimes saw from his room. He liked them; they made friendly chirping sounds to one another when they flew around, and lately one or two had begun to rest on the slim enclosing wall that lined the edge of the balcony when he was standing there. He kept meaning to find some bread or something to give them, to encourage them to visit more often. They made him feel a little less lonely when they came.

Krelig tilted his head and released a bolt of red energy toward the bird.

"Don't!" Calen shouted without thinking, simultaneously sending a bolt of his own, willing it to intercept Krelig's deadly little spell before it reached its intended victim. The mass of color flew from his fingertips without conscious thought, and only afterward did Calen notice what he'd sent and why. Orange for neutralizing; yellow for healing, in case his spell was too slow to stop Krelig's but fast enough to heal whatever damage was done before it was too late; purple for motion and speed, which he guessed he'd included from some desire to make his spell move more quickly through the air. And it seemed to be working—his spell collided with and engulfed Krelig's, consuming it into nothingness, and the bird, sensing the invisible forces clashing just a few inches away, gave a troubled cry and darted swiftly in the opposite direction.

Calen looked warily at Krelig. The mage looked back, seeming more curious than angry. "Friend of yours?" he asked.

"There was no reason to kill it," Calen said defensively.

"No reason not to," Krelig said, with the empty, careless cruelty that always made Calen's stomach turn. But he still didn't seem angry. That was good. After a moment he added, "You made your spell faster."

"Yes." It hadn't really been a question, but Calen answered anyway.

"Did your former master teach you to do that?"

"No. I didn't — it just sort of happened. I only realized afterward what I'd done."

"Hmm. Could you have made it slower? Could you have made *mine* slower?"

Calen paused, considering. "I — I think so."

"Try now." Krelig released another bolt of red energy, but this one, Calen was relieved to see, was aimed only at the stone wall. Calen cast again, this time attempting to cast *into* Krelig's spell instead of just trying to knock it aside or destroy it. He still used purple energy, but the intent was different, and so the effect was different as well. The colors were the *types* of magic energy, what a given spell was created out of, but each color could be used in countless different ways. He tried to shape the

19

magic into something that would infuse Krelig's spell and slow it down without otherwise altering it. He thought it worked, at least a little: the red bolt hit the stone with a small explosion, leaving behind a tiny crater, but not as quickly as it would have otherwise. At least . . . he thought so.

He looked at Krelig. The mage was nodding. "It should have hit a little sooner than that. Good. Try it again."

They continued for the better part of three hours, experimenting with speed and slowness. Calen was fascinated. He'd never thought about trying anything like this before. When Krelig finally declared the morning's lessons over, Calen was exhausted but exhilarated. He loved this feeling; despite the circumstances, despite everything, he loved it. It was like coming around a corner and discovering a whole new world, full of possibility. Every time.

"We'll be having company soon," Krelig said, just as Calen was about to head back down into the castle.

"Company?" he asked, turning back.

"The first of those mages who are choosing to join us." Krelig was leaning on the battlement, looking out at the surrounding countryside. "The first of those ready to cast off the shackles of the Magistratum and help to bring about the new order." He glanced at Calen and laughed. "Don't look so shocked, boy! There are more discontented mages than you might imagine. Some will be too afraid or beaten down to admit it, even to themselves, but others will see that this is their chance to change everything. To remake the world into a place better suited for our kind."

"What — what will happen to those who don't choose to join?" Calen knew perfectly well what would happen to them, but he wanted to see what Krelig would say.

Krelig's voice went very mild, and Calen was instantly sorry he'd asked. "What do you think, Calen? Do you think it will be safe to leave our enemies free to walk among us? Do you think we can all agree to live in peace together? Do you think they will stay safely locked in their cage of a fortress while we do as we wish with the rest of the world?" He turned back to look out over the wall again. "You are not that naive, my boy. Don't waste my time asking questions you already know the answers to."

"Sorry, Master. Do you know when they'll arrive?"

"Soon, I think. I've been . . . sending invitations. I believe that some of them have been accepted."

He fell silent, and Calen crept quietly away before he could do anything else to annoy the mage or draw back his attention.

He had known that Krelig planned to assemble whatever like-minded mages he could to join him, but somehow Calen had thought that wouldn't happen for a while yet. Did this mean Krelig was getting closer to starting his attack against the Magistratum? Calen hoped not. He wasn't ready.

I need more time.

He was learning so much, every day. Getting stronger, and better, and quicker. He wanted to leave, more than anything, but he had to stay long enough to make it worth it. The more he learned, the stronger he got, the better his chances of being able to help bring down Mage Krelig. Of stopping him from carrying out his evil plans. Stopping him forever, so none of them would ever have to worry about him again.

Because if they didn't, Krelig would take them back to the days before the Magistratum existed, when mages were free to use their abilities for whatever purposes they wished, without any rules or constraints of any kind. He would stand atop the rubble of the broken Magistratum and the fallen bodies of his enemies and demand that all nonmages bow to his will. That all kingdoms recognize his authority over them. And if they refused, he'd destroy them, too.

And he could. Calen didn't know if anyone realized how incredibly powerful Krelig truly was. Calen hadn't been able to imagine many mages willingly joining Krelig's cause, but he knew — firsthand, didn't he? — that Krelig had ways of convincing people to do what he wanted. And even a small army of mages under his control would be more than any kingdom could stand against. But most of them would probably try anyway, because who wanted to submit to rule by a sadistic, crazy, evil mastermind? Trelian would certainly not go down without a fight.

But it would still go down. And Meg and everyone else he cared about would go down along with it.

He had to learn enough to save them. He hated it here, hated Mage Krelig and hated being away from Meg and hated thinking about what the others must believe of him now, but the learning would be worth it. *Was* worth it. Worth the pain and the punishment and the loneliness and everything else. Or it would be, once he was ready. Which would be ... soon. But not yet.

Not quite yet.

There was still too much left to know.

CHAPTER TWO

"A GAIN."

Meg was on her feet before the whole word was out of the captain's mouth. On her feet and racing toward where Jakl was waiting, ready to run this drill a hundred more times if that was what she wanted. As soon as she touched his back, the dragon launched himself forward and shot into the sky. Meg let him go for a few seconds of pure, blissful speed before turning him back around toward where the soldiers waited below.

"Not bad," Captain Varyn said gruffly once they were near enough to hear him. Meg couldn't help grinning. She knew by now that "not bad" was about as close to a compliment as she was ever likely to get from the man. And besides, she could tell that that had been their fastest time yet.

Meg couldn't imagine when she might actually be called upon to leap up from the ground like that and fly away on Jakl's back on a moment's notice, but she supposed the Commander of the King's Army wanted her to be ready for anything — and he'd never had a dragon to work into his plans before. So they practiced running, flying, leaping, hiding, sneaking, diving, carrying, and every other thing Captain Varyn and Commander Uri could think of. Meg didn't mind. She was still just so glad that they were letting Jakl and her fight at all. Well, that they *would* let them fight. So far it had just been drills, and practice, and training. The war had already started, but not for her. Not yet. But soon.

It had better be soon.

Not that she was so eager to put herself in danger — she wasn't *crazy*. But every day they waited, more of their soldiers were fighting. Fighting and sometimes dying. Adding a dragon to their forces would be a huge advantage. She couldn't understand what they were waiting for.

The past couple of months had been an adjustment for everyone, but she thought that the soldiers were getting a bit more used to having a dragon in their midst. They had already been used to seeing him around the castle, but that was different from seeing him up close. Or from being expected to ride on his back, which Captain Varyn had required most of them to practice (with Meg's assistance) at least a few times. And a few days ago, he'd had Jakl practice plucking soldiers from the ground and flying short distances with them dangling from his claws.

That had been kind of fun. Well, not for the soldiers, probably. But Jakl had enjoyed it.

The best thing about training was that it helped her not think about other things. Like, for example, her supposed best friend, who had abandoned her and gone flying off with their very evil and terrible enemy for reasons no one could begin to understand.

But she had to let herself think about him sometimes. Because she had to find him. She had to find him and get him back home, where he belonged.

Captain Varyn dismissed them for the day, and Meg sent Jakl off to nap and get something to eat. She wanted him rested and fed and ready for later. She was going to do something very foolish. She didn't want either of them to be tired, or distracted by an empty stomach.

She gave her practice armor to Devan, who smiled shyly at her and gave her a quick little half-bow when she thanked him, as he always did. She smiled back and then shook her head at him as he jogged away. Sometimes she thought the soldiers were almost as perplexed by her presence as they were by Jakl's. There weren't any other women in their ranks, let alone princesses. For the most part they seemed to have settled on sort of intentionally forgetting that she was a princess during training, which suited Meg just fine — it wouldn't do for anyone to waste time trying to be polite and deferential to her in the middle of a battle! But once training was over, they remembered again and had trouble figuring out how to behave. She trusted they'd get it all sorted out eventually.

Pela, ever the perfect lady-in-waiting, was standing patiently beside the castle steps, today's stack of important papers in hand. She gave Meg a summary as they walked inside.

"I have the latest reports on the war; your parents want you to be prepared to discuss them at breakfast tomorrow morning. There's the usual pile of petition letters and"— she gave Meg a sympathetic glance before continuing —"your history tutor sent over a new list of reading assignments."

Meg made a very unprincess-like face. Her parents had agreed to cut back on her lessons during the current crisis, but not to stop them entirely. Meg usually liked history, but although she understood her tutor's inclination to shift their current focus to studying other wars and conflicts, she was getting a little tired of endless reading about death and destruction throughout the world's past. There was more than enough of that happening right here in the present.

Pela went on, relaying a few more notes and messages, but as soon as Meg's door closed behind them, she dropped the hand holding the list and looked at Meg beseechingly.

"Princess, this plan is very foolish."

Meg sighed. "I know, Pela."

"Are you certain you will not reconsider?"

"Yes, I'm certain."

Pela nodded, but managed to convey a vast amount of disapproval along with the acceptance. "Very well. In that case, I have laid out your clothing and arranged for your evening meal to be brought up to your rooms."

"Thank you," Meg said. And she meant it. She wasn't sure how she would have gotten through the past several weeks without Pela's quiet, able assistance. And kindness.

"Please — just be careful," Pela added.

"I will. I promise."

Pela's mouth twitched in a very interesting manner, but she had it back under control again so quickly that Meg couldn't really be sure what she had seen. She presumed, however, that Pela did not quite believe that Meg was capable of being careful.

It was probably not such an unreasonable opinion.

Pela helped her change out of her training clothes and then ducked back out, leaving Meg to spend the remainder of the afternoon going through the letters and other documents that her parents had sent for her to read. Training to fight in the war was one thing, but they still expected her to keep up with her responsibilities as the princess-heir as well. Meg understood, but she wished that the news weren't so uniformly grim and discouraging. Lourin and its allies were advancing steadily, and every day brought more reports of Trelian's soldiers falling back. They were outnumbered, waiting on reinforcements from Kragnir that hadn't yet arrived, and they were losing ground. Meg knew that her father had still not abandoned all hope of negotiating an end to the fighting, but she didn't think it was likely to happen. Meg suspected that lingering hope was the main reason she and Jakl hadn't yet been allowed to join the war effort. She thought they had waited long enough, but it wasn't her decision to make. She had her orders, and currently those orders were to continue training and nothing more.

And you always follow orders, do you?

Meg tried to ignore that voice she kept hearing in her head. The one that pointed out how her current plan was a direct violation of everything she had promised her parents about being more responsible and less impulsive and able to follow orders and do what she was told.

It's not impulsive, she told herself. *I've given it a great deal of thought.* That was true. But somehow she didn't think that really made much difference. She knew, she *knew* it was almost certainly the wrong thing to do. But she didn't know what choice she had. Mage Serek refused to do anything. She'd pestered him relentlessly, cajoling, pleading, demanding, screaming . . . until he had finally banished her from his quarters entirely. Banished her! For trying to make him do what he should have been doing anyway. Well, if he wasn't going to try to find Calen, then she would just do it herself.

Even though you know it's a terrible idea, the smarter, more responsible part of her added silently. That part always sounded a little like her older sister Maerlie. Maerlie, who was far away in Kragnir, married to the prince there and far more sensible in every way than Meg. Meg missed her terribly. Having Calen in her life had helped her not feel Maerlie's absence quite so strongly after she left. But now she had neither one.

"That's what I'm trying to fix," she said out loud. She didn't know if it was worse to have conversations with yourself out loud or silently inside your own head. Either way, she didn't want to listen. She'd made her decision. And it wasn't really *that* much of a risk. She would be careful. She'd take Jakl up so high that there would be no danger of being spotted by enemy soldiers. She just had to start looking. Jakl's eyes were sharp; he'd be able to see even from a great distance. So they'd start going out and looking for signs of where Calen might have gone. And once she found him, she could start figuring out how to get there, to bring him home. It would all depend on where he was, she supposed.

And whether he wants to come back, that voice in her head said.

Of course he wants to come back! Meg closed her eyes. She had to stop arguing with herself this way. She was beginning to worry about her sanity.

She made herself focus on her work, and for a while she succeeded. But then there were no more papers left to read, no more summaries or responses left to write. She sat by the window and thought about Calen until it was time to go.

"There," Pela said, tying off the last of the laces that cinched Meg's boots tightly around her calves. She rose and stepped back, looking pleased at her work. And it *was* her work; Pela had decided that Meg needed a whole wardrobe of riding clothes now that she would be out in public on her dragon so much of the time. Meg had left her to it, which she was discovering was usually the smart thing to do when Pela had her mind set on something. The result was an impressive array of outfits that were practical, comfortable, and somehow still very flattering, despite being mostly variations of tunics and trousers. There were even a few fancy-dress versions, "in case you're ever riding Jakl as part of a ceremony or formal event," Pela had explained at Meg's incredulous reaction. Those were really very lovely. She almost hoped that she had an occasion to wear one sometime.

The one Pela had selected today was what Meg secretly thought of as the thief-in-the-night outfit. She had no doubt Pela had had it made with just this sort of sneaking around in mind. Pela didn't approve, not remotely, but apparently she also didn't expect that Meg would always listen to reason. So she had provided at least one set of clothing in which Meg could sneak around in style. There were long tapered sleeves that wouldn't catch on Jakl's occasional rough scales, and clever leather pieces set along the inner thighs and calves that helped keep Meg firmly in place on Jakl's back. There were even matching black leather gloves and a black hood to hold and conceal Meg's long blond hair.

"Now we must get you outside without incident," Pela said briskly. It was late, but there were always servants about, and some of them wouldn't hesitate to inform the king and queen if they saw Meg stealing out for what could not possibly be any good reason at this time of night. Pela preceded Meg down the halls, checking around corners and making sure the way was clear, until they reached Jakl's paddock. Jakl, of course, was ready and waiting, eager to go. He was always up for flying, especially at night, but Meg thought that he was also eager to help find Calen. Jakl knew how much Meg wanted to find him. And she thought that the dragon had come to love Calen in his own way, too.

Meg turned to thank Pela once more for her help, but Pela brushed her words aside. "It's my pleasure to assist you, Princess. You know that. Now, be swift, and do what you must do, and come back safely."

Meg nodded and was about to climb up onto her dragon's back when she heard what sounded like a strangled squeak behind her.

She turned back around. "Pela, was that —?"

Meg's words died her in her throat.

Pela was standing frozen on the path. She'd only taken a couple of steps before finding her way blocked by the dark figure standing before her.

It was Mage Serek.

He was standing right in front of Pela, but his attention was fixed on Meg. His eyes were alight with anger.

Meg stared back at him defiantly. He was *not* going to stop her.

She waited for him to shout at her, but for a long moment he didn't say anything at all. When he finally spoke, his voice was eerily calm. "What exactly do you think you are about to do?"

"I'm going to find Calen."

He uttered a harsh laugh. "You're going to find Calen. You're just going to fly off on your dragon and *look* for him?"

"Yes!" she said back angrily, practically spitting the word at him. "*Someone* has to."

"And you think you're just going to look down and see him standing there, waiting for you to come rescue him?"

The contempt in his voice was very irritating.

"Mage Krelig has a hundred giant disgusting slaarh," Meg said. "Do you think they will be hard to spot?"

Serek shook his head. "Do you not quite grasp the size of the world we live in, Your Highness? What are the chances that you're just going to happen upon the place where Krelig is hiding?"

"Small," Meg conceded hotly. "But better than nothing. And I'll take any chance over no chance. I don't care how long it takes, how many nights I have to spend —"

"How much you risk yourself and your kingdom in the process," Serek added.

Meg flinched inwardly. She didn't like to think about that part.

"You're not stopping me," she said instead. She climbed the rest of the way up to Jakl's back.

"*Get down from there, idiot child!*" Serek snapped. He sprinted toward her, nearly trampling poor Pela.

Jakl whipped his head down, snarling, knocking the mage to the ground. Serek twisted around to face her, but he didn't try to get up. Jakl was still growling ominously, head lowered, his eyes fixed on Serek's.

"Careful, Mage Serek," Meg said softly. "Jakl knows exactly how important this is to me."

"As do I," Serek said, his voice controlled again, despite the dragon staring him in the face. "But this is not the way."

Meg looked at him, a thought occurring to her. "How did you even know that I'd be out here? Have you been *spying* on me?" She didn't suspect Pela for a second. Pela might try her best to discourage Meg from doing stupid things, but she would never betray her.

"No," he said. "*I* thought you had more sense than to try something this foolish and dangerous. Clearly I was wrong. Anders had a vision."

Meg wasn't sure whether she wanted to laugh or cry. "Anders had a vision about *this?* Why can't his gods-cursed glimmers show him something useful, like where Calen is, or how we can defeat Lourin, or —?"

"You know he can't control what he sees," Serek said. "Although I disagree that this one wasn't useful. At least I got out here in time to stop you."

Now Meg did laugh. "You're not stopping me," she said again.

"Princess, be reasonable! You can't possibly —"

Meg narrowed her eyes at him. "You don't get to tell me what to do. You've given up on him. I have not. I'm going to find him and prove to you exactly how wrong you are. About everything."

"Princess —"

"If you stay very still, Jakl probably won't crush you." *Let's go,* she thought at her dragon. She was done listening to Serek.

Jakl launched himself upward. Meg spared one glance back for the mage, who was still on the ground, staring after her. And then she turned back around and closed her eyes and let herself get lost in the flying.

Not for too long, though. It was tempting to just let go and feel the wind and the night and not think about anything, but she had a job to do.

From the dismal reports, Meg knew some of what she would see before she opened her eyes, but it was still a shock. The damage stretched farther than she'd imagined. Empty husks of buildings littered the landscape everywhere she looked. Farms had been burned, roads destroyed, and people killed, although she hoped that most of them had gotten to safety before Lourin's army had arrived. Many of them had taken shelter within the outer walls surrounding the castle, in lands set aside for exactly this kind of emergency. But not all of them. Some didn't want to abandon their homes. Some wanted to stay and fight to stop the enemy soldiers from destroying what they'd spent their lives building. And some had surely been murdered by Lourin soldiers for their trouble. She tried not to picture Trelian's people — *her* people — falling and dying at the hands of the enemy. Innocent people, caught up in a war that should never even have started.

That was the worst part of all. Everything — all the blood and death and pain and destruction — it didn't mean anything. It was all so *stupid* — they weren't even fighting about anything real!

Lourin had attacked because Trelian had violated its promise to keep its dragon (*her dragon*) safely contained and on the ground. But her parents had explained to King Gerald a million times why they'd had to break that promise, and anyway, the whole reason for the original promise was meaningless, since it was based on Sen Eva's lies about Jakl and his supposed attacks. But even though Sen Eva was dead now, her evil influence was still hurting Trelian. King Gerald didn't believe them, or didn't care, or both, and he wouldn't respond to their repeated pleas for talks. He'd persuaded the leaders of his neighbor kingdoms, Baustern and Farrell-Grast, to join him, and as Meg knew all too well from those cursed reports, things were going very, very badly for Trelian at the moment.

But not for long. The Kragnir soldiers would soon arrive, and that would turn the tide. That, and whenever they finally let Meg and Jakl do something more than train.

She stared down at the ruined countryside and felt angry tears trying to squeeze out of her eyes.

How had everything become such a disaster?

One problem at a time, she told herself. Right now, she was looking for Calen. But the more she surveyed the lands around her, the more ridiculous her entire plan seemed. Serek was right, of course. The world was a very big place. And at present it was filled with fighting and fires and danger and enemies, and she should *not* be flying around waiting for someone to see her and attack. And Calen could be anywhere. *Anywhere.* She knew that. She just . . . she just felt like she should be able to find him. By force of will alone, she should be able to tell where he was.

But she couldn't. She realized that some part of her had thought she would get up here and just have a sense of where to go. But clearly she just didn't have any sense at all.

They flew on a while longer, but nothing changed.

We should go back, she thought at Jakl.

He turned without the faintest hint of surprise. He'd been feeling her feelings this whole time. He probably had known that she would give up before she knew it herself.

She wondered if Serek would be waiting for her. She wondered if he'd told her parents. Maybe they'd all be waiting there for her together. To tell her how foolish and careless she had been.

I know that already.

But when they reached the field by Jakl's paddock, it was Mage Anders who was waiting.

Jakl landed, but Meg stayed on his back.

"Hello, Anders," she said as neutrally as she could.

"Hello, Princess." He nodded at her clothing. "That's a really good sneaking-around outfit. Not suspicious at all."

Meg rolled her eyes. "Did Serek send you?"

"Not exactly. Although he is the reason I'm here. Well, one of the reasons." He waited a moment, seemed to realize she wasn't going to come down just yet, then looked around and found a nearby rock to sit on. "Well," he continued, "how did it go? I don't suppose you found Calen?"

"No."

"Ah, well. I was rooting for you. But I do agree with Serek that it was probably not the best plan."

"It's better than no plan!"

He considered. "Maybe. Maybe not. A bad plan could actually make things worse instead of better, you know. But in any case, what if there were another plan? One that might have a better chance of success?"

She looked at him sharply. "You have another plan?"

"Yes!" he said. "It's a good one, too. My idea, you know."

"But you — you didn't believe —"

"I don't think Calen's a traitor," he said. "Neither does Serek."

"Yes, he does," Meg said bitterly.

"He thought Calen was a *risk*, as did I, but I don't think he ever truly believed that Calen wanted to join Mage Krelig. And he's still a risk, but I think he's less risky here with us than if we leave him in Krelig's hands. Once we get him back, we can figure out whether he's dangerous or not. But first we have to get him back. Serek and I are in agreement on that point."

"He's not dangerous!" Meg said, a little more loudly than she'd intended. "And why didn't Serek *say* he had a plan?"

"I think he was working up to it when your dragon knocked him down and you flew away."

Meg shook her head. "Well, he should have gotten to the point more quickly. He knows I don't have a lot of patience."

"True," Anders agreed.

They were silent for a moment.

"So what's this idea?" she asked at last.

"Come and we'll show you," he said, getting to his feet.

Meg hesitated a few seconds more, then slid down from Jakl's back. "If this is a trick, I'll let Jakl eat you," she said.

"As you wish," Anders said amiably. "But it's not a trick. We need your help to make it work."

She was about to ask what kind of help he meant when Pela burst into the clearing, having clearly run all the way up the path from the castle.

41

"Princess!" she said breathlessly. "I'm sorry! I didn't expect you back so soon! I would have been here to meet you!" She looked at Anders in obvious confusion.

"It's all right, Pela," Meg said. "Come with us, and I'll explain on the way."

Pela nodded, then stepped into place beside Meg. They followed Mage Anders back into the castle.

Serek's study was full of birds.

Well, maybe not *entirely* full of birds, but it had already been crammed with books and strange objects and containers and things, and now every remaining available bit of space seemed to have been taken over by big, black, noisy crows in wire cages.

"Um," Meg said.

"I'll explain in a moment," Anders told her.

Serek, who was sitting at his desk, looked up as they came in. "Princess," he said evenly.

"Mage Serek," she said back, in the same careful tone.

"Oh, stop it, you two," Anders said. "We're all on the same team!" He walked over to one of the cages and leaned over to peer inside. "Isn't that right?" he asked the bird looking back at him.

Pela smiled. "Who's your friend, Mage Anders?"

"I call this one Blackie," he answered, giving the cage

a little pat. "Actually, I call most of them Blackie. It's hard to tell them apart. Except that one over there with the one white feather on his wing. I call that one George."

"Let's get started," Serek said. He gestured toward a small table surrounded by four wooden chairs. "Princess, would you sit?"

If Mage Serek was going to act like their altercation in the field had never happened, Meg decided she could do the same. She took one of the chairs, and after a moment Pela sat in the one to her left. Serek took the one across from her.

"Are you going to do the kind of spell that you and Calen used to find Maurel when she was lost?" Come to think of it, why in the world hadn't they done that sooner? But Serek was shaking his head.

"Krelig will have protected himself against any straightforward location spells. Remember, Sen Eva *wanted* us to find Maurel that time. Krelig . . . I do not think he is ready to be found. We believe he needs some time to prepare for his next move. And to try and get from Calen whatever it is he expects to get."

"Do you have any idea what his next move will be?" Meg asked. "Or—or what it is he wants from Calen?"

Serek and Anders exchanged a look.

"We expect him to attack the Magistratum in some way," Serek said.

"What's left of it, anyway," Anders put in. He made a face. "It's kind of a mess at this point."

Serek closed his eyes briefly in a way that somehow clearly suggested he was praying for patience. "We don't know what form that attack will take, however. And he'll probably attempt to win over as many of us to his side as possible first."

Pela uttered a nervous little laugh. "But — but surely the other mages would not . . ." She trailed off, looking back and forth at their somber faces.

"There are many who do not believe we can successfully stand against him," Serek said. "Some of those might decide to join him rather than die fighting him. More than some, perhaps."

"But that's cowardly!" Pela exclaimed.

"Yes," Anders agreed. "But still true. Mages aren't soldiers, Miss Pela. There's no requirement for bravery. Or good character, or sense, or intelligence . . ." He paused a minute, then continued: "Or pleasant appearances, or tact, or taste, or good grooming habits —"

"Or patience," Serek said, closing his eyes again.

"All mages have to be is good at magic," Anders went on. "Good at magic and able to follow the rules. And there are plenty who struggle with that second part. And if Mage Krelig wants to throw all the rules away . . . that's going to be pretty appealing to certain among us."

Pela just shook her head, clearly dismayed.

"And Calen?" Meg prompted.

"You know that Calen has some very special abilities," Serek said. "Mage Krelig no doubt seeks to use those abilities for his own ends. If enough of us do stand against him, I believe we can win. But if Calen's talent gives him an extra advantage . . ."

"But Calen wouldn't really help him!" Meg said, exasperated. *He wouldn't.* "He must just be . . . he must just be pretending. . . ."

"Maybe," Serek said, then held up his hands in response to Meg's darkening expression and added, "Probably. Almost certainly. But Mage Krelig can be . . . very persuasive. He persuaded Calen to go along with him in the first place, didn't he? Who's to say he won't have ways to ensure Calen's continued cooperation?"

"But —"

"I don't believe Calen *wants* to help him. I don't believe Calen is a traitor. But do I believe that he might be caught up in something bigger than he can handle? Do I believe he might not be able to avoid helping Krelig in the end? Yes, I think those things are possible."

Meg clenched her fists. "But —"

"Which is why," Serek broke in, "I think we need to find him and do everything we can to get him back. Soon."

Meg forced herself to take a few deep breaths. *Calm down,* she told herself. *He wants to help, so just calm down and listen.*

"All right," she said at last. "So how do we do that?"

"Magic!" Anders said, spreading his hands wide on either side of his head and waving them around dramatically.

Everyone ignored him.

"As I said," Serek went on, "Krelig will be protected against any standard sort of location spell. So we've been trying to come up with alternatives that are more . . ."

"Sneaky," Anders put in.

Serek paused, then conceded, "Well, yes. More sneaky. Something he won't have anticipated or prepared against. And we think we have found a good approach."

"It was my idea," Anders reminded them.

Meg looked around the crowded study doubtfully. "You're going to attack him with birds?"

"We're going to use the birds to find Calen and try to communicate with him."

Meg blinked. "You can do that?"

"Magic!" Anders whispered, waving his hands around again.

"We think so," Serek said. "We believe that if we can infuse the birds with a strong enough sense of who Calen is and — most important — a strong enough desire to find him, they'll be drawn to wherever he is. And once they find him, be able to give him a message. At least to let him know that we are looking for him, and that we want to bring him home."

Meg didn't quite understand the infusing part, but the rest of it sounded . . . well, it sounded a lot more promising than her plan of going out every night and having Jakl scan the ground for signs below them. "But how can I help with that? I can't do any magic." She glanced at Anders and waved her hands in the air experimentally. He grinned at her.

Serek rolled his eyes. "Don't encourage him." Then he looked at her seriously, leaning forward across the table. "You can help because you know Calen better than anyone. And . . ." He hesitated, seeming to search for just the right words. "Ability is important in magic," he said at last. "Ability and power and knowledge: all of those are essential. But the most essential part of casting any spell is intention. Desire. The force of will that drives the magic to do what you want it to do. As much as I want to bring Calen home — and I do sincerely want that, very much — I think it is safe to say that no one wants to bring him back home more than you."

Meg swallowed, feeling suddenly on the verge of tears. Serek was certainly right about that last part. She nodded, not quite trusting herself to speak. Pela reached over and took her hand under the table. Meg squeezed it gratefully.

Serek held her eyes a moment more, then sat back, apparently satisfied. He gestured to Anders, who turned and opened up the cage beside him. The crow *quorked* quietly and fluttered its wings a little, but otherwise seemed undisturbed by the sudden attention. Anders held it gently with both hands and carried it over to them, then placed it in the center of the table. The crow tilted its head and regarded Anders silently from its new location.

"Blackie seems to like you," Pela murmured, smiling.

Anders blinked at her, seeming surprised. "Of course he does. Everyone likes me."

Pela laughed, and for once Meg appreciated Anders's strange good humor. She looked back at Serek, feeling more or less back in control of herself.

"All right," she said. "How do we begin?"

CHAPTER THREE

CALEN TOOK A BREATH AND TRIED again to clear his mind. The spell wasn't a difficult one — or, at least, it *shouldn't* have been — but it was hard to concentrate through the pain.

You won't be in pain once you heal yourself. Come on. Try again. He nodded, not caring how crazy it was to nod in response to something he said to himself inside his own head. He couldn't spare the mental energy to care about anything other than focusing enough to cast this spell. He looked again at the angry red welts that lined his left arm. There were more across his back and the back of his legs. They pulsed excruciatingly with every heartbeat, some of them leaking blood at the places where his skin had been entirely stripped away.

Don't think about that. Don't think about anything. He tried closing his eyes, but he could still see Mage Krelig's wild face, streaks of red magic flying from his outstretched fingertips, the last thing Calen saw before he recovered his wits enough to run. The mage had been in a foul mood all morning, but his sudden fury and lashing out had seemed to come from nowhere.

Because he's a crazy person, remember?

I know.

Calen closed his eyes and worked at gathering the energy for the healing spell. He tried to will himself not to feel the pain, to imagine how good he would feel once the spell was cast and his body was healed. Slowly, he felt it beginning to work. Yellow and green energy materialized in a gentle cloud around his arm, penetrating the wounds and encouraging his skin to knit back together. He wanted to make it happen faster, but resisted trying to speed up the spell. It was hard enough keeping his concentration steady as it was.

Once his arm was healed, he moved on to his back. Then his legs.

Finally, exhausted but now suffering only the lingering memory of the pain, Calen relaxed. He lay back on his bed and gave himself a few minutes just to be still, breathing, relishing the feeling of not bleeding anymore.

Then he tried to think about what had just happened.

Not that it was always possible to make any sense of Mage Krelig's actions — he often behaved erratically, surprising Calen with sudden anger or, almost as often, surprising him by not being angry when Calen expected him to be. But usually Calen could at least identify the trigger of the man's rages. This time there hadn't been anything at all.

Yes, there was. You're still not learning quickly enough.

That wasn't quite it, though. It wasn't about the learning, exactly — it was about that great reserve of power Krelig seemed to think Calen had inside him. Power he thought Calen was willfully refusing to let out. But Calen had done everything right today — he'd mastered every spell, he hadn't been slow — and then suddenly Krelig had just attacked.

I have to get out of here.

He knew that was true. But he didn't like to think about it very much. For one thing, he had come to realize just how difficult it was going to be to get away. Krelig left him alone for hours at a time, but he always seemed to know where Calen had been. If Calen tried to leave on foot, he had no doubt that Mage Krelig would be able to find him without any trouble. Calen didn't even try to make himself believe that his invisibility spell would fool Krelig for a second. It had fooled him once, briefly, but that was back when Krelig was still on the other side of the portal, and even then, he was able to sense that there was magic at work in the room. If he could sense that much while peering through a window from *another world*, he certainly wouldn't have any trouble sensing what Calen was up to when he was right here.

Calen had thought about trying to steal a slaarh and ride it back to Trelian, but that idea had so many things wrong with it, he could barely count them all.

The only idea that seemed to hold any promise was his jumping spell, the one he'd used to travel to where Maurel had been taken by Sen Eva. But he would only be able to go short distances at a time, only transport himself to spaces he could actually see before him, and the land around the castle was dense with trees. He wouldn't be able to see very far at all. Which meant that it would probably be very easy for Mage Krelig to catch up with him.

There was one more option, but he knew it wasn't one he should even think about. That was the idea of jumping all the way back to Trelian. He was pretty sure he could do it, in theory; he'd transported both Meg and himself a great distance that first time when he'd cast the spell by accident. But Serek and Anders had explained later on that Calen had been very, very lucky. That there were all kinds of terrible things that could happen when a mage transported himself to a place he couldn't see. Not the least of which was that something else, or even someone else, could already be in the place you were transporting to. Which meant that when you appeared, you might . . . overlap. You could end up partially inside a wall. Or a person.

In his head, Calen heard Anders's gleeful voice whisper: *half-embedded*. He shuddered.

No. He couldn't try that. Even if he was desperate. Because even if he was willing to risk his own life, he couldn't know that he wouldn't be risking the life of someone else.

Unless he could know for sure somehow that the place he was transporting to was empty . . .

No.

Besides, he was pretty sure that Krelig had some sort of wards placed that would prevent him from transporting himself out of the castle. Probably also wards that would alert him if Calen just walked out. Calen had tried to detect any such wards, but so far he hadn't had any luck. He could see his own wards when he cast them, but then even those faded into invisibility once the spell was done.

Well, you have to figure out something, he told himself angrily.

Of course, the reason he hadn't figured anything out so far was also the other reason he didn't like to think too much about leaving. He hadn't learned enough yet. He was sure there was so much more he could learn from Mage Krelig—maybe once he learned enough, he'd be able to cast his way out. His way home.

He just wasn't ready.

But you might not have much time. Not if he's losing his mind completely. If he gets mad enough, he might just kill you.

I know.

Calen got up from his bed and went out to his balcony. Some of the little cheerful birds were there, perched along the outer wall. He'd started remembering to tuck away pieces of bread from breakfast, and he took one out now, holding it out in one hand toward the nearest bird. The bird hopped cautiously toward him, paused, then darted closer and snatched the bread from his hand before flitting back away. Calen laughed.

"I'm not going to hurt you, little friend," he said. He watched it finish off the bread, then leaned his forearms on the wall and looked out over the treetops. A dark shape flying in the distance made him catch his breath for a second, but he realized almost immediately that it couldn't possibly be anything as large as a dragon. After a moment, he could make out the shape more clearly: it was just a crow.

He watched it swooping in seemingly aimless patterns above the trees. Looking for good places to find a snack, maybe. *Sorry, crow,* Calen thought. *I'm out of bread for today.*

He went back inside. He was about to lie back down on the bed when he heard a deep ringing sound, like a bell, only he knew it wasn't really a bell. It was something Krelig did to summon Calen to him when he wanted him.

Calen looked unhappily at the door to the hallway. He did not want to go back out there. But he had to. Disobeying was not really an option. Especially not when Krelig was already angry.

Maybe he won't be anymore. That was a possibility. His moods shifted so quickly, after all. He might be all smiles by the time Calen reached him. And if he wasn't, well, this time Calen would be ready, at least. He'd been caught too much by surprise earlier to do anything other than run. He thought that he could get a shield up in time to block Krelig's attack for a few seconds, if he went in ready to do so. Long enough to get back out the door, at least.

Unless he's really trying to kill me next time, he thought miserably. He didn't think he could hold out even a few seconds against Krelig at full murderous strength.

Calen pushed that idea away and made his way down the hall and back toward where he could sense Krelig waiting. The bell sound was usually, as now, accompanied by an awareness of Krelig's presence in a certain direction, so that Calen could make his way directly to where his master was as quickly as possible.

Never keep a crazy man waiting, Calen thought to himself, crazily.

He had to stop doing that.

You've been talking to yourself in your head a lot lately.

I know.

When he arrived at the right place, Calen cleared his mind and tried to be ready. Then he took a deep breath and pushed open the door.

"Ah, Calen! There you are, my boy." All smiles.

Calen started to relax, but as he stepped into the room, he realized that Mage Krelig was not alone. Five other mages sat in chairs that had been arranged in a semicircle around where Krelig was sitting. They were looking at Calen curiously.

"Come in, come in!" Krelig said, gesturing at Calen enthusiastically. "Our guests want to meet you."

Calen stepped cautiously forward. He hadn't seen anyone other than Krelig in . . . weeks? Months? He had lost track of exactly how long he'd been here, he realized.

It was strange to be around other people again. What were they doing here? For a second his heart seemed to stop inside him, caught in a sudden terrible fist of hope. Could they be here to try to get him out?

Then he remembered Krelig's announcement about expecting company.

Oh. Of course. He was an idiot.

They were here to join Mage Krelig. Traitors to the Magistratum.

Just like you.

Shut up. I am not a traitor.

He studied them more carefully, as they were studying him. Three men and two women, their faces all marked to various degrees, identifying them as mages and reflecting their levels of experience and ability.

"*This* is the boy everyone was fighting about?" the younger of the two women asked. She had blazing red hair tied up in a loose knot behind her head. Calen guessed she was only a year or two older than he was, but the extent of the tattoos on her face was impressive. He'd seen mages much older than her with a lot fewer marks. He didn't much care for her tone, though. And who was she calling a boy? She wasn't exactly anyone's grandmother!

"I know he doesn't look like much," Krelig responded

infuriatingly, "but he's quite powerful. Not able to access all of it yet, but we're working on that, aren't we, Calen?"

"Sure," Calen said, his eyes still fixed on the others. A few of the mages seemed almost embarrassed to be there. Or to be seen there, maybe. They all seemed uncomfortable, anyway. Except the obnoxious girl.

Krelig went on, seemingly oblivious to the tension among everyone else in the room. Or just not caring. He spoke directly to Calen, as though the others weren't sitting right there. "These few are just the beginning. More will follow soon. You will see."

Calen nodded, not trusting himself to speak.

"Mage Krelig," one of the men said hesitantly, "what should we — what will —?"

Krelig glanced at him sharply, as if he'd forgotten the other mages already. "Yes, yes," he said. "We will talk about all of that soon enough. For now, I think you should rest. You must be tired after your long journey." He turned back to Calen again. "Take our guests upstairs and show them to their rooms."

The obnoxious girl snorted. "Is he your apprentice or your servant?"

Krelig turned slowly back around. He looked at her until her smirk disappeared. Then he said, "He is whatever I need him to be. You would do well to follow his example if you desire a permanent place in my little army, my dear."

She looked down and away, not speaking. But she didn't seem very chastened; her smile didn't return, but her mouth twisted slightly, and Calen could see one of her eyebrows arched in a somewhat skeptical expression. He felt a mean little smile tug at his lips. That was definitely not the right response.

"Do you?" Mage Krelig asked softly.

Her eyes snapped back up. She looked around, confirmed that he was talking to her, and asked finally, "Do I what?"

"Do you want a permanent place here?"

"Sure. Of course."

"Sure of course what?"

The other mages were beginning to look even more uncomfortable. Calen stood patiently, knowing he should be worried that the girl was ruining Krelig's good mood, but he was too glad to see her getting taken down a peg.

She looked around again and uttered a defensive-sounding laugh. "I wouldn't have come if I didn't want to be here. It wasn't easy, you know! I don't really know what you expect me to say —"

She broke off with a gasp and clapped a hand to her

arm. When she took her hand away, Calen saw a deep red line across the skin there. She stared at it, then back at Mage Krelig.

"Do you think I care what you had to do to come here? Do you think anything you had to endure could possibly compare to hundreds of years of exile, having to claw your way back to this world by casting across time and space and relying on the assistance of incompetent, unskilled, ignorant—" He broke off, seeming to recognize for once that he was sliding into a rant. He took a breath, then continued. "Now. I'm going to ask you one more time. Do you desire a permanent place here, Mage Helena?"

She finally seemed to start to understand. She glanced again at the red lash on her arm, then back up. "Yes. Yes, Mage Krelig. I want a permanent place here. I—I desire that very much."

He didn't answer at first, just gazed at her with his deceptively calm eyes. "Good," he said at last. "I was beginning to wonder if you really wanted to be here at all. You don't ever want to make me wonder about you again."

"No," she said at once, all swagger and scorn gone from her voice. "No, Mage Krelig. I won't. You won't need to wonder about me. I promise."

He nodded, then smiled. "Excellent!" He gestured carelessly at her, and Calen saw the healing energy fly toward her a split second before she gasped again and the wound closed itself up, disappearing as though it had never existed.

"Now, Calen." Krelig nodded toward the door Calen had so recently entered through.

"What rooms should I give them?"

"I don't care. Any rooms you want."

Calen turned and walked out, not waiting to see if they were even out of their chairs yet. Soon enough he heard their hurried footsteps on the stone floor behind him. He led them to the opposite side of the castle from where his own room was. He wanted them as far away from him as possible.

When he reached the entrance to the long hallway he'd selected, he waved vaguely in the direction of the several closed doors that lined each side. "You can take any of these rooms you like." Then he started back the way they'd come.

The obnoxious girl — Mage Helena — stepped up beside him. "Is he always like that? So — so volatile? I didn't —"

Calen whirled to face her. "Don't speak to me," he said coldly. "I'm not your guide or your ally or your friend.

You'll figure out what it's like here soon enough. Either that, or he'll probably kill you. But don't expect me to make your life any easier. Or to be any part of it at all."

Her mouth opened, but he strode off before she could say whatever she was about to say.

This was not good. Now that some mages had started to arrive, how quickly would others follow? Did it mean that Krelig was going to be ready to do something soon? Calen had to escape before that happened. Before *any-thing* happened. Before his presence here could actively help Mage Krelig in any way.

He thought about his jumping spell again.

No.

I know. I know. But . . .

No. Jumping to places he could see would take too long. And jumping to places he couldn't see would be too dangerous. He had to think of something else. He had to.

He'd learned so much since he'd been here. He'd got-ten better, and faster, and he could cast new, more difficult spells and more than one at a time and protect himself against more of what Krelig cast at him, but nothing he'd learned seemed immediately applicable toward help-ing him get away. Which was probably not an accident. Mage Krelig was not an idiot. He knew Calen hadn't wanted to come here. He must suspect that Calen would escape if he could. Unless he was crazy enough to believe that Calen might have completely changed his mind.

But Krelig didn't seem to care about Calen's motivations. He just wanted Calen here so that he'd be able to use Calen's abilities in whatever way he could to help destroy the Magistratum and set up his terrifying new world order. He seemed to take it for granted that now that Calen was here, he'd remain. At least for as long as Krelig wanted him to. And why not? Where could he go? How could he possibly escape? He didn't even know where they were, let alone how to get back home.

Calen went through the door into his room and out onto his balcony. He looked out at the treetops and the sparkly glimpses of the river through the forest and the birds and the slowly moving clouds and tried not to despair. He would figure something out. He would. He had to.

He'd thought about trying to contact Meg through dreams, trying to re-create some less-terrible version of the dream spell that Sen Eva had used to try to influence Wilem and drive Meg insane. But he was too afraid that something could go wrong. And that whole experience had literally been a nightmare for Meg. He couldn't really bring himself to consider violating her mind in that way, not after how horrible it had been for her before. His intentions would be different, of course, and he hoped (gods, he hoped) that she'd be glad to hear from him . . . but not that way.

Which left . . . what? The summoning spell he'd used to contact Serek in the past was too obvious; Krelig had certainly blocked against that, and even if he hadn't, he would know — Calen was certain he would — if Calen attempted it. He needed something Mage Krelig would never have thought of himself, and so wouldn't be on guard against.

Some of the little birds came to see if Calen had brought any bread for them.

"Sorry, friends," he said. "No more bread today. I'll have some more tomorrow." They couldn't understand him, of course, but that didn't stop him from talking to them. He supposed it was slightly less crazy than talking to himself, anyway.

Not much, though.

Shut up.

He saw the crow from earlier again, circling over the trees. Or maybe it was a different crow; it's not like he could tell one from another, really. He tried to remember if he'd seen any crows around here before today. Mostly he just remembered the cheerful colorful birds, and maybe a hawk or two, which he remembered because he worried that they might attack his little feathered friends.

And this crow was acting so . . . odd. Circling and circling, but not over a single spot, as he'd seen carrion birds do when there was something dead on the ground below, waiting to be eaten. *What are you up to, Mr. Crow?* Idly, Calen sent a tendril of white energy toward it, crafting a little impromptu spell of the sort he'd use to investigate an object or search for information. He used something similar when he was trying to find Krelig in the morning for lessons, but that was purely about location. This one was more about a general sense of what the crow was about. He didn't expect to be able to read its mind or anything like that — even if crows had enough thoughts in their brains for there to be something *to* read, he didn't know any kind of spell that could see inside someone else's head. Even Mage Krelig didn't seem to know that kind of spell, or he surely would have used it on Calen by now. And on everyone else, too.

But it was an interesting exercise, anyway, and Krelig did expect him to work in between lessons — not just practicing what he'd been taught, but attempting things he hadn't been taught, thinking creatively, trying new things. Calen half smiled, thinking of how different

Krelig was from Serek. Serek hated when Calen was creative with magic. He always seemed to expect that Calen would accidentally blow up the universe. Maybe Mage Krelig just wasn't particularly concerned about the fate of the universe. He probably thought blowing it up would be an improvement. He did want to tear down everything and start again, after all.

Calen pushed these thoughts aside and concentrated on his bird spell. He wasn't sure what he expected to find out — maybe a sense of where it had been, or where it meant to go. . . . He watched as his tiny tendril reached its distant, circling form.

It altered course at once, flying straight at him.

Calen watched, fascinated. He hadn't been attempting to draw it closer. Had it been attracted by the magic in some way? It kept coming, finally landing awkwardly on the wall right before him. The little birds scattered nervously, but the crow paid no attention to them. It tilted its head and looked Calen right in the eye.

Then it opened its beak and he heard Meg's voice, speaking his name.

CHAPTER FOUR

MEG WALKED STIFFLY OVER TO THE water station. She'd never imagined she would ever need a break from riding her dragon, but then, she'd also never imagined some of Captain Varyn's more creative ideas for training drills. For the past two hours she'd been running Jakl through vigorous flying formations while trying to hold fast to "unconscious" soldiers riding along with her. Thankfully, they weren't really unconscious, and could grab hold when her own grasp slipped. And even more thankfully, they were all wearing safety harnesses with ropes securely fastened to the dragon's own harness, in case *their* grasps slipped, too. Every muscle in her body ached from the strain of staying on Jakl's back while trying to keep the soldiers from falling. She'd only had to work with one at a time, but even that was hard. They were heavy!

"Nice work up there," Zeb called as he trotted past her. She didn't know how any of them could have the energy or flexibility for anything faster than a slow, stiff walk, but maybe it was a lot easier to be the unconscious soldier than the girl trying to hold him in place on top of a flying dragon. Zeb was one of the ones she'd successfully held in place until she could drop him back off where the rest of his team had been waiting. She gave him a tired but grateful smile and kept walking. She needed that water.

Captain Varyn came up beside her as she was finishing her second cup. "Not bad," he said.

Meg snorted, then choked, getting water up her nose.

"Thanks," she said, once she'd recovered. "I dropped a few, though, didn't I?"

He shrugged. "Not perfect, no. But not bad. To be honest, I thought you'd drop more of them. You're stronger than you look." He looked at her appraisingly. "Or just more stubborn than I gave you credit for."

Meg laughed. "I am pretty stubborn," she admitted.

"It's a good quality in a soldier. Can be, anyway, if it's about the right things."

"I'm not a soldier."

"Sure you are. You are as long as you're training with my men and following my orders, anyway. Maybe it's only temporary, but that doesn't change anything right here in the present." He took her cup and filled it again. "Drink up. You've got another hour of training yet."

Meg fought back a groan and stood up straighter. "Yes, sir!"

He grinned at her and jogged (jogged!) away. But then, he hadn't even been one of the unconscious soldiers. He'd gotten to stay on the ground shouting commands at the rest of them.

Meg finished her third cup, then turned back to where the others were already reassembling. They weren't a very large group — only about fifty all together. Captain Varyn had told her early on that the commander wanted to keep the dragon company on the smaller side. For one thing, not that many soldiers had volunteered, at least at first. But more important, they were meant to be a small, quick, flexible unit, able to work together and adapt to changing conditions easily. The larger the group, the harder it was to change direction or alter course midstride.

Captain Varyn opened his mouth to say something, then closed it again, staring past Meg. The rest of them, Meg included, turned to follow his gaze.

A pair of soldiers was running toward them. Running . . . awkwardly. One was visibly limping.

"Captain!" they said together, lurching to a semblance of attention when they arrived. Meg gasped before she could stop herself. Their uniforms were splattered with blood.

Captain Varyn waved a hand almost angrily at them. "At ease, soldiers. Report!"

"Attack on our company," said the one who'd been limping. "Captain Halse sent us back, to warn you. We received a message just before they hit us. It —"

"Stop," Varyn said, holding up a hand. "Come with me, both of you. I think this needs to go directly to the commander." He turned to Meg and the others. "That's the end of training for today. Get your gear cleaned up and report to your barracks to await further instructions." Then he started at a run for the castle. The pair of soldiers fell in behind him.

The rest of Varyn's company broke up, murmuring in reaction, heading toward the armory or to collect gear that was still out in the training field. Except Devan, who approached to help Meg unfasten her leather breastplate without his usual smile.

Meg thanked him and turned toward the castle. She wished that Varyn had let the soldiers finish. A new attack anywhere was bad, but she had a feeling that the content of whatever message they'd received was worse. She had to get cleaned up and find her parents. Her soldier duties might be over for the morning, but she suspected the princess-heir had a busy day ahead of her.

By the time she reached the king and queen's small audience chamber, Captain Varyn and Commander Uri were just finishing their report. Meg slipped quietly through the door and closed it behind her, then sat in the chair beside her mother. The queen gave her a quick, worried almost-smile, then turned back to listen. But she reached over and took Meg's hand as she did so. A second later, the door opened again, and Mage Serek came through.

"Ah, good," said King Tormon. "We can update you and Princess Meglynne at the same time."

Serek nodded and took a seat. He and Meg had maintained a civil (if not exactly friendly) relationship since that first night in his study. She still didn't think Serek truly believed in Calen the way he should, but he *was* trying to bring Calen home, and maybe that was all that mattered. Meg had been visiting Serek and Anders every evening to help with the bird spells, watching them send more and more crows out into the night sky. None of them had returned yet, but Anders assured her it was too soon to worry about that. She hoped he was right.

"The short version," the commander said, "is that Lourin forces have blocked the pass from Kragnir. King Ryllin has apparently been trying to get a message to us for days; this is the only one that's gotten through."

Meg's stomach tightened in worry. This was bad. They needed those reinforcements!

"How—?" Serek started, but Captain Varyn broke in, seeming to know what he was asking.

"A Kragnir scout managed to climb down from the mountains off the main road. He circled around, stole a horse, and rode south with Lourin soldiers chasing him the whole way. He ran straight into Captain Halse's company and was able to deliver the message just before the Lourin soldiers caught up. Luckily, Halse has a good head on his shoulders and sent men back to the castle with the news while the rest of them stayed to fight. Otherwise, we still might not know."

"We're discussing possible courses of action," the commander continued. "We don't exactly have men to spare with the fighting here as bad as it's been, but we can't hold out much longer on our own. We need Kragnir, and soon."

There were other kingdoms, of course, but they were either too small to be able to help or too far away, or both—like Prolua, where Meg's eldest sister, Morgan, had gone to live when she married the prince there. They'd received letters from her and from the royal family she was now a part of, expressing sympathy and concern, but Prolua's lands were very tiny and very far, and they barely had an army at all. Kragnir was the only ally

Trelian had who was close enough and strong enough to make a difference. And now they weren't coming.

Stop it, Meg told herself firmly. *They will figure something out.*

But they didn't. The discussion went on and on, without any clear progress toward a solution. Meg tried to sit quietly and listen; she knew full well that the others were far more experienced in war than she was.

But she had never been very good at sitting quietly.

"Father," she interjected finally, when she couldn't take one more round of *here are all the things we cannot do*, "perhaps it's time for Jakl and me to fly out with the rest of the company? Surely the seriousness of this current crisis —"

"We appreciate your willingness to help," he said, "but we are not yet at that point."

Judging from their faces, Commander Uri and Captain Varyn didn't entirely agree. But they didn't speak up to support her, either.

"But —"

Her mother squeezed her hand. "Meg, please," she said. "You need to be patient. When the time comes, I'm sure —"

"The time *has* come!" Meg said, pulling her hand

away. She was speaking too loudly, letting too much emotion show, but this was infuriating. "What are we waiting for? What's the point of having me train to fight if you're never going to let me do anything?"

"I am not putting you in danger unnecessarily," her father said. "There may still be a way —"

"I'm *already* in danger," Meg countered. "We're all in danger! We're losing this war, if you haven't noticed! You promised you would let us help. Was that just — just a lie? To placate me? Jakl and I are ready; you can ask the captain —"

"That's enough!" the king shouted. "If you cannot hold your tongue *and* your temper, then I suggest you remove yourself from this room."

Meg stood up. "I suppose I'd better do just that, then," she said coldly. "Because I can't continue to sit here and listen to you make excuses for why you won't do what obviously needs to be done."

"Meg!" the queen said, clearly scandalized that Meg would speak that way to the king in front of the commander, the captain, and the mage.

Meg turned on her heel before she could say anything worse, and stormed out.

Stupid, she thought at herself angrily as she stomped her way down the hall. They would never listen to her if she couldn't stay calm and speak in reasonable tones. She knew that. But she couldn't help it when they were being so stubborn and foolish!

Jakl was stirring, feeling her anger, and she had to send him the now-familiar shorthand *stupid human stuff* through the link before he would relax again. The dragon had learned that Meg sometimes got angry or upset when she wasn't actually in immediate danger, but he couldn't always tell on his own when that was the case. There wasn't anything he could do right now to help her. She just had to calm down.

Knowing exactly how bad everything was getting but not being able to do anything about it was maddening. And it just kept getting worse. Pela, who had suffered through many of Meg's previous rants on the subject of how she and Jakl weren't being allowed to help, also insisted that Meg had to be patient. But how could you be patient when your best friend was gods-knew-where doing gods-knew-what, and soldiers were fighting and dying in a ridiculous war over *nothing*, and —

No. This wasn't going to help her regain control. She was going to *not* think. Just for a little while. She would find a place to sit and be calm and not think about all of those things.

She paused at the outer door, considering, then

headed toward the gardens. She hunted down the most isolated corner she could find and fought the urge to pace angrily around on the grass. Instead she made herself settle down under a tree and close her eyes. Right now all she needed was quiet. Just some quiet. Just some time to not think or worry or be upset or scared or angry.

Meg tried to clear her mind and focus on the feel of the tree behind her and the grass beneath her. She concentrated on her breathing, taking long slow breaths in the way Calen had taught her when she had first been struggling to manage the way the link with the dragon amplified her emotions. She breathed and tried not to think about how much she wished Calen were here beside her right now.

A sound very close by broke into her awareness, and her eyes flew open. For one confused moment her heart leaped upward and she thought, *Calen?* But no, of course it wasn't.

The boy in front of her was older, and taller, with lighter hair and strikingly handsome features. Nearly blindingly handsome. It used to enrage her, how handsome he was. Now it was merely . . . irritating.

"Hello, Wilem," she said.

"I'm sorry to have disturbed you," he said. "I didn't realize you were here."

She looked around at the secluded corner of the garden. It was a cul-de-sac at the end of a tree-lined passage enclosed by a stone wall — he couldn't have been passing through on his way to anywhere else.

"Where were you going?" she asked.

He smiled slightly and pointed at where she was sitting. "Right there, actually. I come here to think sometimes. I didn't realize you did the same."

She smiled back, despite herself. "It's my first time."

"I'll leave you to your thoughts, then." He turned to go.

"No," she said before she could think better of it. She suddenly didn't want to sit here alone. "It was your spot before it was mine. And I wasn't succeeding very well at thinking, anyway. Or not-thinking, which was really what I was trying for. You might as well stay."

He hesitated, then nodded. "Very well, if you wish." He eased himself slowly to the ground. Very slowly. Meg suddenly noticed the bandages on his arm. He was clearly favoring one leg as well.

"What happened?" she asked, sitting up straighter. "Are you all right?"

"Yes," he said, shifting his leg out carefully on the ground. "Just a little roughed up. My company was attacked earlier."

"Are you in Captain Halse's company?"

He blinked. "How did you —? Oh, of course you would have heard what happened. Yes."

"Shouldn't you be in the infirmary?"

"They patched me up and sent me on my way," he said. "I'm fine, really. Not like some of the others. We were lucky that the group from Lourin was a small one. And we surprised them more than they surprised us."

Meg had known that Wilem had joined the Trelian soldiers — *was* a Trelian soldier now, she supposed — but as he wasn't in her own company, she didn't know very much about what he did or where. There were a lot of other things she wanted to ask about what had happened, but she didn't ask them. Like her, Wilem had obviously come here looking for solitude, not someone to pester him with questions.

He leaned back against the stone wall, and they were quiet for a time. His presence didn't exactly help her to not-think, but at least he was a distraction from her other concerns.

Wilem's situation had changed a great deal since he was first taken in as a prisoner. He was permitted to move freely about the castle grounds and no longer had guards placed at his door, although Meg knew they all still kept an eye on him, out of habit if nothing else. Her parents had decided that he'd earned these additional freedoms through his efforts to help rescue Maurel from his mother and his request to join the soldiers who were fighting to protect the kingdom from Lourin and its allies. He wasn't exactly *not* a prisoner, but he'd reached some strange in-between status that everyone had just slowly begun to accept and eventually take for granted. He didn't seem to mind not being able to leave. And really, Meg wasn't sure where he would go if he could — his mother was dead, and she had been his only remaining family. He'd grown up in Kragnir and probably had friends there, or former friends, but he might not be welcome back there after what he and Sen Eva had done. He'd betrayed Kragnir as well as Trelian, after all. At least here, a lot of people knew what he'd done to try to atone for his crimes, and some had seen firsthand his realization that his mother had deceived him in order to gain his cooperation. They'd also seen his subsequent voluntary surrender.

Perhaps someday, if he were permitted, he'd prefer to go somewhere where no one knew him or his past at all.

Meg was still trying to sort out how she felt about him. She'd gone from swooning over him like an idiot to hating him for his betrayal to . . . wherever she was now. She didn't think she could quite say she'd *forgiven* him — could you ever forgive someone for plotting to

kill your sister, whatever he thought his reasons were?—
but his actions since then had been consistently selfless
and admirable. He'd been willing to sacrifice himself to
save Maurel, and now he was actively helping in the fight
against Lourin. She no longer suspected that he was
waiting to turn on them again.

Not-hate. That's what she was feeling, she decided.
At least, that was the part of what she was feeling that
she could be certain of.

"How is your not-thinking going?" he asked after a
while.

"Still not very well, I'm afraid." She paused, then
added, "And it's probably not what I should be doing,
anyway. Not-thinking, I mean. But I was tired of trying
to think and failing at that, too. It is very frustrating to
realize that some problems cannot be solved by thinking.
That no matter how much you think about them, you
cannot . . ." She trailed off, shaking her head.

After a moment, Wilem said, "I think some problems
are too big for any of us to solve on our own. But I also
believe that we must —"

"Please don't say that we must be patient. I cannot
bear to hear that one more time."

He smiled. "I was going to say that we must be hopeful. The one sure way to fail is to let ourselves lose hope."

"Oh." Meg thought about that for a bit. "I suppose that's very true. Although not always easy."

"No," Wilem agreed.

"And I wish being hopeful didn't necessarily involve so much waiting!"

"Have you — have you had any word from Calen?"

"No. We don't know where he is. And if he's tried to contact us, he hasn't succeeded."

"I know that I don't know him very well, but from everything I've seen — I believe he'll find a way. He seems very resourceful. And determined."

"He's an idiot, is what he is," Meg said.

"I'm sure he had his reasons. . . ."

"I'm sure his reasons were not nearly good enough for the choice he made."

Wilem took a minute before replying. "Sometimes there are no good choices. Sometimes you can only make the least terrible choice available to you."

"Hmm." Meg supposed that might be so. But she didn't care. He still should have made some other choice. He should at the very least have told her what he was doing, and why. And he should have found a way to come home by now.

Suddenly she couldn't bear sitting still anymore. She got to her feet. Wilem started to do the same, but she waved him back down. "Don't be ridiculous. You're injured; you don't need to stand up. I believe I've done all the not-thinking I can for the time being." She started to walk away, then stopped and turned back. "Thank you for — for what you said."

He looked up at her, his gaze steady and serious on her own. "If any of my words brought you comfort, Princess, then I am glad."

Meg nodded at him, not sure what else to say, and headed back along the path toward the castle.

It wasn't yet her usual time to visit the mages, and she knew that Serek and Anders were almost certainly busy working out ways to try to contact Kragnir by now, but Meg went to see them anyway. She needed to feel like she was doing something. Maybe she could help somehow. As she walked down the corridor toward Serek's study, she met some of the visiting mages coming the other way. She recognized them as the first group who had arrived at the castle, although there had been several others since. These men had been here for many weeks now, but kept very much to themselves — she still didn't know any of their names. They nodded politely at her but did not stop as they passed. Meg's parents had invited them to stay at the castle as long as they wished, as they tried to figure out what to do to solve their own problems regarding the divisions within the Magistratum. From what little Meg knew, the other mages wanted Serek to lead some sort of resistance, a group separate from the Magistratum proper to fight Mage Krelig and perhaps form some new governmental structure within their organization. Serek did not seem to want any part of this.

Meg was glad; her parents needed him here, to help Trelian, and she needed him working to find Calen. She knew that the situation with the Magistratum was very serious — Calen had told her that much before he left — but she didn't see why Serek had to be the one to solve it. There had to be at least twenty other mages here now. Let them be the ones to do whatever needed to be done.

She reached the study door and knocked. It promptly swung open, revealing Anders on the other side.

"Good afternoon, Princess," he said. "Come in, come in!"

Meg stepped forward, but before Anders could close the door again, they heard a voice call, "Wait!" from back the way Meg had come. Meg turned to see Maurel hurrying awkwardly down the hall toward them. After a second, Meg realized why Maurel was lumbering so strangely — she had Mage Serek's enormous gyrcat in her arms. She was holding the poor animal under its front legs with her hands clasped around its chest, its lower body and hind legs dangling without support.

"Maurel, what are you —?"

Meg broke off as Maurel pushed past, walking right up to where Serek was seated at his desk.

"I'm sorry," Maurel said, depositing the creature unceremoniously on top of a pile of papers. "He keeps *doing* it."

"Doing what?" Meg asked, completely mystified.

Serek looked like he was trying not to look amused. "Lyrimon has apparently developed a particular affection for your sister."

Maurel turned to Meg, half-embarrassed, half-defiant. "I keep finding him in my bed! He turns his colors off and blends in and I don't even know he's there until I feel something furry against my ankles. It's not my fault. I'm not trying to steal him, I swear."

"I don't think anyone would ever accuse you of that," Meg said. "Who would want to steal that cranky thing?"

Maurel frowned. "He's not a cranky thing! He's a good kitty. He just . . . he just needs to stay in his own home." She turned back to Lyrimon and gave him a gentle pat on the head, then pointed at him. "Stay!" she said firmly. Then she marched out.

Lyrimon promptly jumped down from the desk and started to follow her. Anders closed the door before he could.

"Sorry, my furry friend. The little princess said *stay*. So stay you must."

Lyrimon looked at Anders and growled ominously. Then he vanished.

Meg stared. "Where — where did he go?" Calen had told her the gyrcat could do that, but she thought he'd been exaggerating.

"Oh, he's still there," Serek said absently. "You just can't see him."

Somehow that wasn't very comforting. Meg found a chair and sat cross-legged upon it, tucking her dress around her knees and ankles.

"So," Anders said, walking over to sit across from her. "What brings you here at this hour, Your Highness?"

"Is it too early to send another bird?" she asked. "I can't bear all the waiting."

"It's better after dark," Anders said. "More dramatic."

Meg looked at him, uncertain as to whether he was joking. It was never easy to tell with him. She waited for Serek to jump in with a sardonic comment, but before he could, the door banged open again. Meg thought she caught a glimpse of a half-visible cat-shape rushing out as the mages she'd passed in the hallway earlier crowded back in.

"Serek," the one in front said, "it's started. Mages have begun leaving the Magistratum to join Mage Krelig."

Serek had gotten to his feet as soon as they had entered. "How many?"

"Maybe only a handful, for certain. So far. But you know there were some only waiting for someone else to be the first."

Serek nodded grimly. Anders leaned forward toward Meg. "You'd best be on your way, Princess. This will be Magistratum business, and nothing you need to hear."

Meg wouldn't have minded staying; even listening to bad news about the Magistratum seemed preferable to having to go back to waiting around and doing nothing. But she knew they wouldn't let her stay. Best to leave now, before Serek threw her out less gently than Anders was attempting to do.

"All right," she said, rising. "I'll come back later."

Anders glanced at the other mages, then back at her. "I don't think we'll be sending a crow tonight, I'm afraid. We'll try again tomorrow evening."

Meg felt frustration swelling inside her but managed not to say anything she might regret. At least Anders was honest with her. And there were so many crows out there already. . . . Surely skipping one night couldn't make much difference. She just wanted to be doing everything they could, every second. But she knew there were other important things going on, too.

She left, closing the door behind her. She didn't really need to think about where to go next. Jakl was the only one who could make her feel any better now.

Meg felt him become aware that she was coming and couldn't help smiling as she felt his pure, uncomplicated happiness in response. She caught herself walking more quickly, then gave in and ran the rest of the way.

The dragon was sitting up alertly, waiting for her. As always, seeing him brought a surge of joy and pride and awe. She knew what he looked like, of course, and she could always feel him through the link, but being with him in person amplified everything — she always felt slightly more alive, slightly more *there*, when she was with him. And he was so beautiful! She thought he'd just about reached his full size, and he towered over her, wings folded tightly behind him, green scales glinting in the afternoon sun.

Beautiful, she felt him send at her proudly through the link, and she laughed.

The occasional words still caught her off-guard a lot of the time. She didn't think he was really speaking in the way a person would speak, though. The words came, as far as she could explain it to herself, in little packages of emotions that *meant* the same things as what the words represented, and she could understand those meanings and interpret them as words. Or something like that, anyway. She guessed it didn't really matter exactly how it worked. He seemed to pick up on certain words or phrases she used often or that she felt particularly strongly about. And especially ones having to do with him. He was ridiculously vain, she'd discovered. Although perhaps that was her own fault, for admiring him so much.

"Yes, beautiful," she said out loud, closing the last of the distance between them and sitting down at his feet. He sank down around her, repositioning himself fluidly to support her back and curl into the smallest circle he could manage, which wasn't all that small. "And enormous. When did you get so big? I remember when you were barely bigger than Lyrimon."

That made him send back a strange blend of embarrassment and contempt for his former tiny size, which made her laugh again.

"All right," she said. "I'll try to keep in mind how gigantic and strong and fierce you are now." And he was all those things, of course. But also capable of astounding gentleness when he chose. And filled with love for her, which always made her feel safe and protected and just . . . really, really good.

Even now, when everything else was so very much *not* good.

"Oh, Jakl," she said, her smile fading. "I wish none of this were happening."

He nudged his head even closer, putting the tip of his snout in her lap. She laid her head down against him and closed her eyes, letting herself be comforted as much as she could. It would all get sorted out somehow. It had to. They'd end the war and get Calen back and stop Mage Krelig from doing all the evil, terrible things he was planning to do, and everything could go back to normal. Whatever that meant. She was having a hard time remembering.

She stayed there for the rest of the afternoon and into early evening. The sun was just starting to disappear into the horizon when Jakl raised his head abruptly at the same moment Meg felt his alarm through the link.

"What is it? Is someone —?"

He uncurled himself and leaped to his feet just as she heard the shouts and screams begin. But it wasn't until the sky grew bright with flaming arrows that she understood.

They were under attack.

CHAPTER FIVE

THE SHOCK WAS SO GREAT THAT Calen nearly fainted. Or maybe he did faint. The world had seemed to go away for a few seconds — his vision went gray and then white, and then he was sitting on the balcony floor, staring at the bird, who had jumped down from the railing to stand in front of him.

His first thought when his wits returned was that he must have truly gone crazy at last.

But he didn't feel crazy. He felt . . . he felt . . .

Oh, gods. Thank the gods. Meg hadn't given up on him. She was trying to find him.

She was still his friend.

The bird hopped impatiently before him. "Calen," it said again. *Meg* said. Through the bird. How was she doing that?

She couldn't be doing that. Not on her own. Which meant that Serek hadn't given up on him, either.

His relief was so enormous that he had to fight an insane urge to grab the bird and kiss its ugly, feathery head. And then he had to bite his fist to keep from laughing. At himself, at the bird, at everything. Oh, gods.

All right. Good. Really good. This was really, really good. But what did it mean, exactly? What did he do now?

Good question. He didn't see a note attached to the bird's leg in the way that birds sometimes carried messages. Maybe they had been afraid of the bird delivering its message to the wrong person. This bird had zeroed in on Calen as soon as it had become aware of him. It must have been spelled to speak to him and him alone.

He leaned forward and asked quietly, "Meg? Can you hear me?"

The bird just looked at him. He supposed that was too much to hope — that the bird could somehow let them communicate directly, in the moment.

"Can you say anything else, bird?"

"Calen!" it said, still using Meg's voice. "Calen, Calen, Calen!"

Okay. Probably not, then. So the purpose of the bird must have been . . . to find him. To find him and let him know that they were looking for him.

And to give him a way to send a message back.

He thought about how something like that might be accomplished. Unfortunately he could only see the colors of active spells as they were being cast; there was

91

no hint that he could see now of what Serek might have done to make the bird able to find him or able to carry Meg's voice. He had to assume that the bird must be able to find its way back home again; maybe Anders had used one of his sequence spells to send the bird to find Calen and then, once it found him, head back to Trelian. So all he had to do was figure out how to give it a message to carry back.

A paper message was too risky. Even if he'd had any paper. If by some chance Mage Krelig saw this bird on its way home, it had to appear to be just a regular crow with nothing special about it at all. Hopefully the mage wouldn't be able to tell that it had any kind of magic attached to it. He hadn't noticed it on the way here, anyway. At least — at least as far as Calen knew. He looked anxiously over his shoulder toward the door that led to the hallway.

No. He couldn't worry about that. He had to seize this moment. He had to trust that Mage Krelig was distracted with the other mages or whatever had been making him so angry this morning or any of his usual crazy things. Or that Serek and Anders had done something to make the bird pass unnoticed. Or at least less noticeably.

Stop worrying, and start thinking. The voice in his head sounded a little like Meg. It made him smile again.

All right. Thinking.

White energy for communication, obviously, but what else? Should he try to make the bird sound like him? How had they *done* that? He shook his head. First things first. He had to make it say something other than his name. If it returned and just kept saying the same thing they had trained or spelled it to say when it left, they would never know it had found him.

He tried nonmagical means, just to see. But he couldn't get the bird to just repeat something he said. It only cawed at him, or said his name in Meg's voice, over and over.

After a few more minutes of thinking, he tried his original information-gathering spell again, the one he'd tried sending at the bird in the first place. Maybe there was something he could find out that way.

Luckily the bird seemed perfectly content to stand there while he tried all these things. "Good bird," Calen said, because it was true. He wished he had some bread left to give it. He wished he had a whole feast of all of its favorite foods to give it, in fact. If this bird really helped him get home, he was going to make sure it was kept in . . . well, whatever crows liked best, for the rest of its life.

Slowly, he reached toward it with another tendril of

questing white energy. He got back a sense of . . . speed, he thought. Speed and sky and flight. Well, all right. He could have guessed that part. He reached a little deeper, trying to direct the magic to find out what was different about this bird. What had happened to it? What had Serek and Anders . . . ? *Come on,* he thought pleadingly, then suddenly remembered his candles and heard Mage Krelig's voice, telling him that a mage didn't plead with the magic to do his will. He demanded it.

Tell me! Calen commanded his spell, sending it forward more forcefully. He was no longer trying to tease out little hints of information; he was insisting that the magic show him what was there to be discovered. He didn't want to hurt or alarm the bird, and he didn't want to push too hard . . . but he discovered that he didn't have to. The shift in his intention was enough. Almost at once he felt his attention drawn to the bird's head. Or — not its head, exactly, but the space around it. Very faintly, he could see . . . what was that? A tiny ball of energy, seeming to float just above the tiny feathers that rimmed the bird's bright eyes.

He sat back, amazed. That must — that must be the spell that Serek and Anders had cast. But — but he couldn't see colors after the initial casting. He could only see magic when it was first happening.

Well, not anymore, apparently, said the Meg-like voice in his head. *Be amazed later. Right now, use it to cast your spell and send the bird back home!*

Right. He nodded to himself, not even caring anymore about what that said about his sanity. Then he tried to examine the ball of energy more closely. There was a mix of colors — white, of course, as well as purple, blue, green, black. . . . He studied them, trying to sort out how Serek and Anders might have used them, and why. He'd never done anything like this before. He'd identified the colors in magic countless times, and could often reason things out afterward, if the spells and colors were straightforward enough. He could cast counterspells very quickly based on the colors he saw in another spell, but that was more instinct than reason. This was the first time he'd been able to spend more than a few seconds looking at the colors of a spell. He couldn't quite see how they were all connected to one another, but he could see the relative amounts of each type of magic energy used, and given what he knew about what the crow had been able to do . . .

It took some trial and error, and many, many whispered words of thanks to the gods for the crow's continued patience and cooperation, and also to Serek and Anders and to the bird itself and any bird-gods that might exist and be listening as well, just on general principles, but eventually Calen thought that he had it. He could see enough of what the mages had done to figure out his own version, something that would give the bird speed and strength and purpose and would let him give it a message to carry back. Not quite the same spell that Serek and Anders had used, but close enough. And maybe ... maybe even better.

He picked up the bird gently in both hands, and began.

Later, when it was time to go down for dinner, Calen stood for a long moment in his doorway, trying to pull himself together.

He was still reeling from the relief of knowing that his friends — his *family* — wanted him back and were trying to help him, *and* from the astounding realization that it was possible, at least some of the time, for him to see the colors of spells that had already been cast. And on top of that, he was now feeling so hopeful and impatient and excited for the crow to make its way back home.

But what he was feeling right that moment more than anything else was terror that Krelig would be able to tell.

He had been terrified of Krelig from the start,

certainly, even if he had to try to hide it to avoid the mage's anger whenever Calen actually showed his fear. And he'd been determined to find a way home from the start as well. But now that the crow had come, now that he'd heard Meg's voice and sent a reply and it seemed that escape might truly, actually be possible . . . now the idea of Krelig finding out and stopping him was absolutely unbearable. It hadn't been nearly as bad when it had all just been vague dreams of how he would somehow, someday get away. Now it was actually beginning — he had taken the first steps toward getting back where he belonged. Which meant that now there was a real plan, a real *chance*, for Krelig to discover and destroy.

Calen swallowed and tried to slow down his breathing and his frantically beating heart. He had to act normally. He had to go down there and get his food and not draw attention to himself and not seem in any way any different from the person he had been when he left the mage's presence earlier that day. Sometimes the man was too crazy and distracted or just too uninterested to notice anything going around him. But sometimes he wasn't. Sometimes he was very perceptive indeed.

Well, being late to get his food was not going to help him stay inconspicuous. He forced himself to take a step into the hallway. After that it was easier to take another.

And another. And then he was walking, and then he was at the end of the hall, and then the stairway. And eventually he was all the way down in the dining hall.

His covered plate was waiting in its usual location. But there were five other plates beside it.

For a second, he couldn't make any sense of it. And then he remembered. The other mages! He'd completely forgotten about them.

They weren't there yet. He wondered if Krelig had bothered to tell them how meals worked around here. Probably not. Almost certainly not. Well, Calen wasn't going to go fetch them. They could figure it out, just as he had. He took his plate and carried it to one of the long tables, sitting in the corner with his back to the room in a way that he hoped would discourage any of the others, should they eventually show up, from thinking he wanted company.

He ate without noticing the food, his mind continuing to dart against his will to thoughts of the crow. *Stop it*, he told himself firmly. *Stop thinking about it!* But that was far easier said than done.

He was just about to stand up and carry his plate to the counter when he heard someone enter the dining hall behind him. He turned to see which of the mages it was, and his heart sank. It was Mage Krelig.

He never came to dinner when Calen was there. Never. Why tonight, of all nights?

Maybe because he senses that something is wrong, the voice in his head said. It didn't sound like Meg anymore.

He can't. He can't know anything.

Krelig didn't seem angry, but of course, that meant nothing. Calen waited to see if maybe Krelig had gone to fetch the other mages after all and was just leading them in, but no one else entered behind him. He walked straight over to where Calen was sitting and sat across from him. He continued to sit there, silently, just looking at Calen.

Calen thought carefully about what to say. What would he have said if this had happened yesterday? Would he have asked whether something was wrong?

Maybe?

"Is something wrong?" he asked, and immediately wished he hadn't. Mage Krelig's eyes narrowed suspiciously.

"I don't know, boy. Why don't you tell me?"

Calen fought panic. This could be about *anything.* Or nothing. *Don't give yourself away, curse you.*

"Did you — did you want me to bring the other mages down for dinner? I didn't know . . ."

"Don't play the fool with me," Krelig said. His voice was doing that scary calm thing that sometimes preceded violent action. "Something is different about you. I can tell. What is it?"

"I don't know what you're talking about."

Mage Krelig didn't move, but Calen saw the red energy a second before he felt the blinding pain in his head. He screamed and jerked backward, knocking over his chair and falling to the floor. The pain stopped as suddenly as it had begun. Mage Krelig was still seated, still looking at him calmly.

"What is it?" Krelig asked again.

Calen was suddenly furious. *Good!* he thought frantically. *Use that—fury is better than fear.*

And it was.

Without another second of thought, he sent his own red-energy spell at Krelig. He wasn't quite able to do it without moving his hand, though, and Krelig's eyes widened as he realized what Calen was doing. He blocked the spell easily, but seemed caught off-guard by it all the same. "What—?"

"You want to know what's wrong? I'll tell you!" Calen said, pushing himself up off the floor. "What did you bring those other mages here for?"

"What? You knew—"

"I knew you were going to get other mages to turn against the Magistratum. I didn't know you were going to bring them here and turn this place into a boarding-house! I didn't know you were going to parade me in front of them and tell them how unimpressive I was. You brought me here because *I* was the one you needed, the one who was going to help you. I didn't want to come, I *never* wanted to, but you *made* me! You took me away from *everything,* made them all hate me — and now you're just going to bring in a bunch of other mages and — and . . ."

Krelig stared at him in astonishment, then burst out laughing.

Calen just stood there, breathing hard. He had no idea what that meant. He had no idea where that little speech had come from, either, for that matter. He had just been trying to think of something, anything to distract Krelig. He didn't really feel that way. Did he?

"Oh —" Krelig said, as soon as the laughter subsided enough that he could speak. "Oh, Calen. Is that — is that really what this is about? Are you *jealous?*" He started laughing again, but not quite as uncontrollably this time. He pointed at the chair. "Sit down, sit down. Let me explain some things to you."

Calen righted his chair and sat back down at the table, eyeing the mage warily.

Still chuckling, Krelig wiped at his eyes and then

made a little gesture with his hand, which made a goblet of wine appear before him on the table in a burst of purple energy. "You're not being replaced, my boy, although I'm touched to know that you would care so much." His tone conveyed just enough sarcasm to suggest he knew that Calen didn't really care in any way that indicated affection or loyalty, but Calen thought the older man was a little affected by Calen's outburst all the same. Maybe just by the idea that there was anything at all keeping Calen here other than his inability to leave.

"You are the one I need — make no mistake. My visions were quite clear about that. With you by my side, I cannot fail. Without you . . . my success is not guaranteed. I would probably still achieve my goals . . . but not definitely. Not for certain. And I'm not about to leave anything to chance. Not this time." He paused, and Calen wondered if he was remembering whatever had gone wrong the last time he'd faced the other mages, all those years ago, when they'd beaten him and exiled him forever. Or what they thought would be forever. For a moment, Krelig's face went still and he seemed to be looking inward, at something he did not like at all. He almost looked . . . afraid. And then he gave his head a little shake and refocused on Calen. His expression cleared, and he went on as though he'd never stopped.

"Believe me when I say that I need you with me, Calen. I will never cast you aside. You and I are going to do great things together; never fear." His eyes glinted with apparent excitement at those great things, and he took a sip of his wine. "But that doesn't mean we don't need others to stand with us. We are powerful, you and I, more than any of these other so-called mages, but we can still use them to our advantage, to make us stronger — do you see?"

"Yes, but —"

"Of course," Krelig went on, his smile fading, "we're only going to do great things together if you stop resisting your full power."

Calen felt his hands curl into fists almost of their own volition. He was so tired of this conversation.

"I am *not* —"

"What did I tell you about saying no to me?"

Calen knew he should be scared, but all he could feel was anger. Anger at being threatened and beaten and tortured when he didn't learn quickly enough. Anger at everything Krelig was planning to do to the people and the world that Calen loved. Anger that Krelig knew so much, *so much*, and it was all going to waste.

"Then stop telling me I'm resisting!" Calen shouted. "If you'd stop saying things to me that aren't true, I wouldn't have to say no to you, would I?"

Krelig's eyes blazed with fury. "You insolent —"

"What are you going to do — hurt me? Like this?" He lashed out, sending another blood-red spell at his new master. Krelig blocked it even as he remained otherwise completely still, apparently mesmerized by Calen's behavior. "And this? And this?" He climbed out of his chair and backed away, not to run, but because he suddenly felt too confined, he needed more room, he needed more space around him to draw in the energy. Krelig just sat and watched him, anger and astonishment and an odd sort of curiosity warring in his expression.

"I'm tired of being punished for nothing!" Calen went on. He kept sending bolt after bolt of energy at Krelig. He didn't care that they weren't landing, that Krelig would be able to block anything he sent before it so much as grazed him. It felt so good just to be sending them. To just let go of all the fear and caution and attack with everything he had. It felt more than good. It felt wonderful.

He fired again and again, and when he next spoke, he heard his voice grow stronger and louder with each phrase. "Stop telling me I'm not trying!" he screamed. "Stop telling me I'm resisting! Does it look like I'm resisting to you?" He punctuated that last question with a swirling ball of fiery red-black-orange and sent it straight at Krelig's hateful face.

He watched it shatter into pieces against the shield that Krelig had, somewhat hastily, flung up to block it.

Calen stopped then, abruptly spent. He didn't think he could manage to light a candle right at that moment. He stood, the room silent except for his own labored breathing and the pounding of his heart. But it still wasn't fear that was causing it. He stood, not afraid, waiting to see what Krelig would do.

"No," Krelig said finally, his voice soft, but not quite in the way it tended to be when he was most angry. Calen didn't hear any anger his voice. It sounded more like . . . wonder.

Krelig leaned back in his chair. Incredibly, he grinned. "No," he said again. "It doesn't look like you're resisting at all. Not anymore."

Calen blinked. Then, in a great rush, he realized what the man meant.

He thought again about how good it had felt to let go. To *let go.* To stop . . . doing whatever he'd been doing before. Holding back. He hadn't known it; he'd been sure that he was trying as hard as he could . . . but Krelig had been right. He had been holding back.

But not anymore.

The spells he'd used to attack Krelig in the last few moments had been stronger than anything he had ever tried to cast before. They still hadn't touched Krelig, but that didn't matter. They had been . . . fuller. More complete. For the first time, he had truly accessed his full power.

Before he could help it, he found himself grinning back.

It was true. He was a lot stronger than he had ever imagined.

Krelig had him sit back down and actually got him a drink of water.

"Felt good, didn't it, boy?"

"Yes," Calen said. He took a long slow sip from the cup Krelig offered him. There was no point in denying it.

"It will be easier now," Krelig said. "Now that you've accessed it once, you will be able to do so again. *That's what real power feels like, Calen. You are beginning to discover just how strong you truly are.*"

He walked back around the table and sat facing Calen again. All traces of his earlier anger and suspicion were gone.

"We've come far together, the two of us, and we will go farther still. There are so many wondrous things in store . . . and I can see how much you enjoy the learning.

You can't conceal that in the slightest. How much you like what you can do, how much stronger you're becoming. I know exactly how that feels. You love it as much as I do. And now you'll love it even more."

Krelig drained the rest of his wine and stood up. "Embrace the path you're on, my boy. Trust me: the less powerful will never be able to accept or understand you. Not now, and certainly not when you reach your full potential. I'm glad to hear you've started to accept that your former friends won't want you back at this point. These things may seem like terrible prices to you now, but in time you will see that they were really just burdens, holding you back. I will show you what it means to have true power, and you will come to know that it is worth everything you give up in order to get it."

He walked away.

Calen sat, chilled, shocked, confused, exhilarated, listening to the sound of Krelig's fading footfalls.

If Krelig had said those things to him yesterday, Calen might have begun to believe them. But his friends hadn't given up. They did want him back.

Do they really? asked the voice in his head. *Are you sure? What if they get you back, and then they realize you're not the same Calen that they knew? That they loved? What if you come back and they realize you'll never be the same*

again? Might they turn you away then? Once they see what you've become?

Shut up! He hadn't become anything. He was the same person he'd always been. Or — at least — not different enough to count as being someone else. He was still himself. They would see that. He knew they would.

He made himself get up and take his plate to the counter. He left the other plates sitting where they were and turned to go back to his room. He had plenty to keep him busy, which was good, because he didn't want to think about this anymore. He had to think about what he had done, exactly, to access his full power. He was glad to be too tired to cast anything right now, because the temptation to experiment was nearly overwhelming, and Calen didn't think he was ready for that. Soon, maybe. But not yet.

He had to think some more about his plan to escape, now that things were in motion.

His plan to get back to Trelian, and Serek, and to Meg. Who did still want him to come home. And would still be glad when he got there, no matter what Mage Krelig thought. And no matter how much stronger he might be.

They will be glad, he said again in his head, defiantly.

The voice in his head didn't say anything in response.

CHAPTER SIX

MEG WAS UP ON JAKL'S BACK before her mind had time to finish the thought. The dragon launched into the air, and they raced toward the sounds of battle. People swarmed below them; soldiers ran toward the fighting as everyone else ran for the castle. Another volley of arrows illuminated the scene, and Meg stared down, trying to sort out what was happening. The arrows were coming from beyond the outer wall, but there seemed to be fighting inside the wall as well. *Breached*, she thought with shock. *The wall's been breached. There are enemies inside the walls.*

The shock turned to appalled anger, and Jakl roared in response to what she was feeling. What they both felt, now. There was a momentary pause in the action below as everyone looked up.

Meg grinned savagely. *That's right*, she thought. *You're in trouble now.*

The fighting renewed almost at once. The soldiers below were too close together; she couldn't easily pick out Trelian's men versus the invaders. But the enemy archers were on the other side of the wall.

Jakl banked sharply and circled around. When the next volley launched, he let loose a stream of dragon-fire that incinerated the arrows midflight. By the time they swung around again, the archers were aiming at the dragon instead of the soldiers. Meg realized belatedly that she didn't even have her training armor on, let alone anything intended for actual battle. She was still in her dress from earlier this afternoon.

Up! she thought, and Jakl shot upward, out of range. The arrows arced harmlessly below them.

Jakl swung back down immediately and sent another stream of fire — this time at the archers instead of just the arrows. *Attack my castle, will you?* Meg thought at them. She laughed as, nearly as one, they turned and ran. Jakl inhaled for another blast, but Meg stopped him. Trelian soldiers were streaming out after the fleeing archers, and all of them were headed for the trees beyond the cleared lands directly around the castle grounds. She didn't want to risk hurting any of their own soldiers or setting the trees on fire. Instead she directed Jakl back toward the other side of the wall.

The fighting there seemed to be dying down; it appeared to have only been a small group of invaders.

Not that that made it any less terrible that they had managed to get inside the walls. But it looked like Trelian's soldiers had it under control now. Meg had Jakl circle around again, trying to see if there was anything else they could do. She saw Mage Serek and Mage Anders, apparently casting some sort of spell at the gate and the walls on either side. *A little late for that,* she thought bitterly.

Jakl set down again at her silent direction, and she looked around from this closer vantage point for any other way that she could help. She knew that Jakl would keep alert for any approaching danger, but the remaining invaders seemed well occupied with Trelian soldiers, and she didn't think it likely that any would try to take on the dragon. She saw Captain Varyn drive his sword into an enemy soldier, pull it out, then swing around to fight someone else. She saw a few others from her own company, and plenty she didn't recognize.

And then she saw Wilem.

What was he doing? He had no business fighting, with his injuries! She stared, unable to look away, as he moved awkwardly on his bad leg while trying to fend off the sword of an attacker. At least his injured arm wasn't his sword arm. He swung without hesitation, meeting the other man's sword thrusts with his own, but she didn't see how he could keep it up much longer when his leg was obviously not strong enough to fully support him. The invader seemed to be thinking the same thing. He drove Wilem relentlessly backward, striking with less care but greater force as Wilem's limp became more pronounced.

Meg didn't know what to do. Jakl couldn't help here; he'd end up setting them both on fire. No one else seemed close enough to help, and Meg hadn't had any ground-fighting training at all. Which she suddenly decided had been a very stupid decision on someone's part. She was just thinking that maybe she could still do something to distract the other man — throw a rock at him, *something* — when Wilem surprised them both with a quick swipe to his enemy's thigh. The man staggered, and then Wilem buried his sword in the other man's throat.

Meg gasped as the soldier fell, one hand starting to reach for the sword but never completing its journey. Wilem dropped to one knee, clearly having used the last of his strength for that killing blow. *Now* someone noticed, Meg saw with exasperation. Another Trelian soldier came running over and helped get Wilem back to his feet. They exchanged some quick words, and then the other man supported Wilem as they moved slowly back toward the castle.

Meg looked around, abruptly aware that she hadn't been paying attention to anything else for several minutes. But the last of the enemy soldiers seemed to have been subdued. Many were clearly dead, but perhaps some were only unconscious and could be questioned later. She hoped so. They needed to find out how these men had gotten inside the walls!

Captain Varyn came toward her, and Meg slipped down from Jakl's back to meet him. He looked tired but undamaged.

"Not bad," he said with a ghost of a smile. "That was quick thinking, taking out the archers."

"Thank you, sir."

"Emergency war council in ten minutes," he said. He looked down, then added, "You might want to find some shoes."

Meg looked at her bare feet as he walked away. That was what she got for wearing princess clothes. Her shoes must have fallen off somewhere along the way.

She sent Jakl back to his paddock with thoughts of love and gratitude and admiration and stepped carefully toward the castle to find her nice, sturdy boots.

Pela was sitting in Meg's room when Meg got there. She jumped to her feet when Meg opened the door.

"Princess! Are you all right?" And then, scandalized: "Where are your *shoes*?"

Meg laughed. She couldn't help it. Pela was always so refreshingly herself. "I have no idea. I thought I'd put my riding boots on. The brown ones."

"With your dress?" Pela stepped closer. "Oh, and it's a bit dirty, isn't it? We should —"

"No time," Meg said. "Emergency war council, and I need to be there."

"But it would only take a second —"

"Pela."

Pela sighed. "Very well, Princess." She opened Meg's wardrobe to get out the boots. "But not the *brown* ones," she muttered to herself.

Meg surrendered enough to let Pela choose the pair that she thought would look least offensive, and to let her quickly tie Meg's hair back in a simple knot, since its former, more elegant arrangement had come entirely undone while she was flying around.

"I suppose that was your first real taste of what fighting in the war will be like," Pela said around the hairpins she was holding in her mouth.

"I guess that's true," Meg said. She hadn't really thought about it that way, but of course Pela was right.

"How do you feel?"

Meg opened her mouth and then closed it, unsure how to answer. How did she feel? She hadn't been afraid, she realized. Racing toward the battle, all she could think about was getting there, helping to protect the castle. Flying and letting Jakl loose his fire at the enemies had felt . . . good. But it was a complicated kind of good. She thought about Wilem's sword driving into that other man's neck. She didn't think that she and Jakl had actually killed anyone. She could have, she thought, in that moment; she had been so angry . . . but now she was relieved that it hadn't been necessary.

"I'll let you know when I figure it out," Meg said finally. She stood up. "I need to go now."

"Of course, Princess. I'll see you when you get back."

The emergency war council consisted of Meg, her parents, Commander Uri, Captain Varyn, and Captain Naithe, who was the Captain of the House Guard. Serek and Anders had gone to help the medics tend to the injured.

"I think we're all in agreement," the king began, "that what happened this evening should not have happened." He looked around at the rest of them. "How did they get inside?"

"Mage Serek reported that all of the mages' wards are still intact," Captain Naithe said. "They checked everything along the wall and added new layers of protection, but there was no sign that anyone had tampered with any of their spells."

"And all of our men were at their assigned posts," the commander added. "At present, I cannot see how it was possible for them to get inside, Your Majesty. But we will get to the bottom of this. We did manage to capture a few of the invaders alive, but none of them are talking yet. In the meantime we've increased the guard all along the perimeter, but that's only a temporary solution. I think that if tonight's events have shown us anything, in addition to our defenses not being as secure as we imagined, it is that we cannot go on much longer as we are now. We are stretched too thin. We *must* have Kragnir's reinforcements." He looked at Captain Varyn, who nodded slightly, then back at the king. "We need to send Captain Varyn's company to Kragnir to deal with the blockade. Including the princess and her dragon."

Finally, Meg thought. She looked at her parents, but they weren't saying anything.

"You must see that they're right," Meg said. She couldn't believe they were going to argue with her about this again. Not after what had just happened.

"Meg—" her mother began.

"Merilyn," the king said softly, "we knew this day would come."

116

Her parents looked at each other for a long, silent moment. Then Meg's mother nodded, dropping her gaze.

Meg took her mother's hand. "You can't keep me safe by keeping me here," she said gently. "Look what happened tonight. And this is what I've been training for all this time."

"Yes, I know," her mother said. She looked up. "I know. And you're right, of course. It is still a hard thing, though. To send your daughter off to war."

"I'll have Jakl to keep me safe," Meg said. "You know he won't let anything happen to me."

"You saw how well they did tonight," Captain Varyn said. "They're ready. Both of them. I would never suggest sending them if they were not."

The queen nodded again. "Yes. Thank you, Captain. And you, Commander. Our kingdom could not be in better hands."

"I do have one condition," King Tormon said then. "The commander and I have discussed this before, and it has been an additional reason I've been reluctant to send the dragon out with the soldiers. He must be kept under control."

"What does that mean?" Meg asked.

"It means," her father said, "that although I know Jakl could simply set fire to all the enemy soldiers in his path, we cannot allow him to do so. *You* cannot allow him to do so. Your dragon is a tremendous advantage, and we need to let our enemies see that . . . but we also need to make sure that they don't fear him so much that they decide he must be destroyed at any cost. If we appear to be reckless with his power, if we allow ourselves to become what King Gerald already accuses us to be, then our enemies will see the dragon as a reason to continue the war rather than a reason to surrender. Do you understand? If they perceive him to be a weapon we will use without any restraint, without any regard for human life, they will not be able to stop until they kill him."

Meg sat back, trying to take this in. "So . . . you're saying he needs to be just scary enough to make them want to give up fighting, but not so scary that they cannot feel safe until he is dead."

He smiled at her, but it was not a happy smile. "Yes, my daughter. Exactly. Are you sure you can keep Jakl under your control? A battlefield is not a training field. You will be in danger, and I know that Jakl would do anything to protect you. Can you make him understand that protecting you means not completely destroying those who stand against us? Those men . . . they are our enemies. But they are also men, and they are fighting at the command of a king who acts without reason. We must continue to act *with* reason, no matter what happens. We need to be able to repair our relationships with Baustern and Farrell-Grast, at least, when all of this is over. And perhaps someday with Lourin as well. We cannot make them hate us beyond all reconciliation."

"I understand," Meg said. "And I'll make Jakl understand, too."

The king nodded. "Very well, then. I trust in you, Meg."

"We'll leave at first light," the commander said, standing. "I'll send a list of what you should bring, Your Highness. I hope you understand that we must all travel light. . . ."

Meg rolled her eyes. "I won't try to pack *all* of my fancy dresses. Don't worry." Captain Varyn cleared his throat, and Meg realized that her response might have been bordering on insolence. "Apologies, Commander. I will be grateful for your guidance in exactly what to pack."

The two men took their leave. Meg realized that she was still holding her mother's hand.

"Captain Varyn won't put me in any unnecessary danger," Meg said. *There will be more than enough perfectly necessary danger to go around*, she added silently.

"We're both very, very proud of you," her father said.

119

"But . . . please be careful. As careful as you can be, any-way, given the circumstances."

"I will. I promise."

There didn't seem to be very much else to say after that. It was an odd role reversal; it wasn't so long ago that her parents had been the ones telling Meg that every-thing was going to be all right. But ultimately they all knew that this was necessary, and besides, it was a prin-cess's duty to put the safety of the kingdom before her own. They had raised her to believe that, after all. They couldn't change their minds about it now.

She headed back to her rooms to tell Pela.

"I suppose they won't allow me to come with you," Pela said, sighing.

"No," Meg said. "And I wouldn't allow it, even if they would. It would be too dangerous."

"But who will . . . ?"

"Pela, I won't have to be making any decisions about what to wear or how to arrange my hair. The only thing I'll need to put on in the morning is my armor. They are going to send us a list of what to pack. And I'm hopeful that I won't be gone for very long."

"Well," Pela said briskly, "we do know that you'll need good riding clothes, at the very least." She got up and turned to the wardrobe, no doubt already calculating in her mind how many different outfits she could convince Meg to bring with her. She had just opened the doors when a clatter at the window made them both jump.

"What in the world?" Pela asked.

There was a dark shape on the other side of the glass.

Meg supposed she should be wary, especially given the evening's events, but she wasn't. Her heart was nearly leaping out of her chest, but not in fear. Or at least, not only in fear.

She ran to the window and opened the latch.

A big, ungainly crow pushed its way inside and fluttered awkwardly to the floor.

The girls looked at each other, then back at the bird.

"Blackie?" Pela said uncertainly.

Meg felt terrible, painful hope crushing her heart. She struggled to control it. *It might not be from him,* she thought. *It might not mean anything. It could have gotten lost, or maybe the magic wore off and it forgot what it was supposed to be doing, or . . .*

"Meg!" the bird croaked. In Calen's voice.

Meg fell to her knees beside it. Pela rushed over to join her on the floor, decorum forgotten.

Thank you, Bright Lady. Thank you, thank you, thank you!

"Meg!" it said again. And then: "Gods, Meg. I've missed you so much. And I'm so sorry."

Meg stared, her hands flying up to cover her mouth. The birds they sent out had only been able to say Calen's name. Meg felt tears welling up and didn't bother to try to stop them. *Oh, Calen.*

"Tell Serek and Anders that I'm sorry, too. And that if they have any brilliant ideas to get me out of here, I'm listening. I have one idea myself, but I don't think it's a very good one. This bird should be able to find me again. I don't know where I am, but the bird does now."

Five minutes later, they were knocking at the door to Serek's study. Meg hoped the mages weren't still at the infirmary. She had managed to stop crying, but it was hard not to start again. She was very nearly overcome with relief and hope and impatience. It took Anders forever to answer, and when he did, he looked annoyed.

"Princess, I told you, tonight is not—" He stopped abruptly as Meg held the bird up in her outstretched hands and looked at him meaningfully.

"Ah," he said. "Yes. Well, then. Um." He seemed to be thinking. He looked over his shoulder, then opened the door a bit wider and ushered them quickly into Calen's room, which was separate from the main room of the study. "Stay here, if you please. Quietly." He pointed at each of them, including the bird, then closed the door.

Faintly, they could hear him go back to where the other mages were presumably still in conference with one another. He said something that Meg couldn't quite make out, but she could hear Serek's irritated response just fine. "Leave? Anders, what are you —?"

"Sorry!" Anders said jovially and more loudly, speaking right over Serek's objections. "Had a vision! Can't explain. Everybody out. Not you, Serek, of course. Everyone else. I know, I know — we only just resumed our conversation, but now we must stop again. Terribly frustrating. We'll come find you in a bit."

There were confused and angry-sounding grumbles and the clomping of several pairs of feet walking out into the hallway. Then the main door closing.

"Did you really —?" Serek's voice began once they left.

"No," Anders said. "But you'll understand in a moment."

And then the door to Calen's room opened again, and Anders led the three of them into the main study. Serek's eyes widened when he saw the bird.

"Where did —?"

"It came right to my bedroom window," Meg said. She placed it down on the table. "Go on," she said to the bird. "Say your message again."

She didn't know if it understood somehow or was just trained — spelled? — to repeat its message whenever she addressed it. But it spoke the same words it had earlier, still in Calen's voice.

Serek sat down hard in his chair. Anders just stared.

Meg felt the tears starting again, but didn't care. "He's all right," she said. "He's all right and we found him and now we can get him back."

Serek and Anders didn't move.

"What?" Meg asked, frowning at them. Why didn't they seem happy? "It worked! Your bird spell worked! It found him, and he was able to send a message back! Wasn't that the idea?"

Serek rubbed a hand across his face. "Yes. Yes, of course it was. It's just —"

"That's a very advanced spell," Anders put in. "We'd hoped he would be able to send some sort of message back, some indication that the bird had found him, but this — I couldn't have done this."

"Is it truly that much harder to make the bird say a few sentences than it was to make it say one word?" Pela asked.

"Yes," Serek and Anders said together.

"Oh," said Pela.

"And he sent the bird back to you," Serek continued. "It should have returned directly here, where it was released. Somehow he altered its directions enough to do that, and managed to embed the spell with an entire message. . . ."

Meg still didn't really understand. "Well, so . . . that's good, isn't it? Now we have much more information than if he'd only sent back a single word, or no word at all. We know he's okay, and we know he wants to come home. . . ." Of course he wanted to come home. She wasn't sure why she'd even said that. "Why aren't you happy about this?"

The mages looked at each other. "We are happy, Princess," Serek said at last. "It's just . . . a bit of a shock, that's all. Calen . . . Calen couldn't have done this when I last saw him. He's clearly learned a lot since then."

Oh. "Well . . . that makes sense, though, doesn't it? If Mage Krelig took Calen away in order to use his ability, he'd probably have to be teaching him things. It doesn't mean . . . I'm sure Calen's just doing what he has to while he's there."

Serek and Anders exchanged another glance.

"Stop that!" Meg shouted. "You heard his message. He wants to come home. He doesn't want to be there, even if he is learning things. If he wanted to stay he never would have sent the bird back to us."

"Sorry, Princess," Serek said. "I'm sure you're right."

"Well, almost sure," Anders said. Serek gave him a look, and for a wonder, the older mage subsided.

"We need to try to figure out what Calen did, exactly, and what we can send back to help him escape," Serek went on. "Now that we've made contact, we must move very quickly. Every communication presents a risk that Mage Krelig could discover what Calen is doing. We need a plan. Very soon."

"Tell me how I can help," Meg said at once.

"Tomorrow," Serek said. "First I think Anders and I need to spend some time examining the bird." They all looked at the crow, who had apparently gotten bored with the conversation and was now pecking at a tiny spot on the table.

"All right," Meg said. "Then, in the morning—"

"Princess," Pela broke in quietly. "You won't be here in the morning."

Oh. Right.

Everyone was looking at her now. Except the bird.

"Where are you going?" Anders asked.

"I'm going to Kragnir," Meg said. "To fight in the war. Jakl and I leave with the soldiers at first light."

"Ah," Serek said. He rubbed his face again.

"Well," Anders said, "that's sure to be exciting!"

"But I can't go *now*. I need to be here. I . . ." Meg let her words trail off. She had to go, of course. She knew she did. And . . . it might be a little while before she came back, she realized. She'd been letting herself imagine that this whole Kragnir business wouldn't take very long at all. But how could she know? They would have to get there, fight the Lourin soldiers, *win the battle*, and then get back home. It might be weeks before she returned.

But — *Calen*. She wanted to cry. Again.

"We can manage without you," Serek said finally. "You were essential for finding Calen in the first place, but now that this bird knows how to find him, we'll be able to contact him again."

"But what about going to get him? I thought — you'll need Jakl, to go and bring him back. . . ."

"Not necessarily," Serek said. "And in fact, that would probably not be our best choice in any case. I think secrecy is going to be important. If Mage Krelig saw or sensed your dragon approaching his hiding place . . . that could make things very difficult for Calen. And for Jakl. And for you."

That was probably true, she supposed. But . . .

"There's no sense arguing, Princess," Pela said gently.

127

"What is, must be. I will help them as much as I can in your stead."

"Thank you, Pela." She looked at the mages. "Pela can help. Please allow her, if you see a way."

"All right," Serek said. "We can't do anything until we try to decipher this spell, but then — yes, all right. Thank you, Pela, for your assistance."

"Make sure to tell Calen not to send his next bird to me!" Meg said. She was almost sorry to have remembered, but having the crow find her in the middle of a battlefield wasn't going to help anything. Even if it would let her hear his voice.

"Yes," Anders assured her. "We will."

It will be all right, Meg told herself. She had to trust Serek and Anders to take care of this. And of course they could; it's not like she was the one who was going to be casting the spells. . . . She just thought she'd be here to help. To know what was happening. To make sure that they looked out for Calen's best interests. To make sure that Serek, especially, didn't change his mind.

She took Pela's hand in the hallway as they walked back to her rooms.

"Don't let them lose faith in him," she said. "Promise me. Don't let them start to think that they shouldn't bring him home after all. I don't care how much new magic he's learned. He's still Calen."

"Yes, Princess," Pela said. "I know. I promise."

And with that, Meg let Pela lead her the rest of the way without speaking. She would go to sleep, and then she would wake up and report for duty. And she would do everything she could to help end the fighting as quickly as possible so she could get back home.

CHAPTER SEVEN

ONE OF THE THINGS MAGE KRELIG wanted to use the other mages for, it seemed, was target practice.

They hadn't learned the rules yet. One or another of them was constantly making some misstep, inspiring Krelig to use the unfortunate transgressor as an example for the rest. Today it was Darelin's turn. She was a moderately marked young woman with long brown hair that she liked to twist into different elaborate shapes from day to day. This afternoon it was a pretty arrangement of looped coils that ended up looking something like a flower. Or . . . it *had* been pretty. Before.

Krelig had apparently neglected to tell their guests that they were not allowed to cast any divination spells. Calen had known that rule from the start; Krelig had told him that he was never to attempt any kind of divination, ever, along with a great assortment of other instructions and restrictions, right at the beginning, when it was all

Calen could do to keep himself from drowning in confusion and despair and terror. Some of Krelig's rules had obvious reasons behind them. Some didn't. If you were smart, you followed them all anyway. But it did help to know what they were.

As soon as Darelin entered the training hall, Krelig had called out to her from where he was leaning against the far wall.

"What magic were you just practicing in your room before you came down here, Mage Darelin?"

She froze in the entranceway, then hesitantly answered, "Just — just a card reading, Master."

Calen stared at her, aghast, but then quickly realized from the confused expressions on other mages' faces that many of them had not known about that rule. He generally didn't feel much sympathy for the other mages, no matter what Krelig did to them. They were here by choice, he reminded himself often, and deserved whatever they got. Usually. But he couldn't help feeling a little sorry for Darelin right then.

"There will be no divination of any kind," Krelig said. He was standing up straight now, facing her across the room. The mages near her started edging carefully away. "No readings of stones," he added, speaking calmly and sending a red bolt of magic at Darelin that knocked her backward against the wall. "Nor blood," he continued, walking toward her and hitting her with another red spell. "Nor cards." He was standing over her now, looking down at her cowering form.

"But — but *why?*" she asked, daring to look up at him in confusion.

Calen closed his eyes briefly. That was not the right response.

"Why?" Krelig repeated in a harsh falsetto, mimicking her inflection. "Why? Because I have no need for your mediocre readings and portents. My own sightings have shown me everything I need to know about what lies ahead." He pointed at her, and she gasped and began slapping frantically at her own head a moment before the smell of burning hair reached the rest of them. "I will not have anyone trying to seek out some alternate future, some less favorable reading to try to interfere with my plans."

"I wasn't!" Darelin protested, still trying without success to put out the magical fire that was slowly consuming her looped strands. "I swear, I only wanted to help, I —"

"*Do you think I need your help?*" Krelig asked this last in a furious whisper, but they could all hear him in the otherwise still and silent room. Darelin's only response was her desperate sobs of pain and fear. Krelig stood looking down at her for a minute more, then shook his head and turned away. He sent one last spell as he did so, and Darelin screamed as the rest of her hair went up in a *whoosh* of flame.

"You may heal her scalp," Krelig said offhandedly to the first other mage he noticed. He walked slowly back to his place against the wall as the other mage rushed forward to heal Darelin. He couldn't do anything about her hair, though.

At Krelig's impatient glare around the room, the rest of them hurried to form the half circle in which they usually began each training session. They all averted their eyes from Darelin's bald head as, still crying softly, she took her place in the line a moment later.

Calen continued his private lessons with Mage Krelig every morning, but afternoons now involved all of the mages who had come to the castle. Krelig had them practice casting at one another, defending against more than one magical assault at a time, working in teams, and working alone against the rest of the group. Serek had always refused to teach Calen how to fight or even how to effectively defend himself with magic. Now Krelig wanted him to learn all he could about it, and despite everything, Calen was happy to.

Because he needed to know how to fight and defend himself, of course.

But also because he was really, really good at it.

He was still testing the new limits of his ability. The strength of his spells still varied, but there was no question that even his weakest attempts were now much more powerful. Calen knew that Krelig had taught him enormous amounts since he'd been here, but he had thought he was still far behind most other mages. And he was, in terms of experience and practice — those who had been training for years and years, who had started younger than he had and who were much older now, those mages had accumulated a wealth of life experience that no amount of training could replace. And yet all the mages who had arrived to join Mage Krelig so far (and more of them kept coming, nearly every day) seemed slow and clumsy to him. At least, a lot of the time. Calen knew some of this was because of his ability to see the colors — it helped him to react more quickly, and certainly to defend himself more effectively. But it was also because he was much more powerful than they were.

That was sometimes a frightening thought. He wasn't exactly sure why; he wanted to be powerful, didn't he? He *needed* to be powerful to be able to help defeat Mage Krelig.

But sometimes he was afraid that he was starting to enjoy these lessons a little too much.

The other mages always got the worst of it in the group lessons, and today's was no exception. Krelig paired Calen up with Helena against a group of ten other mages. Calen still didn't like her; she always had something to say and was particularly fond of showing off. She practically crowed anytime she bested one of the others. She was talented, though. He had to give her that. He thought she was the strongest of all the traitor mages Krelig had recruited so far. She and Calen stood back to back, and the other mages surrounded them in a large circle, firing anything they wanted as long as it wasn't actually lethal. Krelig was quite clear about how he would feel if they killed one another off without his express permission.

Calen and Helena had cast a combined form of shield that was stronger than either of them could cast alone. The other mages were having a hard time breaking through it, although once they started teaming up in their attacks, more of the spells started coming close. Calen tightened his focus as a particularly nasty-looking red spell came hurtling at his face. There was purple mixed in as well, and he could tell that it was meant to cause some kind of painful disfiguring. That was allowed;

it was the kind of thing Krelig could fix afterward . . . if he chose to.

Calen knocked it aside but then stared as it circled around and started toward his face again. Somehow the mage who had cast it had connected it to Calen in some way. Made it seek him out even after it had been pushed off course. That was fascinating, but he would have to think about it later. Right now he just wanted to stop it from reaching him. He felt the shield beginning to flicker and weaken as both he and Helena grew more tired. That wasn't good. Even with his new reserves of power, he couldn't keep going forever. And he used up a lot of energy in his morning lessons with Krelig. The mage who had sent the targeted spell — his name was Cheriyon — must have sensed the weakening shield, because he grinned and sent a second targeted spell after the first. Calen knocked them both aside again with his own spells, but they continued to turn back to find him every time. He had to find a way to — there!

Deep within the swirl of purple and red was a thread of white — something in that thread was what told the spell to keep trying to find Calen. If he could send a counterspell just at that part, with new information inside it, he might be able to . . .

He knocked the spells off course a few more times

as he tried to reason out his approach, then fired his own tight beams of white and orange and purple not at the entire spells, but just at those threads of white. He watched the spells connect, and then smiled, gratified, as they turned as one and flew back at Cheriyon. The mage felt his own spells coming back at him and screamed. Too late, he tried to raise a shield against them, but his surprise and panic made him react too slowly. The spells slammed into him, both at once, and the rest of the mages all stopped what they were doing to watch as his skin began to slide right off his face, as if he were melting.

It looked horrible: painful and disgusting and just — just awful. Calen felt sick knowing how close he had come to being the one who suffered that fate. Sick, and angry. Why would anyone want to do that to another person? Krelig made them practice fighting each other, and he rewarded innovation and creativity, but he hadn't directly ordered them to be monsters.

They all continued to stand there, staring. No one dared to interfere, of course. Krelig waited a few more seconds and then, mercifully (for all of them — the gargly shrieking was getting hard to take, and Calen was sure he was going to have nightmares about what was happening to the man's face) sent a healing spell at Cheriyon. Calen watched carefully to see how the healing spell was put together. It wasn't just yellow energy; there was orange to neutralize the original spell, and green, probably to help regenerate the skin that had melted off. A kinder person would also have included some blue to reduce the pain. Cheriyon screamed even louder when the healing spell hit him, then seemed to pass out. He fell backward onto the floor, his skin still remolding itself into shape around his bones.

The other mages had also watched the healing spell carefully; they all wanted to know what to do if someone ever sent that spell at them! But without the colors, the others had to rely on their varying abilities to sense the magic being used around them, which was more difficult the more complex the spell. It was like they were blind, Calen thought sometimes with pity. And yet from what Calen could tell, Krelig had honed his own sensing ability to be just as sharp as Calen's. So maybe it was just a matter of power and ability after all.

"That's enough for today," Mage Krelig said. "Someone get him back to his room." He gestured in Cheriyon's general direction, then turned and walked out. The rest of them looked at one another for a moment, and then Lestern, who had arrived the same day as Cheriyon, sighed and walked over to the fallen man. Calen could still see the last vestiges of Mage Krelig's spell at work around his face.

Lestern stood there looking down at Cheriyon, frowning. Then purple energy started gathering around his hands. A few seconds later, he pointed his fingers at Cheriyon, and the spell lifted him several inches off the ground. When Lestern turned and began to walk away, the unconscious Cheriyon floated silently after him.

Calen watched them go. That had been odd — the way the purple energy had appeared around his hands so long before he began to cast the spell. Usually the energy appeared only at the moment it was being gathered and cast. Maybe Lestern had just been casting really slowly?

"Those two are a real pair, huh?"

Calen turned to see Helena standing beside him.

"Not friends, exactly," she went on. "Cheriyon's too much of a worm to have friends. But they look out for each other all the same. You can see it sometimes. Like now."

Calen grunted noncommittally. Helena had started trying to have conversations with him lately, but he had no desire to talk to her. He turned to go.

"Wait," she said. "Thanks for showing me how to do that shield spell today. I've never tried anything like that before."

139

Calen paused, on the brink of walking away . . . then turned back around. This was the most polite she'd ever been to him. It seemed unnecessarily rude to ignore her when she was thanking him. "It was a good spell, with both of us," he admitted. "Saved us from the melting skin thing, maybe."

She raised an eyebrow at him. "It saved us from a lot of things, but not that. I saw what you did. You found some way to turn Cheriyon's spells right back at him. How did you do that?"

"How much can you sense, when other people are casting?" he asked her in turn, dodging the question. Krelig had forbade him from discussing how he used the colors with anyone else. Not that he had any intention of doing so. Everyone knew he could see them, or that he *claimed* to see them, but he didn't think they fully understood exactly how he could put that ability to use.

"Not as much as you," she said grudgingly. "But a lot. More than most of the others. They seem so slow sometimes! I hate when Mage Krelig teams me up with them." She looked around, as she almost always did when she said Krelig's name; Calen thought she did it without even realizing it.

"Yeah," Calen said. "Me, too." It was true. Helena was really the only one who could keep up in most ways.

But he still didn't like her. He supposed, however, that he could be civil. And maybe he'd be able to learn some things from her as well.

They started walking toward the dining hall; it was getting close enough to dinnertime that it didn't really make sense to go back to their rooms. After a moment, Calen asked, "Was it hard, getting here from the Magistratum? I didn't — I think you know that I got here in a very different way from the rest of you."

She shrugged. "Yeah. I mean obviously it wasn't something any of us could talk about openly, wanting to come here. And everyone there was getting so paranoid, accusing everyone else of being a traitor. . . . We couldn't use magic to get out. We spent a lot of nights in the woods, cold and dirty, trying to get far enough away that they wouldn't sense us casting before we could even light a cursed fire. I was just with Mage Dothier at first. We met up with Chan, Pelerio, and Scoral a few days out."

Calen hesitated, then asked what he really wanted to know. "But why? I came because I had to, and while I'll admit now that it's been worth it" — he sent a silent apology to Meg for the lie, or maybe for the fact that he wasn't entirely certain it really *was* a lie — "I never would have dared to come on my own, I don't think. What made you . . . ?"

"You don't know what it was like, after you and Mage Serek disappeared," she said. "Things went a little crazy. People accused Mage Brevera of killing you, then accused you and Mage Serek of . . . well, all kinds of things. And I started to realize that it was only going to get worse. The council had lost control; everyone was forming these little groups, traveling in packs. . . . it was awful. And then . . . Mage Krelig started sending us dreams."

"Dreams?"

"Recruiting dreams, I suppose. I don't know if everyone got them; it wasn't the sort of thing you felt comfortable talking about. He spoke to us. To me. About how the Magistratum was dying, and why did I want to be a part of it anyway, when I could be so much more . . ."

"That sounds like him," Calen agreed.

"Finally Dothier told me one night that he was thinking of coming to join Mage Krelig. He claimed that he thought the accusations against Krelig might be as false as some of the other ones, for all we knew. I don't know if any part of that was true, but either way . . . we could see that the Magistratum was falling apart, and if Mage Krelig was going to end up winning anyway, why not join him now, when it could do us some good? Come over as allies instead of conquered enemies?"

"That . . . makes some sense, I guess," Calen said.

"Yeah," Helena said. She didn't sound entirely like she believed it anymore, though, Calen thought.

"How did you know where to come? If everyone knows where we are, why haven't they attacked us already?"

She shook her head. "Not everyone knows. In fact, hardly anyone does. We didn't know, not for a while. Once we got out, we started trying to reach out to Mage Krelig magically, to let him know that we wanted to join him. Eventually he must have heard us. Suddenly Scoral just knew which way to go, and then in a few more days we were here."

They walked in silence for a little way. Then Helena stopped and looked at him.

"He's — he's really crazy, though, isn't he? It's not just that he's so much more powerful than the rest of us. The way he gets when he's angry, the way he gets carried away with the discipline sometimes . . ."

Now Calen had to fight the urge to look around. It wasn't safe to say things like that out loud. You never knew who was listening, even when there wasn't anyone nearby. But it wouldn't be safe to tell her that out loud, either. Calen looked at her as significantly as he could. He held her gaze steadily as he said, "No, he's not crazy. He's just . . . different from the rest of us. You'll see.

143

You just need to do what you're told, and learn as much as you can. He's going to lead all of us back to where we belong in the end."

He kept looking her right in the eye. He didn't know why he was trying to warn her. She must know, anyway, that it was dangerous to talk that way. He knew she was terrified of Krelig; she had been ever since that first day that he'd reached out and cut her, so casually. She'd never quite regained that same overconfident swagger that had so immediately annoyed him.

She looked back at him, wide-eyed. Then she nodded. "Of course. You're right. I just . . . find him so intimidating, I guess. I'll just keep trying to learn, like you said. I've already learned so much."

"Yeah," Calen said. He started walking again, and she fell into step beside him. "Me, too."

That night the crow appeared again on his balcony.

This time when it spoke his name, it was Serek's voice that he heard. Calen was a little disappointed, although he knew that was stupid. And mostly he was ecstatic to know that his message had reached them. But it had been so good to hear Meg's voice that first time. He wanted to hear it again.

This message was longer than the first; it looked like

144

they'd used another version of his own message-spell this time. Mostly the message just said that they were glad he was all right and that they were working on a way to get him home. He thought they must not have gotten very far, though, because they asked what his one idea was. He'd been afraid of that. His idea made him very nervous. But they didn't have a lot of time. He suspected that Serek and Anders knew that as well as he did.

It also said that he had to send the bird back to Serek and Anders, not to Meg this time. It didn't say why, though. He thought about whether to follow those instructions or not. He liked the idea of Meg being the one to receive the crow. He liked feeling like he was talking to her rather than to Serek and Anders. But they must have put that in there for a reason. Maybe it was too dangerous for the bird to seek out Meg right now. He had no idea what was going on there, after all.

It's not because she doesn't want the birds to come to her, he assured himself. She helped the first time. She would still be helping if there wasn't a good reason not to. Just because he didn't know the reason didn't mean it wasn't a good one.

He stayed out on the balcony the whole time the bird was there. He didn't know why, but somehow it seemed safer in the open air. He thought there was more of a

145

chance of Krelig sensing something if he talked to the bird inside. He hoped that it was safer outside, anyway. He didn't really have any other options.

He gave his new message to the bird, then fed it some of the bread he'd saved from his bird-treat stockpile. "More where that came from," he told it. "Lots more, if you get me back in one piece, my friend."

The bird cawed quietly at him in its own voice and then lumbered off into the dark sky.

Calen's days began to fall into a new kind of rhythm. They still always started with his morning lessons, which he now looked forward to without reservation. He couldn't help it. Every day, every single day, he learned something new. Something significant. Some whole new way of looking and thinking and working with magic. He told himself it was all right to love the learning. He deserved to get something good out of being here, didn't he? After everything he was enduring, everything he had sacrificed? And the stronger he got, the better his chances were of being able to help Serek and the others defeat Mage Krelig. It was all part of the plan. It didn't change anything that he happened to like this part.

It helped that Krelig didn't punish him very often

anymore. He was just as interested as Calen in finding out how deep those new reserves of power were.

And the power itself was . . . incredible. Easy spells were easier; harder spells were easier. He was casting things now that he'd never even imagined being able to cast before.

One morning Krelig showed him how to stop a mage from being able to cast. It was the same spell Sen Eva had used on him on the day Mage Krelig had returned. It was ridiculously simple, or at least, it seemed so now. The only trick was that once someone cast it on you, you needed help to remove it. Krelig had removed the one Sen Eva had cast somewhere during their long, terrible journey to wherever they were now, but Calen had been too distracted by betraying his friends to even notice until much later.

Krelig wouldn't allow Calen to practice on him, of course. But he encouraged him to use it on one of the others during their next group lesson. He also taught Calen how to prevent someone else from using it on him. These moments, when Krelig conspired with him against the other mages, were always . . . confusing. Calen didn't ever want to feel like he and Krelig were on the same side. But he didn't want to be on the traitor mages' side, either. And of course he wasn't on either of those

147

sides, not really. But he had to do so much pretending; sometimes it took him a minute to remember what the truth was.

The group lessons were educational in other ways. The other mages had learned to be wary of him; they knew that he tended to show up with new tricks up his sleeve. And they were beginning to understand how powerful he really was. Sometimes when they looked at him, he could see the fear in their eyes, and he was glad. They should be afraid. A day would come when he could stop pretending, and then they'd find out exactly what they had to be afraid of.

But not yet, he reminded himself regularly. He'd never really come close to losing control during a lesson. He'd just had occasional moments of wishing he could. He hated them so much.

Except for Helena.

That had been hard to accept at first, but he knew that it was true. She and Calen had fallen into a pattern as well. After group lessons, they would discuss what they'd seen and learned, and practice some of the spells they'd watched the others craft, or think of new ways to defend against attacks. He still didn't *like* her, but he couldn't deny that he didn't quite hate her, either.

Evenings varied: if Krelig was there, there might be

additional lessons; if not, there might be more free time to practice on their own.

And every night, Calen sat on his balcony, watching for crows.

One evening, practicing with Helena again after the group lesson had ended, Calen noticed the colors around her hands before she cast, as he had that time with Lestern. Just for a second, maybe two. But . . . early. Earlier than should have been possible.

He paid closer attention for the rest of their practice session. Not every time, but often, he could see the colors gather before she raised her hands to cast. She was like most mages in that she used her hands to direct the magic once she'd crafted the spell. Krelig was the only one Calen had ever seen who hardly ever needed to use his hands. Even he still did sometimes, although most often only when it didn't matter. Calen thought about how he'd struck him across the dining hall table without moving a muscle, but had gestured to summon his glass of wine.

They practiced attacking each other — just with harmless tag spells, nothing that would hurt beyond a tiny pinch — as they often did; Krelig loved to make his mages attack one another, and perfecting their abilities to cast and defend at the same time was probably the most

149

important part of their training. It made sense. When they fought the other mages, the ones who opposed Krelig (*the good mages*, as Calen always thought of them), that's primarily what they would be doing, after all.

Usually Calen and Helena were almost evenly matched in terms of speed when it was just the two of them. Helena got flustered sometimes when she had to fend off multiple attackers at once, but one-on-one, she was often as fast as Calen. Not as strong, not anymore, but just as fast. Sometimes even faster. But tonight was different. He kept seeing the colors seconds before she actually cast something at him. Which gave him a few extra seconds to prepare.

"All right, stop!" she said after he had intercepted her latest attack as soon as she released it. "How are you doing that?"

"Doing what?" Calen asked. They were both breathing hard at this point. Physically they were just standing there, facing each other on opposite sides of the room, but the constant casting and concentration was hard work.

She walked over to him, rubbing a hand against her forehead, which was glistening with sweat. "It's like you know what I'm going to cast before I do!" she said. "Am I giving myself away somehow, all of a sudden?"

Yes, Calen thought. *Gods, that's exactly what's happening. I can see her spells before she casts them.* But he knew, without one shred of doubt, that this was something he should keep to himself.

"Maybe I'm just getting better at reading you," Calen said. "You do sort of make a face before you cast certain things."

She punched him in the arm. "I do not!"

Just like Meg, he thought, with a strange mix of affection and annoyance and a sadness that seemed to pierce right through him. But he couldn't dwell on that; he had to distract her.

He shrugged. "Sorry," he said. "You do. You sort of scrunch up your eyebrows. Especially when you're casting something you think is going to hurt." He paused. "Or, you know, *would* hurt, if you could ever land one on me."

She gave a shocked laugh, raising her eyebrows. "I'll land one on you right now!" she said, punching his arm again, and then the other one.

Calen started laughing, too, fending her off. Or trying to; it was harder to avoid her fists than her spells.

"Okay, okay!" he said. "I'm sorry!"

"Take it back!" she said, still swinging.

He hesitated, pretending to consider. "Well . . ."

151

She lunged at him suddenly, and then they were on the ground. Before he knew what was happening, she was sitting on top of him, pinning his arms to the ground. Gods, she was strong!

"Take it back, *apprentice*! Or I'll make you sorry!"

She was still laughing, but something seemed different now. He didn't think she was angry, not really. Just . . . different. He couldn't quite figure out how, though.

"Okay," Calen said. "I take it back. I do. You don't scrunch up your eyebrows. Ever. They barely ever move at all. Not like your hands, which always twitch just a little before you —"

"Oh, that's it," she said, and started tickling him.

"Stop!" Calen cried through his laughter. It was somehow both excruciating and delightful; he couldn't quite bear it, but at the same time he didn't entirely want her to stop. "I'm sorry! I mean it! I was just teasing!"

"Promise you'll never do it again."

"I promise! I'm sorry!"

She tickled him for a few more seconds, then sat back and looked down at him. They were even more sweaty now.

"How — how did you learn to do that?" Calen had never been tackled and tickled within an inch of his life like that before. In fact, his tickling experience was decidedly on the small side.

"I had five brothers, growing up," she said, smirking. "I know how to get boys to behave."

"I'll say," Calen said. He pushed her off, but gently.

She let herself be pushed, and they sat there on the floor, recovering.

"I don't really have a tell, do I?" she asked after a moment.

"No," Calen said. "Really. I'm not sure why I was so fast before. Just having a good night, I guess."

She looked at him, her expression unreadable. "Yeah," she said. "Me, too."

She climbed to her feet and headed for the door.

Calen stayed where he was, wondering what she'd meant.

CHAPTER EIGHT

MEG WAS AWAKE LONG BEFORE PELA came to rouse her.

Both girls were quiet while Pela helped her dress. Meg was relieved to see that Pela had selected a very simple outfit — plain and practical riding clothes in a color similar to the soldiers' uniforms. Meg smiled at Pela in the mirror as the younger girl finished tying Meg's hair back in two sturdy braids and bound them together with a thick band that matched the rest of her clothing.

"Thank you, Pela. So much. For everything."

Pela flushed, but she couldn't quite hide her own smile. "Think nothing of it, Princess. And don't speak to me as though you're never going to see me again. You and Jakl will cow these Lourin soldiers and be back home before you know it."

"Of course."

After one last going-over to make sure Meg looked as well turned out as she could manage, Pela released her. Meg kissed Pela's hands and turned toward the door. Then she turned back.

"Don't forget what I said," she told Pela.

"I won't, Princess. If you're not back in time, I'll make sure they get Apprentice Calen back home safe."

Meg nodded and then opened the door and walked out.

Jakl was waiting for her in his field, sitting up alertly under the still-dark sky. He was looking forward to getting to fight, she knew.

"Ready?" she asked him. Needlessly, of course. He was more than ready. Meg supposed she was really asking herself. But that was needless, too. She had to be ready, didn't she? It was time to go.

She climbed up, and he flew them over to the soldiers' barracks.

They were early; the rest of Varyn's company hadn't yet arrived. Captain Varyn was there, though, and he came out to meet her.

"You're ready for this," he said, watching as she slid from her dragon's back. "The both of you. I know you're going to make us proud."

"Thank you, Captain."

He looked at her a moment in silence. Then he said, "What the king said last night is correct, of course, Your

155

Highness. It is essential that you keep Jakl in line. But at the same time, you must not forget that we are at war. The men you will face out there on the battlefield are our enemies. If given the chance, they would kill us all. You must not hold back more than necessary. Do you understand? I'll need you and the dragon under control, but still at full ferocity. We *must* clear the way for Kragnir's forces."

"I — yes, sir." Meg spoke with more confidence than she felt. She believed she'd made the situation clear to Jakl through the link last night before she fell asleep. As clear as it was to her, anyway. But it all still felt very . . . complicated. How would she know how far she could let him go? How would she be able to tell where the line was? *You'll just figure it out*, she told herself. *You will do what you have to do. And you'll help Jakl to do only what he must.*

"All right, then." Captain Varyn raised his head to gaze up at Jakl, who was sitting proudly on his haunches. "I hope your dragon is all rested up and ready for some heavy lifting."

"He's ready for whatever you need, Captain."

It turned out that the first thing Captain Varyn needed was for Jakl to carry most of the armor and other supplies on the way to Kragnir, to let the horses travel lighter and faster. Jakl had already practiced carrying supplies (as well as soldiers) in the large cases and carts the castle carpenters had constructed for those purposes. There were several different models, some with wheels, some without, with different interior layouts and sizes, all able to be rigged up to a harness and ferried by dragon to wherever they needed to go. He'd never carried any of them all day for several days in a row before, but Meg had no doubt that he could do it. When she thought the question at him, he was disdainful of Captain Varyn's assumption that this would even qualify as "heavy lifting" for an enormous powerful creature like himself.

As the other soldiers began to assemble, carrying gear and supplies, several came over to speak with her or say hello to Jakl. They'd developed the habit of touching him for luck, and Jakl permitted this with an interesting blend of pride and amusement. Meg had come to know all of them over the time they'd trained together, and liked them in addition to respecting them. They were good men (although some seemed little older than boys, really), and while many had been hesitant about Jakl at first — and about her — she'd watched them change their minds as they saw what she and the dragon could do. She thought they were all, herself included, excited to see how well they could fight together in a real battle.

She noticed some faces missing, though, as she looked around.

"Where are the others?" she asked Zeb as he came up to give Jakl's neck a quick pat.

"We're down five this morning," he said. "Wounded in the fighting last night. Nothing life-threatening, but Captain says they're not to come. They're mad as — uh, well, they're pretty mad about it, Princess."

"I don't blame them," she said truthfully. "I'd be mad, too. Although the captain's right, of course."

"One more score to settle when we get the chance, eh?"

Meg nodded emphatically. "Oh, yes."

When she looked around again, she saw Devan walking toward the supply cart. He blushed when he saw her looking, but held up his bundles of gear to show her that her armor was included in his haul. She nodded to show that she understood.

"Does he *ever* speak?" she asked Zeb. "Or is it that he just won't speak to me?"

Zeb followed her gaze to where Devan was tossing his bundles into the cart. "Ah, he's a quiet one; that's certain. He is *capable* of speech; I've heard him. But he doesn't talk much, and never to girls."

"But . . . why not?"

Zeb shrugged. "Just shy, I expect. He's never said, as

you might have guessed. Top theories among the rest of us are that he never met a girl until he came up to join the army, or that he was raised entirely by women his whole life until he escaped to come here and has learned to be afraid of them." He flashed her a quick apologetic grin. "No offense meant, Princess."

She laughed. "None taken. I just wish he wasn't afraid of *me*."

"Oh, he's not," Zeb said, sounding surprised. "I've seen the way he smiles around you. You should see him with other girls. You're the only one he can be around for more than a second without fleeing in terror."

"Oh," Meg said. "I'm glad to know that. But I'm still going to get him to talk to me one day."

"I hope you do," Zeb said. "Lots of the boys have been betting on how long it will take. I've got a decent amount riding on your success, Princess." He flashed her another grin, this one decidedly less apologetic, and then ran off before she could decide whether she was furious or flattered or both.

By the time first light fully arrived, the supplies were packed and everyone was ready to go. In addition to their own company, they were bringing a pair of field-trained medics and several of their assistants, as well as a cook and a team of camp hands who would take care of the horses and other tasks as needed. When Meg commented on all the extra people, the soldiers near her laughed.

"This is nothing, Princess," Erik told her by way of explanation. "Usually there's a whole army of nonfighting types — Captain's only bringing the absolute essentials this time."

Meg had never thought about it before, she realized — how many people it took to maintain an army in the field. Blacksmiths, leatherworkers, medics, cooks, laundresses . . . there was a long list, apparently. The commander and Captain Varyn were counting on this not being a very long engagement, or else they'd never be able to get away with the small number they were bringing along.

When the soldiers formed ranks, Meg climbed up onto her dragon, checked the rigging once more to make sure the supply cart was securely fastened to Jakl's harness, and waited for Captain Varyn's command to fly out.

The soldiers were on horseback and would travel at least part of the way on the winding roads through the Hunterheart Forest. Meg and Jakl would risk drawing too much attention flying above them there, and since Varyn wanted to maintain the element of surprise as long as possible, he sent them on a separate course, different each day, with instructions on where to meet the rest of the company each night. She was also supposed to fly low enough at certain points to be easily seen by enemy soldiers, helping to mislead them regarding the dragon's true destination. Captain Varyn had gone over the maps with her beforehand, but he'd also sent a soldier along to ride with her, just in case she got lost or ran into any trouble. She couldn't imagine what sort of trouble he anticipated that one soldier would be better equipped to handle than her dragon, but she didn't argue. It was Liame riding with her that first day; he was another quiet one, although nowhere near as quiet as Devan. Meg didn't mind; she liked being alone with her thoughts and her link with Jakl while they flew.

They traveled until near sunset and then met up with the others as they made camp. Meg had a tent of her own to sleep in, and with Jakl curled up outside, there was no question about her safety.

Still, she had trouble finding sleep. Jakl was his usual comforting presence, but she still felt . . . lonely, she supposed. Lonely, and impatient, and anxious.

Why are you so eager to be in battle? she asked herself for about the hundredth time. But she knew why. She had never been any good at waiting. When you knew something was inevitable, even something unpleasant — *especially* something unpleasant — the best course was generally to get it over and done with as soon as possible. And truthfully, the prospect of this battle did not seem entirely unpleasant to her. She *wanted* to fight the Lourin soldiers. She wanted to punish them for what they'd done last night, for what they were still doing with their blockade of the Kragnir pass and the ongoing fighting all around her father's lands, for everything since this stupid war had started. Her people had only just settled the last war with Maerlie's wedding; they deserved more than a few months of peace. They deserved a lifetime of peace. And she was going to help them get it.

She must have slept eventually, because suddenly it was morning. They struck camp, and Meg and Jakl flew out again on their own course with the supplies, this time with Zeb for company.

The journey was supposed to take them seven days, but Captain Varyn had warned Meg that nothing ever went truly according to plan in war (or most other times, either), and in the end it took them twelve. They lost two days to a bad storm that was too severe to ride through and left several fallen trees across the road that had to be dragged away or chopped through before the horses could press on. The other three were spent diverting from their planned route to avoid encountering a company of Lourin soldiers the Trelian advance scouts had discovered. They couldn't afford to waste time or strength along the way; they needed to throw everything they had at the enemies blocking the Kragnir pass.

On the evening of the twelfth day, they prepared for what would happen in the morning. They were still a few hours' ride from where their scouts had told them the Lourin soldiers were. Varyn's plotted course would let them get as close as possible without being seen before they attacked. Jakl would walk with the horses, on the ground — an idea he found entirely incomprehensible, but he understood that it was what Meg wanted, so that's what he would do.

Meg thought she would lie awake a long time that night, but to her surprise she fell asleep almost at once. In the morning, she thought perhaps it was because the waiting was finally over. Gods, but she hated waiting! Today they would finally get to fight. And win.

They left all the extra supplies and everyone who wasn't a soldier behind when they headed out. Jakl found the slow walking ridiculous, but he tolerated it in as good a humor as he could manage. Meg kept catching bits of sarcastic dragon-thoughts about snail-paced horses and poor wingless humans who had to ride them or move

163

even more slowly. *We'll get our chance to fly*, she thought at him. *Just you wait.*

Finally, Captain Varyn called a halt. Everyone dismounted and took a last chance to check armor and saddle girths and anything else they could think to check. Devan came over to silently adjust the fastenings of Meg's leather breastplate, and she smiled at him gratefully. They had wanted her to wear a leather helm as well, but she hated the way it restricted her vision. She needed to be able to see. And besides, the chances of anything reaching her where she would be were very small. Captain Varyn had reluctantly relented.

"All right," Varyn said, his low voice carrying just loudly enough among their tight circle. "Just over that ridge, we're going to encounter the enemy. Your king and your commander have sent us here to clear this pass and let the reinforcements through, and that is exactly what we are going to do. These men think they have an idea of what it's like to fight Trelian. But we're going to show them a whole new side to our beloved kingdom, with the help of our secret weapon." He looked at Meg, and all the other soldiers did, too, many dipping their heads and making the sign of the Lady with their hands. "They all know we have a dragon, but they don't truly understand what that means. Today, we're going to show them."

In pairs and small groups, the men all clustered around to touch Jakl for luck. Even Captain Varyn. Meg found herself suddenly blinking back tears as she saw how reverently they pressed their hands to whatever part of him they could reach, touching fingers to scales, then stepping back to allow others a chance to get close. It was not so long ago that her parents had thought no one would ever accept a princess with a dragon. That her link with Jakl was a curse rather than a blessing. She wished they could see what was happening right now.

And then the soldiers were mounting up and getting into formation, just as they had a million times in training. Meg climbed back onto her dragon, who was practically dancing beneath her, so eager was he to begin. *Easy,* she thought at him, although she understood exactly how he felt. *Very soon now.*

And then it was time.

Captain Varyn gave the signal, and the horses surged forward, and Jakl shot into the sky and over the ridge.

The first thing Meg saw was the enemy, laid out before them. *There are so many of them,* she thought. *So many!*

She'd never seen so many soldiers in one place before. Soldiers and horses and so many other things that her brain struggled to take all of it in. *It doesn't matter,* she told herself. *You have your orders. You know what you have to do.*

And she did. The first thing was just to show off a little. That part was pretty easy. She gave Jakl free rein, and he circled above the enemy soldiers, screaming his battle cry and sending a pure, bright stream of liquid fire into the air above them.

Below, soldiers ran everywhere. The rest of her company came riding hard into the center of the Lourin camp, swinging swords and crying, "Trelian!" and "King Tormon!"—and, she was startled to hear, "Dragon Princess!"

And then the fighting began for real.

Meg tore her eyes away, trying not to think about the blood she had already seen starting to spill. *We have a job to do, and if we do it right, then we can stop the bloodshed once and for all.* She knew that was so, and believed in it. But suddenly she felt reluctant to put this next part of the plan into action.

Jakl, however, was not. He had picked up on her hatred of Lourin, both because of what she and Tessel had suffered at the hands of King Gerald and his people and because of the ongoing war, the fact that King Gerald would not stand down, even though he knew there was no basis for this fighting, that everything was based on

Sen Eva's lies. And more than that, Jakl was made for flying and fighting. He spent a lot of time lying around and getting his scales rubbed, but that was not his true nature, and they both knew it. *This* was his true nature: this soaring, screaming, fire-breathing glory, and he had been waiting for this for far too long.

Meg took a breath and let him go.

Jakl screamed and shot forward, diving at the enemy and searing them with his fire. He was still flying high enough that he barely damaged anyone; this was mostly about scaring them. She wouldn't be sent in to kill unless it was absolutely necessary.

Still, Meg continued to feel reluctant. The anger she'd expected to feel was strangely, disturbingly absent. These weren't the same men who had invaded her home. She knew they were the enemy, but when she looked down, all she saw were individual soldiers. People. Who probably had no more desire to be at war than her own people did.

And then the first catapult nearly knocked them out of the sky.

She felt Jakl twist beneath her and held on for her life as the ball of fire shot past them, startlingly close. They had known there would be catapults, and of course she should have expected Lourin to use them against the dragon, *had* expected it, and yet it was one thing to know something was likely to happen and another to actually have someone try to kill you.

Jakl screamed again and circled around, searching for the catapult that had fired at them.

While he did, Meg scanned the battle below, looking for Trelian soldiers in trouble. If she saw any of their team in difficulty, Jakl either swooped in to pluck them out or picked up soldiers from elsewhere and carried them to wherever they were needed. This was essential, because they were so vastly outnumbered. She knew that if they distracted or disabled enough of Lourin's force immediately at the entrance to the pass, there was a good chance that the Kragnir soldiers would be able to fight through and join the battle, but until then, the Trelian soldiers were on their own. Meg's dragon's-eye view of the fighting let her see where men were most needed and from where they could most be spared. And in between, she let Jakl terrify the enemy, flying low and disrupting their formations, shooting flame just close enough to singe them, sometimes just picking up random Lourin soldiers and depositing them elsewhere . . . like in a ditch. Or a pond. Or at the top of a very tall tree.

Eventually she had the startling realization that she was having fun.

No matter how the Lourin soldiers tried to organize themselves, Meg and Jakl could swoop in and put their plans in complete disarray. She laughed as Jakl darted down and made yet another formation of soldiers scatter, screaming and running for their lives. Jakl could kill them in a heartbeat, and although he hadn't killed a single enemy soldier so far, they surely knew that he could. They ran, as they should, and it was glorious.

Meg and Jakl circled back around so she could look and see where they were needed next. Then the world lurched as Jakl dodged another fireball launched from a catapult. And then another.

They flew higher up, out of range, but that put them too far away to be useful. Lourin had rallied, finally understanding that keeping the dragon at bay was their only hope of success. Meg kept trying to bring them closer, but the catapults were firing faster and faster, and all of them were now directed at Jakl.

They circled again and again, but there was too much enemy fire — they couldn't fly down to assist the Trelian forces.

All right, she thought. *Time for the catapults to go.* She hadn't wanted to focus on them until she had to, since that would mean leaving her fellow soldiers without the dragon's protection, but clearly she couldn't put it off any longer. She couldn't do anything to help with those fireballs flying at them.

Another came hurtling toward them as she watched, and Jakl dodged violently sideways, letting it fly past. He didn't like those things any more than she did.

"The catapults!" she screamed at Jakl. "Now!"

Jakl screamed in response and flew down, swooping between fireballs and targeting first one catapult and then another. They were made mostly of wood, and when the dragon's fire enveloped them, they caught immediately.

Now, if they could just get them all, Lourin would have no way left to keep Meg and her dragon out of the fighting.

They knew it, too. The remaining catapults were firing twice as fast, forcing Jakl to dive and swerve constantly. But he kept circling back, and soon enough he set another one on fire. And then another.

She could see the Trelian soldiers pressing inward, forcing their advantage. The Lourin soldiers were torn between trying to fend off Captain Varyn and his men and trying to protect the catapults. Volleys of arrows came streaming up at them, but they bounced harmlessly off Jakl's scales, and he didn't let a single one get close to Meg.

But the arrows kept coming, and so did the fireballs sent from the catapults. Some of the arrows were on fire, now, too. It was getting harder for Jakl to dodge them. He started to circle up higher, out of range.

No! Meg thought at him. *Keep going! We have to get them all!*

He obeyed, but the remaining catapults were very well guarded now. The arrows came almost constantly. And the fireballs were coming more quickly as well. Meg felt the searing heat of one as it passed mere inches from her head.

But the Trelian soldiers were still advancing, and she could see that the plan was working. The Lourin soldiers were so focused on fending off the dragon that there weren't enough of them paying attention to the men on the ground.

Jakl attacked the catapults with everything he had, twisting in the air to avoid enemy fire and screaming defiance at every turn. Meg held on for all she was worth. Despite everything, the speed and the power and the — what had Captain Varyn said? The ferocity. Despite everything, all of that was wonderful. Jakl was doing what he was born to do, and Meg was loving it every bit as much as he was.

There were only two of the catapults left. If they could take those out, they'd be free to go back to assisting the rest of their company. The arrows were far easier to dodge than the fireballs, and easier still when they were all Meg and Jakl had to worry about. Jakl only had to stop the arrows from hitting Meg, after all. The fireballs were a different matter. Those could hurt him, as well.

Meg pressed herself flat against Jakl's back and urged him onward. He dived, and although some of the archers stood their ground, the majority broke as they saw his enormous, terrifying form coming straight at them. They scattered, and Jakl turned back around before they could regroup. He shot a stream of dragonfire at one of the catapults, and Meg shouted in triumph as it went up in a *whoosh* of flame.

One more to go.

They circled around again. Meg clung to Jakl's back, feeling even more a part of him than she usually did. They were invincible. *Take that, King Gerald!* she thought in exultation. One more catapult, and then it would just be a matter of time. Lourin's blockade forces would be defenseless against Meg and her dragon, and they would be forced to surrender. And then the Kragnir soldiers would be able to join them, and they could all go back home.

Jakl dived again, and Meg closed her eyes and let herself get lost in the speed and the fury and the *flying*. She felt Jakl inhale, preparing to let loose the flame that would destroy the final catapult and turn everything in their favor. And then she felt a searing pain in her right shoulder, and then she realized that she was falling.

Jakl screamed, in fear and pain this time, and Meg opened her eyes to see him racing toward her, diving down, struggling to reach her before . . . before . . .

Before I hit the ground, she thought.

Oh. Oh, no.

She was facing up, and she couldn't tell how far away the ground was. She didn't try to turn. She kept her eyes on her dragon, waiting for him to reach her. Of course he would reach her. She kept her eyes on him, calmly, patiently, not thinking about how far below her the ground might be. Until another bright burst of agony erupted in her left thigh, tearing a ragged scream from her lungs.

Hit, I'm hit! That . . . that wasn't . . . I wasn't supposed to . . .

Everything had gone strangely silent. She was tumbling, turning in the air, and there was the ground;

173

she could see it now. There were soldiers shouting and running and the ground was rushing up at her and she wanted to turn the other way, she wanted to see her dragon, she wanted to not be falling, to not be on fire — was she on fire? She felt like she was on fire. She kept tumbling, the world and the sky spinning around her. It was like flying, but not at all like flying. It was terrifying. Why hadn't Jakl caught her yet?

The ground was getting closer, and everything was getting dark. Meg's last thought was that it couldn't be getting dark; it was still so early. She had to get home, had to be there to make sure the mages didn't give up on Calen. Nighttime was when the crows went out. She had to be home by then.

But the darkness kept coming, all around her. And then everything went black. And she didn't think anything else at all.

CHAPTER NINE

THE CROW CAME AGAIN SOON AFTER.

Serek and Anders had not come up with any other brilliant ideas. Or any ideas at all. Which was a shame, because it meant that they would probably have to go with Calen's idea.

That made him very, very nervous.

Also, he wasn't sure it would work.

Those things did not seem like insurmountable obstacles to Serek and Anders, apparently.

Calen sat on the balcony next to the crow, tossing little pebbles over the edge. The crow pecked at his shirt, looking for bread. Calen ignored him.

His idea, of course, was trying to transport himself all the way back to Trelian. He thought that if they picked a location that they could keep absolutely clear, he could jump into it with little fear of finding himself half-embedded in anyone or anything, even though he wouldn't be able to see where he was jumping to.

It was probably safe enough, assuming they picked the right location. And that nothing unexpected happened at the last minute.

Why would anything unexpected happen? Just because there's a multikingdom war going on, and another war brewing between the Magistratum and Mage Krelig; and oh, yes, you're locked away in some long-abandoned castle with a crazy person and several traitorous mages.

Calen put his head in his hands.

They had to try it. They were running out of time.

Unfortunately, the other problem involved a little more than just talking himself into trying something that terrified him. He was pretty certain that he wouldn't be able to jump from inside Krelig's castle. He was sure there'd be magic of some kind to prevent that kind of thing. Which meant that he'd somehow have to get outside the castle. Which was possible . . . but Krelig would know.

Calen knew this for certain now, because when Cheriyon had walked out two days ago, Krelig had known instantly. Calen had assumed that Krelig had wards around the castle, and simple alarm wards — the kinds that would let you feel when someone passed through them — would have been very easy to maintain, hardly requiring any energy or attention at all from someone that powerful. Krelig had been in the middle of lecturing them about there being no place for fear or timidity in battle or really at any other time either, and suddenly he'd gotten this faraway look and then turned and left the room. The rest of them had waited, looking uncertainly at one another. After several minutes they heard what sounded like Cheriyon's voice raised in desperate pleading, coming from outside.

"By the gods," Lestern said, his voice shaking. "I can't believe he really did it."

"Did what?" Helena asked at once.

Lestern swallowed and looked around at them. "Left. Or . . . tried to leave. I thought he was just angry . . . I never believed . . ."

Helena ran to the window. "I think they're by the front gate," she said. "I can't quite see from here —"

She broke off at the sound of Cheriyon's faint, terrified scream.

And then there was only silence.

Helena moved quickly away from the window.

Several minutes later, Krelig returned and informed them that Mage Cheriyon would no longer be training with them. Then he went back to his lecture.

They sneaked glances at one another, but no one dared ask any questions. Mage Lestern's face had gone pale, but even he continued to behave as though nothing had happened. Calen had assumed that Cheriyon had still been recovering from his harsh lesson the other day, but if Lestern was right, Cheriyon had decided that training with Mage Krelig was more than he'd bargained for. And apparently Mage Krelig had not been willing to let him go.

Horrible as that was, Calen understood the logic. Krelig couldn't just let one of them walk out, knowing where he was located. And if Cheriyon had made it clear that he didn't want to stay . . .

Calen forced himself to pay attention. Cheriyon didn't matter; he was gone. And he'd given the rest of them some valuable, if not especially surprising, information.

The other essential piece of information for Calen had come earlier this afternoon.

Mage Krelig had been having them practice transporting one another. There were ways to protect against being transported against your will, which he also taught them, but he explained that at least at first, their enemies wouldn't think to protect themselves. The no-transporting-people rules were so deeply ingrained in these "mages" (Krelig always said that word in a tone of voice that indicated he didn't think it truly applied) that they wouldn't imagine that anyone would break those rules.

Krelig pointed to several mages and told them to stand in the center of the room. Then he forbade them to protect themselves and explained that the rest of the group would now practice transporting them.

Helena was one of the mages selected.

She shot Calen a panicked glance as she went to go stand with the others. Krelig noticed, and Calen wondered whether Helena would be punished for it. But Krelig only seemed amused.

"Calen," he said, "why don't you go first?"

He didn't tell Calen whom to practice on, and so Calen focused on Helena. He trusted his own abilities far more than he trusted most of the others, and he didn't want one of them accidentally transporting Helena into a wall. He still didn't *like* her; it wasn't anything like that. But she was the best sparring partner he had. He didn't want anything to happen to her.

She stood perfectly still, staring back at him with too-wide eyes. Calen concentrated. And then — he moved her three feet to her left.

She blinked and looked around, seeming surprised to find herself still there. Krelig snorted. "Well, yes, technically you transported her," he said. "But let's try for a little distance next time." He pointed to Mage Barbaryn, an older woman who had arrived just a few days earlier. "You. Do someone else."

She nodded and picked out one of the others — Mage Neehan, a rotund little man with an impressive array of tattoos covering his small, round face. He gulped visibly and closed his eyes tightly and stood there looking like he was waiting to be kicked in the stomach. Barbaryn, perhaps overly influenced by Krelig's criticism of Calen's lack of scope, gazed at her victim, squinted, then looked through the open window, apparently intending to transport him all the way out to the half-visible road that led to the front gate. Neehan vanished but then reappeared with a yelp just beyond the window.

Then began to fall, screaming, toward the ground.

Krelig shook his head, and a second later Neehan rematerialized in the center of the room in a heap, still screaming. Once he realized where he was, he stopped, blushing furiously.

"I don't understand," Barbaryn said in a frightened voice. "I was aiming for the road, but it was like there was a wall . . ."

"Yes, yes," Krelig said. He still seemed to find the

whole thing amusing, which was a relief. "You get credit for ambition, but as you can see, you overshot a little. Let's keep our transportation inside the castle, shall we?"

Neehan had gotten back to his feet. His face was still red, but he seemed otherwise all right.

The rest of the mages took their turns, transporting their victims down the hall or to other locations in the castle. Krelig didn't seem to care if they transported each other to locations they couldn't see, although he did remind them that he didn't want anyone killed by accident during practice, and so they'd better be careful. And they were, although Mage Madali still ended up reappearing with one foot impaled by a table leg. She screamed as she became visible again, clawing at herself and trying to get free. Krelig transported the table away from her, and she collapsed, whimpering. Her friend Allicynth, who had performed the poorly executed spell, ran over to try to comfort her, but Madali, understandably, pushed her away. Allicynth continued to hover nearby, wringing her hands and muttering endless apologies.

"She'll be fine," Krelig said dismissively. "Good object lesson, though. And of course, you can do that on purpose to your enemies. Not many things render someone

181

too distracted to attack you quite as well as transporting him to appear with a piece of furniture running through his head."

Calen was sickened to see many of the mages nodding at this, as though it were a helpful tip they were filing away for later use.

But at the same time, he was thinking about Neehan hitting that invisible wall. He was remembering exactly where the wall had been. Very close to the outer walls of the castle itself. Not the road. Not the gate. Maybe only five feet past the window. Maybe not even that much.

After practice, when he had some time alone, Calen stood by a window where he could see the front gate and looked out to where he thought the barrier might be. He looked, and tried to see. If he'd been able to see Serek and Anders's spell on the bird, then it stood to reason that he might be able to see other spells after they were cast, too.

Was that a slight shimmer cutting through the air? He couldn't tell if he was really seeing something, or just convincing himself that he was.

Calen gripped the edge of the windowsill and focused as hard as he could. He sent the tiniest sliver of white energy; he didn't want anyone else to be able to tell what he was doing. The shimmer might be real. Might. But he had to know for sure. He tried to remember what he'd done to be able to see the spell on the bird. *You commanded it*, the voice in his head reminded him.

Right, Calen thought. *Okay, then.*

He stopped straining to see. He looked out at the seemingly empty air and widened his sliver of white into a fine spray that radiated out from — not his hands, he realized; he wasn't using his hands. From his head. From his mind. *Show me!* he demanded. He knew it wasn't the words themselves that mattered, just the power behind them.

He waited, watching the white energy fly outward, carrying his will with it. And then he saw it illuminate the magic barrier. Which was suddenly, faintly visible. A shimmery black and orange and white curtain, paperthin, but impenetrable to whatever it wanted to keep inside. It surrounded the castle, only a few feet beyond the walls and windows of the upper levels, but much farther out near the gate and along the outer perimeter on the ground. In fact . . . he squinted and saw that the gate itself had several layers of protection. Krelig had known the second that Cheriyon passed through the gate and had been able to catch him before he reached the outer barrier. So just walking — or even running — far enough away to be able to transport wouldn't work. Not down there.

People could pass through it nonmagically, but not without alerting Mage Krelig.

Some magic could pass through it; he and Krelig had both sent magic into the air far beyond the castle during lessons, and Calen had been able to send his information-gathering spell at the crow. And the crow itself had been able to pass through, even while carrying Serek and Anders's spell. But people being moved by magic ceased being moved by magic at its boundary. Which made sense, since surely the whole purpose of it was to prevent any of Krelig's recruits from leaving via magical means.

So all he had to figure out . . .

Suddenly someone's hands were on him, yanking him back from the window and up against the wall.

Krelig—I'm caught—!

But it wasn't Krelig. Calen had a glimpse of Helena's fiery red hair and dark eyes and then she was suddenly closer and then—

And then she—

It took his confused brain several seconds to put it together.

She was *kissing* him!

He tried to push her away, but she blocked his hands and kept her mouth on his. And part of him, he realized, wasn't really trying all that hard to make her stop. It was . . . interesting, the kissing. No one had ever kissed him before.

It was not precisely unpleasant, either.

But it's Helena!

He thought that he should try harder to push her away now, but then he heard Krelig's voice from behind her and the kissing stopped as abruptly as it had begun.

"Really, Mage Helena. I must ask you to stop terrorizing my poor apprentice." Even through his confusion, Calen could tell that Krelig was still amused. Not angry. Thank the gods.

"I didn't hear him complaining," she said, just defiantly enough to avoid being outright disrespectful.

"He looked like he was about to faint."

Helena shrugged. "I thought he deserved a reward for not crashing me into a wall or impaling me on a table leg earlier," she said.

Calen finally found his voice. "I was not about to faint!" he said. "I was — it was —"

They both turned to look at him. Unfortunately, he couldn't think of how to finish that sentence, and after a moment they went back to ignoring him again.

"It's nothing to me if you like each other," Krelig said. "And alliances can be useful, when you're fighting in and against groups. Just see that it doesn't interfere with your training. And that it doesn't become annoying."

Calen tried again. "There's nothing — we're not —"

They didn't even turn to look at him this time.

"You fight well together, and that's something I can use," Krelig went on. "Just remember that your first loyalty must always be to me."

"I know, Master," Helena said, all traces of defiance gone. "Your will above all."

He nodded, satisfied.

"But —" Calen began.

Krelig rolled his eyes and walked away.

Calen turned to Helena, furious.

"What — *why?*"

"Oh, don't pretend you didn't like it," she said. But her eyes were straight and serious on his, and she held his gaze intently. "And I meant it about you deserving a reward. You're powerful, Calen. I'd rather have you on my side than against me."

"But —"

She glared at him, but her voice stayed lightly teasing. "Maybe if you help me work on that transporting spell a little, I'll kiss you again."

Calen stopped trying to interject any sanity into this conversation. It was clearly impossible.

She turned to glance behind her, then leaned in close. But this time instead of kissing him, she only whispered. "He was coming this way. I don't know what you were doing, but I didn't think it was anything you wanted to be caught at. Was I right?"

"Oh. Yes. Uh — thank you." He paused, then added, "So you didn't — you weren't . . . ?"

She smirked at him. "I suppose I did want to thank you a little. But mostly I just wanted to save your skin. You're the only one here I can stand besides myself. If he kills you for 'making him wonder about you,' who would I practice with then? Lestern?" She made a face.

She studied him, then asked, "So what were you doing?"

"Nothing," he said immediately. "Just — thinking."

"Hmm." She looked skeptical, but didn't press him. "Well, I wasn't kidding about wanting help with the transportation spell. Would you practice with me a bit before dinner?" She smirked again. "Don't worry — I promise not to kiss you."

He shook his head to clear it and pushed away from the wall. "All right," he said. "Let's go back downstairs."

She started walking and he followed, trying not

187

to think about how her last comment made him feel vaguely disappointed.

Calen sent the bird back with a message that said he needed more time.

He knew they didn't have a lot of time. More mages were arriving every day. And while Krelig was still sometimes relatively normal — as normal as he ever got, anyway — his violent outbursts seemed to be getting more and more common. He'd set one of the mages on fire the other day for failing to correctly perform a new spell quickly enough. And not just his hand or foot — his whole body. The man had been screaming, the rest of them frozen in fear and horror, and Calen had been on the verge of putting out the fire himself when Krelig had suddenly seemed to come back to some semblance of sanity. He had appeared momentarily surprised to see the man burning to a crisp in front of him, then waved a hand and put him out.

Calen had seen the colors for both the fire and the quenching a few seconds before Krelig had cast them.

It had been happening more and more often, at first sporadically and then more regularly, until he was seeing the colors early nearly all the time. In fact, his biggest challenge at practice now was trying not to react to the early indications of what someone was about to cast. Mage Krelig thought he knew what Calen's special talent was. He *had* known. But now — now Calen seemed to have another special talent. Or a new manifestation of the old one. Or something. Maybe because of the new levels of power he could access now. But whatever it was, he knew it was vitally important that Krelig not find out. No one could find out. Not even Helena.

Because if Calen ever did get out of there, this new ability could be the key to defeating their enemy.

If nothing else, it would give the good mages an advantage that they sorely needed. No matter how much Mage Krelig taught his recruits — and they were still learning at an incredible rate, every day — the older man still knew a million times more than all of the rest of them combined. And he was so *strong*. Serek and Anders and the rest of the non-traitor mages were going to need all the advantages they could get in order to have a chance. Calen had to get back in time to help them.

But he also had to learn enough to make sure he was able to really make a difference when he got there. Seeing the colors early wouldn't matter unless he was able to use those extra seconds to cast the right spells.

Sometimes when he had those thoughts, the little voice in his head asked him when that was going to be, exactly. When would he know that he'd learned enough? Maybe he should take what he knew now and leave before it was too late.

And that was probably good advice. But . . . what if the next thing Krelig taught them was the spell that ended up being the one they needed? What if the next group practice revealed some other mage's self-invented spell that shed new light on something Calen had never considered casting before? What if the next piece of essential knowledge was right around the corner, and he left just one crucial day too soon and missed learning what he needed to learn?

You could keep saying that forever, you know.

I know.

Calen decided that when the crow next arrived, he would set the date and confirm the location for his jump. He was pretty certain that he knew how to do it. He was terrified by what he would have to do, but he thought it would work. And the voice in his head was right. He couldn't keep putting it off.

But then the next day at practice, Krelig taught them a variation on shields that Calen felt sure he would never, ever have thought of on his own. *See?* he said to himself. *There's still so much to learn! How can I leave now? How can I ever leave?*

What?

Wait. Wait, I didn't —

The voice in his head didn't say anything. But it didn't really need to.

He did not feel that way. He did *not*. He wanted to leave more than anything. No amount of learning would be worth staying here with Krelig. Not ever.

Calen took a deep breath and forced himself to focus on the lesson. He couldn't let anyone see how shaken he was.

Clearly, he had to get out of there as soon as he possibly could.

When the bird came again, Calen calculated how long it would take it to get back to Serek and then return with confirmation, based on the time between the bird's previous visits and how much faster he might be able to get it to fly with a little extra magical help. Then he picked his date. Six days from now. No — no, seven. Seven days. Or would eight be safer?

He made himself stop. Seven days.

He spelled the crow and sent it on its way, giving it as much extra speed as he thought would be safe. He didn't want to give the bird more speed than it could handle. But it was hard to hold back.

Calen tried to act as though nothing were different.

191

He had his private lessons, then group lessons. He ate meals with the others in the dining hall; half the tables were full now when they were all there together. He practiced with Helena and tried not to think about whether she would try to kiss him again. That had been . . . confusing. Best to just pretend it had never happened.

She seemed to feel the same way, as far as he could tell.

So, good. That was good.

He thought he'd been doing a decent job of behaving normally, but Helena stopped him as he started back to his room after practice.

"Calen," she said.

He stopped and turned around. They had already said good night; he was surprised to see her still standing where she'd been when he'd first turned to leave.

"What is it?"

She only stood there for a minute, not speaking. Then she came toward him, and he froze, wondering if she was going to kiss him.

She did throw her arms around him, but she only hugged him close. Then she whispered in his ear. "If you're leaving, take me with you?"

He tried to pull away, but she held him fast.

"I — I'm not —" He didn't know what to say. He didn't want to lie. But he couldn't take her with him. Could he?

Could he?

He pushed her a little away from him, but only far enough to look at her. To look her in the eyes.

Could it be a trick? He thought of the way she'd promised Mage Krelig her first loyalty. But then, they all had. You had to, to survive here. He'd done a lot of things to survive here. Done things he wasn't proud of. Said things that weren't true.

She looked back at him, her eyes shining. With tears? Because he was leaving? Or because he might leave her behind? Or because she was about to betray him?

No. He didn't believe that. Maybe it was foolish. . . . It was almost certainly foolish . . . but he trusted her.

And really, there was no reason he couldn't take her with him. One more mage who knew Krelig's secrets — she could be an asset. At the very least, it would mean one less mage to fight against them. And she knew Calen, knew how he fought and what his strengths and weaknesses were, and if he left her here . . .

He pulled her close to him, so he could whisper in

her ear. He supposed they were being careful in case anyone was watching. Or listening. But he didn't mind the closeness so much just for itself.

"I don't know for certain if it will work," he whispered. "But I can try."

"Please," she said, pulling him closer. "Please."

They stood there for a little while longer. And then she abruptly pulled away, wiping her eyes. "See you tomorrow," she said in a lighter voice. "I'm definitely going to block that fire-arrow spell next time!"

"I'll believe that when I see it!" he answered in the same tone.

After another second, they both turned and walked in opposite directions.

Calen hoped he hadn't made a terrible, terrible mistake.

CHAPTER TEN

PRINCESS...

Someone's voice, calling her in the darkness. Calen? No, not Calen. He was too far away. He had left her.

She felt Jakl calling her, too. He never called her Princess, though. He didn't exactly *call* her anything. There was just a feeling that meant *her*, that he connected only with her. He was sending that feeling now, wanting her to come back.

I'm trying, she thought at him. And she was. But everything was so dark. She couldn't tell where she was, or which way to go.

Jakl seemed to feel her trying, seemed to be reaching back toward her. She went to where she could feel him. It was like standing outside with your eyes closed, feeling the sun shining on your face. She moved toward the warmth of him, that feeling of *her* that he was sending so fiercely. She followed that feeling, pulled herself along it like a rope. It got easier, lighter, as she got closer. She could feel him pouring his strength into her, making her stronger, making her able to find her way back, until . . .

She blinked, and the world started to come into hazy focus around her. At first all she could see was an enormous green shape carving out a space against the sky, but she knew who that was, of course. Jakl hovered over her — no, around her — no, both. He was coiled around her as much as his size would allow, his head bent down to be just inches away from her own. When he realized that she was awake, he blew out a hot, snorty breath that lifted her hair back from her face and made her laugh despite the pain.

"Yes, hello," she said, half whispering, half croaking, trying to reach out and stroke his worried face. "I'm here, I'm okay." Her arm didn't seem to want to do what she told it, though.

"Princess! Thank the gods." It was Captain Varyn, a bloody bandage wrapped around his head. He leaned closer to her, fending off a persistent medic's assistant who seemed to be trying to put more bandages on him. "Are you all right? Are you really back with us?"

"Yes," she managed. It was hard to talk. "Hurts, though."

"Don't try to talk," he said at once.

She glared at him, or tried to. *You asked me a question!* But she didn't try to say it out loud.

A tall woman with a white medic's sash pushed Captain Varyn firmly back in his chair, then turned toward Meg. "The difficult captain is right, Princess. You shouldn't try to talk. You've been injured. Your shoulder was badly burned, and we've immobilized your arms and chest to help prevent further pain or injury. You were grazed by one of those fireballs, and then you took an arrow in the leg on your way down. Your throat, I believe, is only hoarse from screaming, and maybe a little from the smoke. Your right ear was very slightly scorched, but the shoulder took most of the fire's damage."

Meg nodded slightly, grateful that the woman was giving her the information she would have been asking for if she could. Some of it, anyway. She looked at Jakl. *Did you catch me before I hit the ground?* He must have. Surely she would be dead otherwise.

Yes, he thought at her, but hesitantly. After a moment he added something that felt like: *Just.*

The medic looked back and forth at Meg and Jakl. The dragon hadn't moved an inch to make room for anyone else to get closer to her, although at some point he must have allowed them close enough to treat her wounds.

197

"Your dragon saved your life," the medic said. "He caught you just before you would have been lost to us. Not gently, but then, I don't suppose he had much choice at that point. He broke your arm in the process —" A flood of shame and sorrow flowed from the dragon through the link. The medic seemed to guess something of this; she placed a hesitant hand on Jakl's neck. "A small price to pay, Sir Dragon," she said. "You saved your lady, and then you saved us all."

What does that mean? Meg thought at him. Strangely, the shame flared up again, though less intensely than before.

Well, if he wasn't going to tell her . . . "What — what did —?"

"Please, Princess," the medic said. "I'm sure the captain will tell you everything, but first you must rest."

Meg tried to protest, but someone held a cup of sweet liquid to her lips, and then everything went fuzzy and dark again. But it was a different dark from last time. Sleep. Not — not whatever that had been before. And she could feel her dragon there with her. That was enough. She stopped trying to resist and let herself go into the darkness.

The next time she woke, she was in a large tent, on a cot. More cots filled the rest of the space, with other wounded people in them — some sleeping, some talking, some moaning, some crying. Many faces were unfamiliar to her. The white-sashed medics and their assistants moved quickly and efficiently among them. Jakl wasn't inside the tent, but she could feel him just outside, so that was all right. She still hurt, but she thought that perhaps the pain was a little less than it had been before. She caught the eye of a passing assistant, who gave her some water. After she drank, her throat felt much better. She handed back the cup and asked him to send for Captain Varyn.

The captain appeared shortly thereafter. He pulled up a chair beside her, looking much better than when she'd seen him last. She wondered suddenly how long she'd been asleep.

"You gave us quite a scare," he said. "I was not relishing the idea of having to tell your parents I'd gotten you killed."

"What happened?" Meg asked. She had so many questions, but that one covered the most ground.

Captain Varyn gave a strange little laugh and ran his hand through his hair, wincing when he grazed the bandage. It had been changed since she'd last seen it; there wasn't any blood oozing through it now. "What happened," he repeated. "Quite a bit. It's hard to know where to start."

"Did we win?"

Now he laughed outright, heartily if not for very long. "All right, sure. That's a good place to start." He grinned at her. "Yes, Princess. We won. We cleared the pass. Kragnir soldiers were fighting through from the other side, and soon after ... uh, after ... well, they finally broke through and came streaming out against the enemy like a swarm of angry bees. It was glorious. Most of them are already well on their way toward Trelian now. I sent most of the rest of our company — everyone except the injured and a few others — riding ahead to give the king and queen and commander the news."

Meg closed her eyes for a moment, overcome with relief. She hadn't ruined everything. She'd been afraid ... but then ...

"But ... how? We still hadn't destroyed the last catapult, and then I was hit...."

"We almost had them by then," the captain said. "You and your dragon were magnificent, Your Highness. They were scrambling, making mistakes, and my men were getting the better of them. They couldn't take their eyes off you for more than a second, and that combined with your destruction of the catapults — well, they couldn't organize themselves to defend against us. Not while maintaining their hold on the pass. We were waiting for that last one to go up; it seemed about to happen, and then the dragon screamed, and we realized that you were falling. Everything stopped at that point. Everything. Both sides — we just stood there, watching. Transfixed.

"I'll tell you, it didn't seem possible that he would catch you in time. And there was nothing we could do — there was no way to help or even to get something to soften your landing. So we watched, and waited, and prayed. I prayed, anyway, and I'm certain I was not the only one. The dragon shot through the air like an arrow, straight down, racing you to the earth. And at what had to be the last possible moment, he grabbed you. Grabbed your arm in his jaws and sort of swung you up and away and then caught you again — it was mostly a blur, to tell you the truth, but the one thing that was clear was that you were still alive. You were screaming bloody murder as he laid you gently down on the ground."

Meg tried to call up some memory of this, but there was nothing there. She looked at Varyn quizzically. "But then — the pass was still blocked. How did we win? They could have . . ."

"The dragon," Varyn said. "He . . . well, he went a

201

little crazy up there, I'd say. He was gentle as a lamb with you, bringing you down to us, but once he saw you were safe . . . I've never heard a sound like the scream he gave as he launched back into the air. He had that last catapult in flames before anyone could even react, and he set most of the men around it on fire as well. And then . . . and then he was everywhere. Raging, screaming, breathing fire — it was clear that he was ready to burn every last one of them to a crisp for hurting you, and they knew it. Lourin soldiers starting throwing their weapons to the ground and dropping to their knees. A few at first, and then the rest of them, faster and faster. He didn't hurt anyone who laid down their weapons, Your Highness. I feel you should know that. He killed a good number of the enemy, but only those who stood and fought against him. And not nearly so many as he could have. And once the rest of them threw down their arms, he came back to where you were and would not leave your side. That's why we had to have the medics treat you out in the field. He wouldn't allow us to move you. Not until after you woke up."

Meg took this in silently. That was what the shame was about: that he had lost control, that he had unleashed himself upon the enemy after they'd hurt her. He thought she would be angry. But how could she be? He'd only been reacting to what they'd done. And he'd accomplished their goal. Accomplished it even without her there to ask him. And he hadn't lost control completely. Even after she left him there alone. He had nothing to be ashamed of.

She tried to send her reassurance through the link. *It's all right,* she thought at him. *I understand. And you did well. You did so very well.*

And he had. She couldn't bring herself to feel happy that he'd killed anyone, even enemy soldiers . . . but as Captain Varyn had said: this was war. And Jakl had made sure that the fighting here hadn't been in vain. And now Kragnir would be able to help them defeat the rest of the enemy back home. Home. Where she needed to be, because —

Calen, she thought suddenly. How long had she been out here?

"What day is it? How long . . . ?"

"You were in and out of consciousness for nearly five days," the Captain said. "And the medics say it will be another few days before it's safe for you to travel." He held up his hands as she opened her mouth to object. "I know you're anxious to get back home. We all are, Your Highness. But we nearly lost you once. There is no way I am going to move you one second before the medics give the word. So you just focus your energy on resting and healing. Kragnir sent down additional medics and supplies, and you are getting the best possible care. We'll get you home as soon as we can. I give you my oath on that. But not sooner."

He left her then, and she lay back, alternately exhilarated and exasperated and exhausted. Well, constantly exhausted; it was just the exhilaration and exasperation that varied. She supposed the resting advice was probably good. She looked down at herself — as much as she could with all the bandages and the blankets. Her right arm had been set free of its bindings, although the shoulder was still tender and tightly wrapped, so she couldn't see how bad the burns were. Her left arm was bound up tightly; that was the broken one. That hurt the worst, but there was a dullness to it that made it bearable. She realized after a moment that Jakl was taking some of the pain from her.

Hey, she thought at him. *You don't have to do that.*

Yes, he thought back. Then refused to send her any further thoughts on the subject.

She let it go. If that would help him to feel better about what had happened, so be it. She wasn't really sorry to be in less pain than she had to be. And it was probably less painful for him, since he was so much larger.

She felt him stir a little at that, and smiled. *Yes, large and fierce and strong. That's you, my lovely. Thank you. I accept your gift gladly.*

She was gratified by his heartened response.

It was six more days before they finally agreed to let her go home. Everyone from Trelian was leaving; those who remained had only been waiting for her to be well enough to travel. The Kragnir medics and their own wounded would stay, until they were able to be brought back up the mountain to the castle.

Meg's left arm was still bound and splinted, her right shoulder and the side of her head were bandaged, and her left thigh refused to support her weight for more than a few steps at a time. Medic Lorena, the one who'd explained what had happened that first day, assured her that her leg would heal fully in time. She might have a scar, but she'd be able to walk and run and move about without limping or feeling pain, and that was what was important. As though Meg would care about a scar! She knew she'd be scarred from the burning, anyway. She was just glad to be alive.

And there had been one definite upside to the delay. On the third morning, she woke to find Maerlie sitting beside her bed.

"Maer!" Meg was halfway to a sitting position before she remembered how badly she was injured. "Ow," she added, lying slowly back down.

"Look what happens when I'm not around to stop you from getting into trouble," Maerlie said, smiling. "You stay still, now. You appear to be rather broken."

Meg satisfied herself with grabbing her sister's hand. "What are you doing here?"

"What do you think I'm doing here? You almost died in my front yard. I had to come see you." That was an exaggeration; it must have taken her at least a full day to make it down here from the castle. But Meg wasn't about to object.

"I didn't almost die."

Maerlie gave her a look.

"All right, maybe I almost died. But I *didn't* die. I'm fine now. Well, okay, not *fine*, not yet, but I will be."

"I know," Maerlie said. "I made them tell me everything as soon as I heard you'd been injured. I didn't even know you were here until after it happened! But I suppose you couldn't have sent word, could you? Secret mission and all that."

"Yes," Meg said. "Sorry."

"*Successful* secret mission. I hear you and Jakl saved the day."

"Mostly Jakl." She smiled at his combined swell of

pride and protest through the link.

Maerlie raised an eyebrow, but all she said was, "Well, please allow me to convey official thanks on behalf of King Ryllin and Queen Carlinda, and of course Prince Ryant and myself."

"Please tell them it was our pleasure." She winced at a sudden twinge in her shoulder, which she suspected rather took away from the effect she'd been going for. "And that we are most grateful for their aid in this war."

Maerlie shook her head. "So formal! You don't sound very much like the girl I left behind."

It hurt a little to hear that. Meg remembered a time not so long ago when she had vowed never to change. But she knew it was true; she wasn't the same person she'd been when Maerlie left. So much had happened since then.

Maerlie stayed until Medic Lorena gently suggested that Meg needed to get some more rest. Meg tried to argue, but it was clear to all three of them that the medic was right.

"I'm so glad you came," Meg said. "Almost worth it, all this"— Meg gestured at her leg and torso with her less-damaged arm —"to see you." Her head was starting to feel a little fuzzy.

"Hush," Maerlie said. "When this is over, you will come for a proper visit, without a whole army of soldiers and medics or any need for such, and we will catch up on everything."

"Yes," Meg said, closing her eyes. "That's a promise."

The soldiers and medics and assistants seemed to pack up the camp in agonizing, exaggerated slowness. Meg knew she couldn't complain, especially since she couldn't help them move any faster. She had firm orders, from both Medic Lorena and Captain Varyn, to sit in her chair patiently and quietly. Jakl was helping where he could, lifting and dragging heavy things when they thought to ask him, but she realized that they were used to doing all of this without the help of a dragon, and so finding ways for him to help might really only slow them down.

So she sat, and she waited, and she tried not to worry about what was happening back at the castle. Had Mage Serek and Mage Anders gotten Calen back yet? Were they at least trying? Meg had faith in Pela and trusted that she would do all she could to keep the mages on track, but there were limits to what she'd be able to accomplish. Meg hoped there was a least a plan in place by now. She didn't know how long it took the crows to travel to wherever Calen was. And back. Maybe there hadn't even been another crow since she'd left. She tried to decide what would be worse — to get back and discover she'd missed a great deal or to get back and discover she hadn't missed anything at all.

Well, the first step was just to get back. Which had required some negotiation. Medic Lorena was firm that Meg could not ride back on her dragon. At first they tried to get her to agree to ride in a wagon with the other wounded, but that was just ridiculous. In fact, it was ridiculous for any of the wounded to ride slowly back in a rickety wagon over the bumpy, winding road through the forest. Meg pointed out that they could load the wounded into one of the special supply carts and have Jakl fly them all home. It would be a much smoother ride, she was sure, far less jostling around, and much faster — they'd be home by the afternoon, instead of days from now.

Captain Varyn saw the wisdom of this at once, and he helped convince Medic Lorena. She did like the idea of the injured soldiers getting home to the infirmary as quickly as possible. Varyn offered her a spot in the dragon's cart to oversee her charges, but she turned a little pale at that and said that one of her assistants would make the trip in her place.

Finally, *finally*, it was time to go. Jakl was already up in the sky, flying in wide, lazy circles, sending her occasional images through the link of what he could see of the countryside around them. One was a lovely view of Kragnir's castle, tall and stately in its nest of craggy peaks. It made her happy to know that Maerlie lived in such a beautiful place.

Once everyone had been loaded into the cart under Lorena's watchful eye, Meg let Jakl know they were ready. He came down to let them fasten the harness and attach the cart, then slowly rose back into the air, this time taking Meg and the others with him. Some of the wounded were unconscious, or in enough pain that they had no interest in anything other than lying still, but the others looked avidly out over the edges of the cart, marveling at their speed and watching the landscape race by beneath them.

Meg looked out as well, but she wasn't thinking about the landscape.

She was thinking about Calen.

What if he's there when I get back? The thought should have made her glad, but somehow it didn't. She puzzled over this for a bit, and realized eventually that it was because she was still so angry. Angry at how he'd left, at how he'd made that plan to try to rescue Maurel without even telling her. He had gone off, possibly to get killed, and he hadn't even said good-bye. And then once she'd caught up, he'd left her *again*.

Didn't he know that he wasn't ever supposed to leave her? People left sometimes; she knew that — people left for all kinds of reasons. But not *Calen*. Calen was not allowed to leave. Things were always better when they were together. For both of them. How did he not know that? She didn't understand how she could be best friends with someone who was so *stupid* sometimes.

She envisioned several different scenarios of his homecoming. In some of them, she ran to him and hugged him. In others, she ran to him and punched him in the stomach as hard as she could. In some he was glad to see her; in some he was resentful to be back.

But she couldn't give any credence to that last idea. He wanted to come back. He'd said so. And anyway, of course he did. She was sure that he had some crazy reason for having gone off with Mage Krelig in the first place, some reason that he thought was a good one at the time. But by now he'd have realized what a mistake it was. By now, he would be desperate to get back home. Where he belonged.

Maybe she'd punch him and then hug him. Or the other way around. She was pretty sure she'd want to do both. She just wasn't sure which she would most want to do first.

Just be okay, she thought silently at him, trying to

send her thoughts out to wherever he might be right now. *Just be okay, and maybe I won't even punch you at all. Just get home safe, and I will forgive you for everything.*

Jakl flew swiftly and steadily onward, bringing her closer and closer to finding out . . . something, at least. Meg tried to make herself feel confident. Calen would make a good plan with Serek and Anders, even if she wasn't there to help make *sure* it was a good plan. And he'd escape, and he'd get back and—she was sure now—she'd only hug him. She wouldn't even punch him a little bit. Not if he made it back safe.

Please.

CHAPTER ELEVEN

WHEN THE CROW RETURNED CONFIRMING THE date and time of his jump to Trelian, Calen sent it back immediately. Again with extra speed. Before he could change his mind.

Which was ridiculous, because of course he wasn't going to change his mind. Had he finally gone completely insane? Just like Krelig?

No. If he had, he *would* have asked for more time.

Which part of him still wanted.

Three days. Three more days to learn everything he could and not get caught. On the night of that third day, he'd be going home.

He wished the crow had gone back to using Meg's voice. He wondered why it hadn't. Where was she? Had something happened? Or was she just too busy to lend her voice to the spells when Serek and Anders cast them?

Did she still want him to come back?

Stop thinking that way. Of course she does.

Calen went back inside, but he was too worked up to try to sleep. Too excited, too afraid, too anxious about not having learned enough yet. He stepped through his doorway wards and walked down the hall. He still had the wing to himself; the castle was large, and so far all the new traitor mages had taken rooms on the other side of the castle, where he'd put the first group. Which was fine with Calen. He didn't want to see them any more than he had to.

Well, except Helena. But that was different. She was different. She didn't want to be here anymore. She'd realized it had been a mistake.

Or she is setting you up to betray you.

But he didn't believe that.

If you're wrong, it will cost you everything.

He was so tired of that voice in his head. *Be quiet!* he barked at it. And for a wonder, it listened.

Calen wandered the castle, not really paying attention to where he was going. Most of the other mages would be in their rooms by now, sleeping, or practicing, or praying, or whatever they did when they were alone. Finding ways to live with themselves while betraying everything that should matter to them. He still couldn't believe how many had come. More than forty the last time he had counted. And he knew there would be more. They knew

Mage Krelig was evil, but they still came. He supposed most of them were afraid of being on the wrong side if Krelig won. But didn't they realize that if they all fought *against* him, maybe he *wouldn't* win?

He kept wandering, and thinking. When he reached the stairs, he climbed up and up and up until he reached the outer battlements and stepped outside. The sky was brilliant with stars. Calen stood there for several minutes before he realized that he wasn't alone.

Mage Krelig was standing near the door on the other side, also looking up at the stars.

"A fine night," Mage Krelig said, walking over toward Calen.

"Yes," Calen said. His heart was pounding, but he thought he was hiding it well. He wasn't doing anything wrong; there was no rule against being out here, but he still felt guilty and afraid.

"Couldn't sleep?"

It was times like these that Calen was most confused by Mage Krelig. He knew that the man was evil and terrible and heartless and wrong in every possible way, and usually that was quite clear from his behavior and speech. And then other times he'd talk to you just like a regular person, and it was hard to know how to respond.

But Calen knew he had to say something. Even when he was in a good mood, Krelig hated it when you didn't answer.

"No," Calen said. "I'm not sure why. Sometimes a walk helps to clear my head. I didn't mean to disturb you, though. I can go —"

"No, no," Krelig said, waving him closer. "I'm glad for the company."

Calen made himself lean casually against the outer wall, just a few inches from where Krelig was doing the same. He kept his eyes on the sky; he didn't want to look down and see how far above the ground they were. Heights still made him . . . uncomfortable.

Which made his escape plan extra terrifying.

Don't think about that now! Not here! Not when he's STANDING RIGHT THERE!

He tried to think of something safe to say.

"Is it the girl?" Krelig asked. Calen just stared at him, completely caught off-guard. Krelig laughed.

"I remember being your age. I know; it's hard to believe, but I was young once, too." He shook his head, looking out again at the night. "Be careful with that one. She's attractive, no doubt, but fiery. Fiery girls are always unpredictable. They usually break your heart in the end."

Calen kept staring, trying not to look as shocked as

he felt. Krelig talking about feelings was about a million times more incomprehensible than Serek talking about feelings.

"Still, it's usually worth it," Krelig added. "You might as well enjoy yourself while you can, my boy. Our time for preparing is almost at an end. Soon enough we'll be at war, and who knows what will happen?"

Calen swallowed, still struggling with this whole conversation. "Well — we'll win. That's what will happen," he said. Surely that's what Krelig believed, anyway.

But the mage surprised him. He laughed again — such a normal, human sound that Calen felt like he was talking to a complete stranger. "I do hope so," Krelig said. "But the gods offer no guarantees, and I haven't had another sighting since I've returned. I know your ability will be a great asset, and I know we are stronger than our enemies. But war is . . . unpredictable. Ha! Like fiery girls. It may seem like everything is going your way, and then suddenly you're lying in tatters on the floor, wondering what went wrong."

Calen tried desperately to think of a response. He couldn't tell whether Krelig was using war as a metaphor for some girl who had broken his heart a thousand years ago, or . . .

Krelig clapped Calen on the shoulder. "Oh, don't be

so serious," he said. "No harm in a few stolen kisses. It's probably good for you. Just remember that when the time comes, the only thing that matters is the fight. You must be able to cast everything else aside. Can you promise me that? I don't mind you having a little fun, but if there's any chance it will distract you from what's really important . . ."

"No, Master," Calen said at once. "I know what's really important." Krelig was still looking at him, and he felt like something else was required. "I don't even — I don't even know if I like her."

Krelig laughed again, actually throwing back his head and guffawing up at the stars. "Yes, that's often how it is with women. Of any age. Just be careful. And remember what's important. You'll be fine. And if necessary, we can always get rid of her. She's a strong one, and I'd hate to waste her abilities . . . but you are my most important weapon, Calen. If I need to sacrifice her . . ."

"No!" Calen said, horrified. "No, it's okay. She's — she's not that much of a distraction. I know what's really important. I promise."

Krelig nodded and pushed back from the wall. "All right, then. Don't stay up too late, my boy. I expect you to be awake at lessons in the morning."

"Yes, Master," Calen said. He watched as Krelig

walked toward the far door and disappeared back into the castle.

Three more days, he thought. *Just three more days.*

Suddenly the time couldn't go by quickly enough.

Calen did get to sleep eventually, and he managed to be alert for his private morning lessons with Mage Krelig. As usual, the lessons were so engrossing that it wasn't hard to put everything else out of his head. Almost everything. He still had to be careful not to give any sign that he knew what Krelig was going to cast before he actually cast it. But that was becoming almost second nature at this point. He thought he was doing a good job of pretending it was just another day. Not two days before the day he'd be leaving this place forever.

Helena could tell, though. He knew as soon as he saw her watching him at group practice that afternoon.

"Stop staring at me," he muttered through his teeth as soon as he could get close enough to her to do so and not be overheard.

"Sorry." She looked away, and then asked, "Soon, huh?"

"Yeah."

She nodded and then seemed to refocus on the lesson. Calen tried to do the same. He made it through the rest of the day without incident. And the next morning as well, despite having trouble sleeping once again. Helena, too, seemed to be acting normally to him. At that afternoon's practice, she made just-audible mocking comments about some of the other mages' spells and rolled her eyes at Calen from across the room, just like any other day. It was strange to realize how much that had used to annoy him, back in the beginning. Now it was a welcome relief to the tension. And some of her comments were actually pretty funny. As long as they weren't directed at you.

But even Helena grew serious as the afternoon went on. Krelig was in another of his foul moods, and no one seemed able to please him. Which of course just made everyone less able to focus, which worsened Krelig's mood even further.

Krelig was watching two of the mages — Joran and Ya'el — sparring with each other at the center of the room. The two of them were casting shock spells — they gave you a sharp jolt when they landed, but nothing too terrible, and it only lasted for a second. Krelig circled them, and Calen was dismayed to see the mage's expression darkening yet again.

"Too slow," Krelig said finally, pushing Ya'el aside and taking her place. He faced Joran, who had gone very pale.

"Are the shock spells too weak to motivate you? Do you need something more dreadful to inspire you to move quickly?"

"No, Master, I —"

"Silence!" Krelig roared. He raised his hands and sent something dark red at the other mage's head. Joran yelped and threw himself flat on the floor, the spell flying over him and exploding against the far wall. It left a small crater in the stone.

Krelig's eyes grew huge and incredulous. "Did you — did you just *duck*?" He spoke in an eerily soft voice that did not match his expression in the slightest. "Did you *throw yourself to the ground* to avoid my spell instead of trying to block it or fight back?" His voice was getting louder now. "Are you a mage at all? Are you? Answer me!"

"Yes!" Joran yelled. He was still lying on the floor, facedown, his hands covering his head. "Yes! I'm sorry, I'm sorry, I'll do better, I'll —"

"It's too late for that. Do you think your enemies will give you a second chance? Do you think they will wait for you to get up from the ground? Do you think they will say, 'Oh, you're *sorry*; all right, in that case, let us start again'?"

"Please —"

It was the wrong thing to say. Maybe, *maybe* if Joran

had tried to stand up for himself, to not show his fear, maybe Krelig would have backed down, or merely punished him. Instead, Krelig shook his head in disgust and sent a far stronger stream of dark red at the cowering mage. Everyone gasped; even the weakest of them at sensing magic energy could feel the deadly power in that spell.

Joran barely had time to scream. He went up in a red burst of magical fire. And then he was just a pile of ash on the stone floor.

No one moved. They had all seen Krelig punish other mages, had all *been* punished to various degrees, and they all knew that Krelig had killed Cheriyon, but this was the first time he'd killed someone right in front of them.

Not the first time for me, Calen thought darkly, remembering how Krelig had incinerated Sen Eva when she'd thrown herself in front of the spell aimed at her son. But he was still shocked into stillness with the rest. Cheriyon had been trying to escape, and Krelig couldn't have allowed him to leave and reveal their location. But Joran had wanted to stay. Joran had wanted to try again, to get better. He'd just been having a bad day at practice.

Krelig stood there for several minutes, eyes closed. Trying to get himself back under control? Did he

222

even realize that he had been *out* of control? When he opened his eyes again and turned toward them, Calen thought he'd tell them that practice was over for today. Instead, he gestured at them impatiently. "Well? Get back to it." He glanced at Ya'el. "Find yourself a new partner."

Everyone hurried to pair up and start casting. They kept going, even when Krelig walked silently out of the room a few seconds later. They kept going even when he didn't come back.

That night, Calen brought Helena up to his balcony to tell her his plan. They sat with their backs against the castle wall, looking out at the sky.

"I can bring you with me if we're in physical contact," he said.

"But . . . how? You saw what happened with Neehan and the barrier. You can't transport through it."

"No," Calen agreed. "We have to get physically past it first without using magic. That's — that's going to be the scary part." He almost laughed. *All* the parts were scary. But this part was probably the worst.

She shook her head. "I don't understand."

Calen nodded toward the faint shimmer that he knew she couldn't see. He could see it now whenever he wanted. Usually he caught glimpses of it out of the

223

corner of his eye even when he wasn't trying, but when he focused on it, he could see it quite clearly straight on. "The barrier here is only a few feet past the edge of the balcony," he said. "We'd need to take a running start, I think, but we should be able to jump far enough to get past it. Once we pass through it, I'll be able to transport us to Trelian."

She stared at him, then out toward the barrier. "How do you know? Just because it was close to the castle where Neehan slammed into it, that doesn't mean ..."

"I can see it."

She turned back to him, staring even harder. "You can? I thought — I thought you could only see colors when someone was casting."

He'd already told her the most dangerous secret; this one hardly mattered at all. And he couldn't expect her to trust him if he didn't tell her.

"That's always how it was before," Calen agreed. "But now — now if I try, I can see active spells even after they're cast. It just started happening recently." He looked at her, trying not to be terrified of confiding in her. "He doesn't know."

No need to explain which *he* Calen meant, of course. Helena's eyes widened even more.

"So . . . that's the plan. Tomorrow night. You have to

be here, and then you'll need to jump off the edge of the balcony with me. And then I'll get us home."

She looked back out past the outer half wall, squinting, then shook her head again. "If you're wrong, we'll both die."

"I'm not wrong."

"But —"

"I'm not wrong."

She took a breath. "All right. I trust you, Calen." She hesitated, then leaned over and kissed him again, more gently than the first time. "Thank you," she said when she'd pulled back. She squeezed his hand. "Thank you for taking me with you."

He nodded, not trusting himself to speak. She stood and went back inside, and in a moment, he felt her pass through the doorway wards on her way out. Calen sat there for another hour or so, looking out at the night.

One more day.

He slept very badly that night. Nightmares kept waking him — nightmares of falling, of not making it past the barrier, of being caught, of ending up half-embedded in a tree or a wall or, in one dream that was so horrible it was almost funny, materializing into the exact place where Lyrimon was taking an invisible nap.

Gods, Calen thought after waking from that one. *I hope they think to make sure he's safely out of the way.* Too late to send a crow-message to suggest it, unfortunately.

He tried to seem awake for lessons in the morning, but it was clear that Krelig could see how exhausted he was.

"I know what this is about, Calen," he said finally.

Calen's heart stopped in his chest, but he fought to keep his face calm. "You do?" *He can't know. He can't. Unless . . . Helena . . . ?*

Krelig nodded. "But you don't have to worry. You couldn't be as disappointing as Joran if you tried. Such slowness is intolerable to me. There's just no excuse. And . . . the *ducking!*" Incredibly, he laughed, as if at a fond memory. "I just couldn't believe it."

"Neither could I," Calen said.

"And besides, I need you. You wouldn't be much good to me as a pile of ashes!"

Calen forced himself to smile. "No, Master."

"I can forgive one sleepless night. But I expect you to be back in top form tomorrow morning, understand?"

"Yes, Master." *Gods, I hope so,* Calen added silently. *Top form, and far away from here.*

The day passed with excruciating slowness.

226

He couldn't bring himself to look at Helena when he arrived for group practice in the afternoon. And then he worried about how that might look suspicious, until he realized that everyone was avoiding looking at one another today. It made sense, after Joran. No one wanted to see their own fear and dismay reflected in anyone else's eyes.

Krelig seemed back in good spirits, and everyone worked extra hard to please him. Calen worried that this might encourage Krelig to kill more mages in order to inspire the rest to better performance, but he reminded himself that this would not be his concern after today. Let the traitors get what they deserved. Although really it was getting harder to think of them all that way. As a group, collectively, he hated them. But he found it hard to wish death upon any one of them individually. Even the truly awful ones — and there were many of those. For every misguided coward who joined out of fear, whom he could almost, *almost* feel sorry for, there were more who came because they wanted more power, more freedom to do whatever they wished. He hoped they were realizing how little freedom being under Krelig's rule would truly give them. He hoped it kept them up at night and gave them indigestion. He hoped . . .

"Calen," Krelig said, startling him out of his thoughts, "come here and demonstrate the proper way to adjust the speed of another mage's spell."

Calen forced himself to focus. He just had to get through this last day without giving himself away. Just a few more hours to go.

Calen and Helena practiced as usual that evening in the empty training hall. It seemed dangerous to do anything that deviated from their normal routine, and besides, they needed to be together tonight so he could bring her with him. Luckily, she'd had trouble with the speed-adjustment spells earlier, and so they had an easy choice for what to focus on and a ready excuse for practicing late into the night. Anyone who saw them would certainly understand Helena's desire to not be too slow at mastering something. And they spent enough time together now that the other mages were used to seeing them in each other's company. There was no reason for any of this to seem suspicious. But Calen worried all the same.

Eventually Helena released her last spell and said, "I'm done for the night, I think. Too tired. But I think I've gotten better, don't you?"

"A little better," Calen said. "Not nearly as good as me, though," he added, making himself smile at her.

"Watch it," Helena said, smiling back. "Unless you want another tickling. Don't think I won't do it."

He held up his hands in mock surrender. "No tickling, please. I don't think I could take it right now."

"Then you'd better be nice to me." She walked over and took his arm, and they started walking back to his room. Every step, Calen expected someone to appear and challenge them.

But no one did.

They reached his room, and he set the door wards behind him as always. The plan was for them to transport to Trelian at midnight. Just a little over an hour from now. He dragged a small, low table over to the balcony.

Helena watched, eyebrows raised.

"Running start," Calen explained. "I thought it would help us get more distance — run toward the balcony, up on the table, then up onto the wall, and push off. . . ."

"And out into nothing," she finished, looking bleak. "I'm terrified, Calen."

"Me, too," he admitted.

She smacked him on the arm. "Don't tell me that! Tell me you're perfectly confident that everything is going to go exactly according to plan!"

He laughed. "Okay, sorry! I am perfectly confident that everything is going to go exactly according to plan."

"Much better," she said, laughing a little herself.

That was when Mage Krelig stepped through the door.

"Master!" Calen said. Oh, gods. What was he *doing* here? Had he heard them talking? Had — had Helena . . . ?

No. He wouldn't believe that. He scrambled to think of how he might try to explain, to pretend he had misheard them . . . but Krelig didn't seem interested in what they had been saying. He was holding something in his hands, looking down at it. Calen looked down at it, too.

It was a crow.

"I found this bird," Krelig said in a strange voice. He looked up at Calen, and his eyes were blank and distant. "Someone has cast a spell on it. A spell that makes it want to find you. Look." He poked it, a spark of white energy appearing just before the point of contact.

"Calen," the bird said in Serek's voice.

"Why would a bird be looking for you, Calen?" Krelig asked. He didn't even seem to see Helena standing beside him.

"I — I don't know," Calen said. He had to stay calm. "Maybe the other mages have been trying to find me? I'm sure they would want to get me away if they thought it would hurt your plans."

"That's what I thought, too," Krelig said. "I thought we would laugh about it together. But then I heard the rest of its message." He poked the bird again.

Calen listened in horror as the bird confirmed that everything was ready for his return.

"It's — it's a trick, Master. I didn't . . . I don't know what it's talking about. . . ."

"I don't believe you," Krelig said, still speaking in that odd cadence with no real expression whatsoever. Calen had never heard his voice sound so . . . empty. "This is not the first message the bird has carried. I can't hear them, but I can tell that there were more. You've been communicating with someone. With our enemies."

Helena was still standing beside him. Calen could grab her hand, but he didn't think they could make it over the balcony before Krelig stopped them. Stopped them and probably killed them both.

"No, I —"

"Don't lie to me, Calen." He looked down at the bird again, and then abruptly snapped its neck and dropped its lifeless body to the floor. When he raised his head again, his eyes were no longer vacant. They were blazing with anger. And pain? "But you've *been* lying. All along. Haven't you?"

"Master —"

"*Stop lying!*" Krelig screamed. Calen saw the red energy begin to gather around the man's hands and without thinking pulled Helena close and threw a shield up around them both. Her face was white and terrified. The spell that came at them was powerful and deadly, but he'd had enough time to prepare, thanks to those few extra seconds of knowing what Krelig was about to cast. The spell shattered against his shield, but the force of it made him stagger back a step. That wasn't good. He realized that he'd never before attempted to block Krelig when the mage was really trying to hurt him. Not like this.

Krelig started walking toward them, casting new spells with every step. Each one forced Calen and Helena back farther. She added her own magic to his, reinforcing the shield, but it was clear that even together they wouldn't be able to hold out against him for long.

"We have to run," Calen whispered.

"We'd never make it," Helena responded. "Not both of us."

Another blast shook them, and the shield wavered for a second before Calen got it back under control. "I don't know what else to do," he said desperately. "We can't keep this up. He's going to break through."

"I know what to do," she said calmly. They were both facing forward, eyes locked on Krelig, but Calen felt her reach around for his hand and then, once she had it, squeeze it tightly. "Thank you for trying to take me with you. If you see Mage Avicia, tell her I'd been trying to get back, okay? Tell her I wasn't a traitor at the end."

"What are you —?"

She let go of his hand and threw herself at Krelig. He'd gotten close enough that she was able to tackle him before he could react to this unexpected, nonmagical attack, and the two of them went tumbling to the floor.

"Helena, no!"

"Go!" she screamed at him. She was tearing at Krelig's hair, pounding at him with her fists, but he'd have her off of him in a second, Calen was sure. "Go now! Don't you dare make this for nothing!"

Krelig pushed her away with a ghastly scream of his own, then started to bring his hands up toward her.

"Calen, *go!*" she screamed. "Go right now, gods curse you! Go!"

He went.

He turned and ran for the balcony, leaping up onto the table and then the outer wall just as he'd envisioned. Behind him, he heard Helena say something that sounded like, "Oh, no, you don't," and then a crash. A burst of red-black energy scorched the air as it shot past, missing his head by inches. He didn't turn around.

He pushed off the wall as hard as he could, sailing forward into the black sky toward the slight shimmer of the barrier. It couldn't have been more than a second or two before he reached it, but it felt like forever. He had time to wonder why he'd listened, why he'd let her do it. He had time to wish he could go back and try to save her. The voice in his head told him that there was no way to save her. That he had to get back to help the others stop Krelig. That he had a responsibility to survive, and to fight. He had time to tell the voice to shut up.

Then he passed through the barrier, flying and falling, and with a final silent apology to Helena, he cast the transportation spell.

Her dying scream echoed in his ears as he vanished.

CHAPTER TWELVE

MAUREL WAS THE FIRST ONE TO reach them, although Pela was only a few steps behind her.

"Meg!" Maurel shouted, climbing up to poke her head over the edge of the cart, startling some of the wounded soldiers in the process. "Are you okay? They said you almost *died!*"

"I'm all right," Meg said, just as Pela reached up and gently but firmly pulled Maurel back down from the side of the cart. Meg saw several medics and assistants approaching behind them. "Who said? How did you —?"

"The soldiers Captain Varyn sent back to bring word of your victory arrived a few days ago," Pela answered. "They said you'd been badly injured but were expected to recover. They weren't sure when you would be returning to us, though."

Meg grimaced. *Expected to recover* was not the most reassuring phrase; her parents must have been in a panic.

"I'll be fine," she said. "Eventually. I should report in. . . ."

"You should go straight to the infirmary," Pela said. As Meg opened her mouth to object, Pela added, "But I knew that was never going to happen, so I had the physicians set up your room for you as soon as we heard what had happened."

"Thank you, Pela," Meg said gratefully. "I — I'll just need some help getting there." But Pela had anticipated that as well.

"I sent word as soon as we saw Jakl approaching," Pela said. She took Maurel's hand and led her off to the side. "Let's give Meg and the medics some room."

Maurel stared as two rather burly assistants carefully helped Meg down from the cart and onto the litter the medics had waiting for her. The rest began helping the other soldiers down from the cart behind her.

"Meg — can't you walk?"

"Not very well just yet," Meg said, wincing slightly as they settled her into place. "It's okay," she added, seeing Maurel's stricken expression. "I'll be able to walk again just fine. My leg just needs a little time to heal."

"And your arm, too? And your shoulder? And your head?"

Meg had almost forgotten about the bandages still covering the burns on the right side of her head. "Yes," Meg said. "Don't worry, okay?"

"Okay," Maurel said doubtfully. She looked at Meg for a moment, then past her at where Jakl lay resting beyond the cart. "Is Jakl hurt, too?"

Meg smiled. "Jakl is fine," she said. "He was very brave and helped us win the battle. I'll tell you all about it later."

"Time to get you inside, Princess," one of the medics said.

"Yes," Meg said wearily. *I have to go inside now,* she sent to Jakl. *I need to rest and let them help me heal. It may be a while before I can come see you, but you know I'll come as soon as I can.*

She felt his grudging acceptance of this information.

Thank you for bringing me home, she added fervently. *I don't know where I would be without you.*

He sent back feelings of gladness and safety and protectiveness and love and *always,* and she nodded and let the medics carry her away.

But instead of heading for the kitchen entrance, which was closest, they took the longer route toward the front courtyard. "Why are we going this way?"

"The king and queen requested that we bring you in through the main hall," one of the medics responded.

"But why?"

"You'll see," one of the assistants said, looking back

237

over his shoulder at her and smiling broadly. And in a moment, she did.

A great crowd of people had gathered in the courtyard. They lined the outer wall and even spilled out through the main gate toward what she could see of the Queen's Road beyond. Soldiers, servants, refugees from the surrounding countryside . . . and more were arriving as she watched.

"Some of them have been here since yesterday, waiting, even though your parents sent the guards to tell them it might be days before you returned," Pela said, leaning in close from where she walked beside the slowly moving litter.

As their small procession finished rounding the corner, a cheer went up, which rose in volume and exuberance as it spread through the crowd. The closer they got, the louder it became, until it gradually changed from a wordless series of shouts to a repeated unified chant: "Dragon Princess!"

Meg stared, agape, for several long seconds, then pulled herself forcefully together. She wasn't feeling quite up to a public appearance in her current physical state, but that didn't matter one bit, and she knew it. These people had gathered to celebrate their victory, to celebrate the successful campaign of Varyn's company, to celebrate Meg and her dragon. There was a time when Meg would never have dreamed this possible — this public, joyful recognition of Jakl's place in the kingdom and undeniable proof that the people of Trelian accepted her fully and freely. More than accepted — they loved her. Clearly they did, the way they were shouting and waving and hugging one another as she went by. She smiled brightly back at them, waving her less-injured arm, ignoring the tenderness of her shoulder, and radiating her own thanks and gratitude. She kept it up the entire length of their slow journey along the narrow inner road and up to the entrance to the main hall, where she saw her parents waiting at the top of the stairs.

Her mother's eyes widened at the sight of her dirty, damaged daughter being carried toward her like an overcooked pheasant on a plate, but she quickly hid her dismay and flashed her own bright smile. Her father was doing the same. The people continued their enthusiastic chanting until the medics and their assistants had managed to get her all the way up the stairs and through the doors. Meg gave her admirers one last wave and blew them a kiss, and then some blessed person closed the doors and she let her hand drop, exhausted, to her side.

"Please, set me down for a minute," Meg asked her carriers.

They complied as her parents rushed over and Maurel struggled free of Pela's hand to crowd in close beside them.

"We're so glad you're home safe," her mother said, touching her good shoulder gently. "And very proud of you."

"Yes," her father agreed. "Well done, Meg. Well done, indeed."

"Thank you," she said. She cast a glance back at the closed doors. "I see that everyone has already heard all about the battle."

"Yes," her mother said. "Varyn's riders couldn't keep the story to themselves, and we didn't see why they should try. These people needed something to celebrate, by the gods. And what we heard certainly sounded worth celebrating."

Meg couldn't help feeling pleased by her mother's words. "I'm glad I could help them there. But I didn't do it alone, you know. Captain Varyn and the others did most of the fighting. And Jakl was magnificent."

The king nodded. "So we've been told. We've also been told that he saved your life. Please give him our very sincere thanks for taking such good care of you."

"You should go thank him yourself," Meg said. "I think he'd like that."

The king looked startled, but after a moment nodded his acquiescence. The queen looked equal parts alarmed and amused at the idea.

They insisted that she could tell them the rest in a little while, and the medics resumed their forward progress. When they reached her room, she saw immediately the adjustments Pela and the castle physicians had prepared. There was a small but high table brought close to the side of the bed, bearing a stack of books and a tray containing a pitcher of water and a glass. The books appeared to be romantic stories of the kind that Pela loved to read — these were probably her own copies. Meg smiled at her lady-in-waiting, touched. There were also baskets of what looked like medical supplies on another table, and another medic standing at attention, wearing that same no-nonsense expression that seemed to be a requirement for the profession. This woman watched closely as the others gently helped Meg onto her bed, which had been covered by a thick sheet. Then she waved them away.

"You too, young Princess," she said to Maurel, who

pouted but allowed herself to be sent away once Meg promised that she could come back later, after Meg had had a chance to rest a little. The medic didn't attempt to send Pela away; Meg suspected that had been negotiated by Pela in advance.

The medic then carefully unwrapped Meg's bandages and examined her injuries, and gave her a somewhat embarrassing but very welcome washing with hot water and soap and a series of wet cloths. After gently patting Meg's skin dry again, she applied some thick salve to her burned shoulder and ear and some other kind of medicine to the wound on her thigh. "We'll send Mage Serek to see you shortly," she said, "in case there's anything he can do to help. But these look very well; I believe all will continue to heal nicely, Your Highness." Then she gave Meg a significant look. "Assuming you rest as you are supposed to."

"She will," Pela said at once. "I'll see to it, Medic Sadie."

The medic bustled about a bit longer, redressing Meg's shoulder and leg, helping Meg into a fresh nightgown, and giving Pela some final instructions before heading out. Meg was glad; she really did want to rest. The top sheet had apparently been to protect the bedding from at least some of Meg's layers of dust and dirt;

it had since been removed, and she was now nestled comfortably under the blankets. Her bed felt like heaven. And she still felt so weak. Even just being carried into the castle had completely worn her out. But first . . .

She gripped Pela's arm as soon as the medic was gone. "Tell me what's been happening. Has Calen —?"

Pela shook her head. "Not yet. Soon, I believe. I'll tell you everything I know later, after you rest. We'll have some lunch brought up for you, and we can talk while you eat."

"No," Meg tried to argue. "I want to know now. Pela —"

"Truly, Princess. There is nothing so urgent that you cannot rest first. Just for a while."

Meg felt her eyelids drooping and suspected this was not a fight she could win. All Pela had to do was wait her out, anyway. She was desperately tired.

"All right," Meg said finally. "Just a little sleep." She could barely get the last words out before she felt herself drifting away.

She woke to the sound of Pela quietly arguing with Maurel in the doorway.

"It's all right, Pela. I'm awake." By the position of the sun, she'd slept plenty long enough for now. And she did

243

feel a good deal better than she had when she'd arrived. There was still pain, but it was tolerable. And she couldn't sleep forever.

Maurel took that as permission and pushed past Pela, bouncing toward the bed. She remembered just in time that Meg was injured and merely sat on the bed rather than jumping onto it. She gave the side of Meg's head, now free of bandages, a long look, but didn't say anything. Meg hoped that her scorched ear didn't look too frightening. She had assumed it was mostly healed, since the medic had left it uncovered.

"So. What has been happening while I was gone?" Meg asked, smiling for her sister and raising herself gingerly up against the pillows. Pela was there in an instant, fluffing and arranging them to just the right position behind her.

"Nothing, really," Maurel said. "Mostly we were all just wondering about you. But then the riders came saying that Lourin had lost the pass and you and Jakl were heroes and the Kragnir soldiers were on their way now and everyone was glad, except that also they said you were hurt, but that you would probably be okay. But they also said it would be a while before you came home, but then you came home the next day."

244

"I wasn't supposed to let Jakl take me home," Meg said, "but then everyone decided it would be okay after all. But I'm not allowed to ride him anymore until I'm all healed up. I can't even go and see him for at least the next few days. Would you go and visit him for me sometimes? I don't want him to get lonely."

"Sure!" Maurel said. "I like him. I'll bring Lyrimon with me so they can be friends, too."

Meg wasn't so sure how well that would go, but decided to let Maurel work that out for herself.

Maurel stayed a bit longer, filling in Meg on what she'd been studying and what terrible injustices she had suffered at the hands of Nan Vera, and then the servants arrived with some food, and Pela suggested that Maurel should go now and let Meg eat. Maurel left willingly enough, saying maybe she'd go see how Jakl was doing.

Meg wanted to get up and sit at the table, but Pela insisted that she stay put. She instructed the servants to lay the tray on the bed. As soon as they lifted the cover, Meg realized that she was ravenous. Which was good, because she had a feeling that Pela would have made her eat regardless.

"So," Meg said, once she'd taken her first few bites. "What has happened with the plan to get Calen back?"

"There have been several crows back and forth," Pela said. "I wasn't there for all of the messages, but Mage Anders assured me that plans were being refined. He wouldn't share the details with me, but I believed him that they were still working hard to arrange Calen's return."

"I hope so," Meg said. "I will insist on more information when they come to see me, though."

"That should be soon," Pela said. "I can send for them as soon as you're finished eating, if you like."

"Yes," Meg said. "That would be very welcome. Thank you, Pela."

There was an immediate knock at the door. Meg wondered if Anders had been outside listening, waiting for the perfect moment to make an entrance. It seemed like something he would do.

Pela went to the door, but she only murmured something and then closed it again.

"Not the mages?" Meg asked as Pela turned back toward her.

"No," Pela said. "It's Wilem to see you, Princess. Might I suggest you have him return later?"

"No, it's all right," Meg said. "Let him come in."

"But —"

"It's all *right*, Pela," Meg said. Pela looked like she

wanted to say something else, but only nodded and went back to the door. After a moment, Wilem stepped hesitantly inside.

"Oh, Princess," he said. "You're not—I can come back—"

"It's all right," Meg said again. "I'm not supposed to leave this bed for some time yet, so I'm certainly happy to have visitors. I'm—I'm glad to see you're well. You seem to have recovered from your injuries?"

"Yes," he said, coming closer. He stood awkwardly a few feet from the edge of the bed. Pela stood back by the door, arms crossed, face carefully blank. "I was very sorry to hear that *you* had been injured."

"Not as badly as I might have been, all things considered," Meg said lightly. Memories of *fire* and *falling* and *screaming* tried to flash across her inner vision, but she pushed them forcefully aside. That was over now. "They tell me I'll heal in time. And Mage Serek may be able to help speed things along. It was worth it, of course. Small price for what we gained."

"I don't know that I'd call it a *small* price, Princess. But certainly we needed that victory." Meg wondered if he realized that he spoke of Trelian's people as "we" now.

"Captain Varyn trained his company well," she said.

He smiled. "Spoken like a true soldier. And I'm sure

he did, and I'm sure everyone in your company helped earn that victory. But you know that they could not have done it without you. You and your dragon, too." His smiled widened. "They said you were glorious."

Meg couldn't help smiling back. He always did have an infectious smile. "Who said that?"

"The soldiers. They're all talking about it. I think half of them are in love with you. And the other half are in love with Jakl."

Meg laughed, but felt herself blushing as well.

"It's good to see you smiling," he said.

Meg wasn't sure what to say back to that, so she didn't say anything. She was still smiling, though.

"Yes, well," Pela said, stepping forward, "the princess needs to finish her lunch and get back to resting."

"Of course," Wilem said at once. "I'll visit again soon, if — if that's all right."

"I'd like that," Meg said, surprised to realize it was true.

He gave her a little bow and then walked out. Pela closed the door quickly behind him.

"Oh, Princess. You should have let me send him away," Pela said, practically wringing her hands.

"Why? There's no harm in —"

"But your *hair!*" Pela burst out.

Meg stared at her. "What — what about my hair?" she asked finally.

Pela swallowed. "I was waiting to tell you until after you'd eaten. I made Maurel promise not to say anything. The fire — it caught in your hair, Princess. We'll need to — to cut it, I think. To even it out."

"Bring me a mirror," Meg said.

Pela did. Meg took a breath and then held it up before her.

Oh.

That's what Maurel had been staring at. Earlier it would have been hidden by the bandages. The left side still looked all right, if rather messy, but on the right . . . her hair was almost entirely burned away on the right side. Some of the back as well. At least her ear didn't look too bad.

"I'm so sorry, Princess," Pela whispered. She sounded close to tears.

"Pela, please," Meg said. "It's not that bad. I mean, yes, it looks *terrible*, but . . . goodness, it's only hair. It will grow back. Better my hair than my head!"

"Of course," Pela said. "I know. I just — I had hoped — you didn't need to let that boy see you that way."

Meg shocked herself by laughing. But she couldn't help it; Pela's dismay was so oddly directed sometimes!

249

"Pela, I don't think Wilem cares what my hair looks like. But if it's distressing you so much . . . let's take care of it right now."

Pela brightened, happy to have a course of action. "Yes, that would be good. It needs a good washing as well. I'll get my supplies."

She didn't need to go very far; apparently she'd had everything ready. She did agree to let Meg move — slowly and carefully — to a chair for this, at least. Meg closed her eyes and let Pela take over. She realized that there had been a time when she probably would have been very upset about having half of her hair burned away. When she would have been mortified at the idea anyone might *see* her under those conditions. But she was still just so relieved to be safe, to be alive, to know that they'd accomplished their mission, that she couldn't work up much emotion over burned hair and a few minor injuries.

Pela took her time, snipping carefully, but eventually she stood back and nodded, satisfied. She brought Meg the mirror.

Pela had cut her hair short all the way around. It was longer in the front than in the back, but somehow that didn't look as strange as Meg would have guessed. The longest pieces came just about down to her nose. The shortest pieces, in the back, were barely half an inch in length. She tilted her head, taking a good look. She rather liked it, she thought. It's not something she ever would have chosen if not for the burning, but she liked it.

She looked up at Pela. "You've done a lovely job," she said. "Truly. I might just decide to keep it this way!"

Pela blushed and retrieved the mirror. "You are very kind, Princess. Of course it will grow back in time, but I do think you look just as pretty with short hair as with long." She helped Meg back into bed, pushed the tray of food suggestively closer again, then turned away and busied herself with collecting her scissors and other supplies.

When the next knock came at the door, it was Serek, accompanied by Anders and Medic Sadie.

"Princess!" Anders exclaimed before Serek could open his mouth. "You've survived! And gotten a haircut!"

"It would appear so," Meg said, smiling.

Serek approached and asked permission to look at her injuries. Medic Sadie assisted him in unwrapping the bandages, and he studied her shoulder and thigh with a thoughtful expression. "These are healing nicely," he said. "I can help them along a little, though, if you would like?"

"Yes, please," Meg said. "Anything to get me out of this bed faster!"

The medic frowned at that, but she didn't object. Serek placed a hand on her shoulder and seemed to concentrate; Meg felt a strange surge of . . . something, and then the little pain that had been there was gone. After a moment, Serek repeated the process with her thigh.

"You'll still have a bit of scarring, I'm afraid," he said. "And you should still stay off your leg as much as possible for at least the next few days. Your arm is set very well — I'm inclined to leave that to heal naturally, I think. With broken bones, accelerating the healing with magic can sometimes be less clean in the end."

"Yes, of course, whatever you think is best," Meg said. She felt a little winded from the healing of her shoulder and thigh. She thought she was all right with not having him do that to her arm just now, too.

Anders had wandered over to the bedside table. "*The Sweetest Dark of Midnight!*" he exclaimed, picking up one of the books. "I love this story!"

Everyone ignored him, except Pela, who beamed at him with approval.

"Medic, I'd like a word alone with the mages, please," Meg said.

The woman frowned again, but obediently collected her things and left.

"All right," Meg said once the door had closed behind her. "When is Calen coming home?"

The mages looked at each other. Meg sighed in exasperation. If she'd had full use of her arms, she would have throttled them.

"Just tell me!"

"Tonight," Serek said. "We hope."

"Tonight!" Meg exclaimed. "But that's wonderful!"

"Yes," Anders agreed. "Unless it all goes horribly wrong."

Now it was Serek's turn to sigh in exasperation. "We don't expect it to go horribly wrong," he said. "But it's a dangerous plan, and so, yes, there is always the chance that something will happen."

"What is the plan?" Meg asked at once.

"Do you remember when Calen transported you and himself to . . . well, wherever you went after Sen Eva tried to . . ."

Meg looked at him. "Did you think I could forget?"

"Ah. No. Of course not," Serek said. "Well, he's going to use a similar spell to transport himself back here."

"He can do that?" Meg asked, surprised. "Why didn't he just do that in the first place?"

"He needed to make sure there was a safe place to

transport to," Serek said. He explained briefly about the dangers of transporting oneself into a space already occupied by a thing or a person. By the time he was finished, Pela looked more than a little green.

"But — but you've worked it out," Meg said. "So there will be a safe place?"

"Yes. We're using his room. It's a place he knows well, of course, and can envision clearly, and that will help. And it will be unlikely that anyone would be in there unexpectedly."

"Make sure that horrible gyrcat isn't around," Meg said at once. Serek looked startled. Anders looked thoughtful, then excused himself. They could hear him out in the hallway after a moment, softly calling, "Here, Lyrimon!"

Meg looked at Serek, confused. "I thought you said it wasn't happening until tonight."

"Yes," Serek said. "Midnight. But no matter how carefully you make a plan, there is always the chance of last-minute . . . complications. So we want to make sure the room is kept clear, just in case. I admit we'd forgotten about Lyrimon. That would, ah, not be good. If he were there."

"I should think not!" Meg said. "All right. I'm coming down there, of course."

"There's no need—" Serek began, but Meg cut him off.

"You know that you can not possibly keep me away," she said.

He hesitated, then nodded. "That's probably true," he said. "All right. But you must stay back where we tell you. No arguing."

"I understand," she said.

When Serek left, Pela came over to sit beside Meg on the bed. "It will be a great relief to have Calen back," Pela said.

"Yes," Meg agreed. "But . . . I'm not sure how I'm going to get down there. Do you think you could help me walk that far?"

"No," Pela said at once. "You can't. You're supposed to stay off your leg."

"But—"

"Don't worry," Pela said. "I'll think of something."

In the end, Pela's plan was not a very pleasing one. About two hours before midnight, Wilem returned to Meg's room. He came in, looked at Pela, sighed, and then looked at Meg apologetically.

"If you'll permit me, Princess," he said. "Pela has asked that I help you get down to the mages' quarters."

"I will be very grateful for your help," Meg said. "But how?"

255

"I'm afraid it won't be very dignified," he said. "Or comfortable."

It wasn't. He had Pela help her stand up, and then, with one more apology, he picked her up and hoisted her as gently as he could over his shoulder. Meg squawked in protest, but both Wilem and Pela assured her that this would be the quickest way. She subsided, but she could feel her face burning a fiery red. She just hoped that no one saw them. And that his leg was truly fully healed. Pela walked ahead to clear the halls of anyone who might still be wandering around, just in case.

Wilem was breathing rather heavily when he deposited her in a chair in Serek's study. Meg didn't blame him. She was impressed that he'd been able to carry her that far. She guessed he'd gotten fairly strong while training with the soldiers, but still.

"If you need help getting back," he said, "just have Pela send for me."

"I would invite you to stay, but . . ."

Wilem shook his head. "It's not my place to be here for this. I know. Just send for me if I can help you again."

Anders watched him leave. "Such a nice boy," he said. "And so handsome!"

Serek was standing outside the door to Calen's room.

If it were anyone else, Meg would have said he was hovering anxiously.

"Where's Lyrimon?" Meg asked.

"Safe with your sister," Anders said. "We told her it was very important that he stay with her tonight. It should be all right. I think Lyrimon was actually purring when I left."

"Lyrimon doesn't purr," Serek said irritably.

"Not for you, apparently," Anders said, winking at Meg.

Meg nodded, satisfied. Then she settled in to wait. Pela sat down next to her and took her hand. Meg didn't expect anything to happen for some time yet, but it was only a few minutes before Serek straightened suddenly and said, "Something's happening."

There was an odd sound, almost like someone shouting from a great distance, and a strange sort of pressure in the air.

Serek rushed forward into Calen's room. Anders was two steps behind. Meg lurched to her feet, ignoring Pela's protests, and limped as fast as she could after them, injury be cursed.

When she got to the door, Serek was kneeling on the floor. Calen was there, sitting very still, his head in his hands.

257

"Calen," Serek was saying. "Are you all right?" He had to ask twice before Calen responded.

"No," Calen said finally. He lifted his head, and Meg gasped. He looked . . . different. Older. And—and so sad. There were tears running down his face.

"Calen," she said. "Calen, what—?"

"It's all right," Serek said. His voice was more gentle than Meg ever would have imagined possible. "You're safe now, son. You made it back."

"I know," Calen said. "But it's not all right." He looked around at them, but Meg didn't think he was really seeing them. His face . . . his face was *haunted*, she thought. That was the word for it. Haunted and full of pain.

"What did he do to you?" Meg asked softly. She wanted to go toward him, wanted to touch him, to make sure he was real, but she couldn't bring herself to move. She was afraid he might disappear again if she did.

His eyes found hers, and now he seemed to see her, but there was no sense of recognition or relief in his expression that she could see.

"I don't know," he said. "Oh, gods."

Then he put his head in his hands again. And stayed that way for a long time.

CHAPTER THIRTEEN

CALEN WASN'T SURE HOW LONG HE stayed there, sitting on the floor of his room, Serek kneeling silently beside him. He knew they were waiting for him to talk to them, to tell them what had happened, to be glad that he was back. But all he could see was Helena's face in his mind; all he could hear was her voice screaming at him to *go, go right now!* And then the sound of her dying as he fled like a coward.

You couldn't have saved her, the voice in his head tried to tell him. But how did it know? What if he could have? He didn't even try!

He wondered if he could just stay here forever, not moving. Not thinking.

Is that what you let her die for? For you to give up now?

And there could be only be one answer to that. Calen forced himself to sit back, raising his head.

Serek was gone. So was Anders and whoever else might have been there when he arrived.

Except Meg.

She was sitting beside him. Not touching him, just sitting close by.

"Hi," she said when he looked at her.

"Hi," he said back. He blinked. "You cut your hair."

"Oh," she said, reaching up to touch it. "Yes. I had to. Half of it was burned away by a flaming catapult missile. Pela was beside herself."

"It looks nice." *Flaming catapult missile?* "I guess things have been happening here, too, huh? Are you okay?"

She shrugged, then winced. "Ow. But yes. Mostly. I was injured a little, but I'll heal. Jakl and I helped win a big battle with Lourin. They were preventing the Kragnir soldiers from coming to help us. They're not anymore."

"Did they just surrender as soon as they saw you were coming for them?" Calen asked, smiling. Gods, he'd missed this. Just talking.

She smiled back. "Not quite. But a whole lot of them surrendered when they saw what Jakl wanted to do to them after they hurt me." She paused, then added, almost reluctantly, "We almost had them before that, though. Jakl and I were taking out all the catapults, and the Trelian soldiers were winning. But then they got me." She paused again, her smile fading. "But Calen — are *you* okay? You don't . . . you don't seem okay."

His smile faded, too. "I'm not. I'm —" He almost

said, *I'm not sure I'm the same person anymore.* He couldn't quite bring himself to say it, though. "It was . . . bad over there."

"I'm sure it was." She seemed about to add something else, but then didn't. Instead she took his hand. "I'm so glad you're back."

He didn't like the stiff way she was moving. "How injured are you, Meg?"

"It's not so bad, really. Burned shoulder, arrow through my thigh, broken arm, scorched ear." She started to shrug again, then clearly thought better of it. "The field medics did a good job, and Serek healed me a little when I got home. He said it was best to let the rest heal naturally."

"Well, *that's* silly," Calen said. "I can fix you right now." He lifted his free hand and sent a swirling stream of yellow, blue, and green energy toward her, seeking out where she was hurt and willing her body to knit itself back together. She gasped, staring at him, then down at herself.

"It's — the pain — it's just gone. Completely. I —" She looked back up at him, eyes wide. "What did you do?"

Now it was his turn to shrug. "I healed you."

"But Serek said —"

Serek and Anders suddenly appeared in the doorway.

"Calen," Serek said, looking back and forth between them, "did you just —?"

"I healed her," Calen said. "The injuries weren't very complicated."

Meg stood up, seeming to marvel at the way her body handled the experiment. "It's like I was never hurt," she said to Serek, amazed.

"That's —" Anders studied Meg, then raised his eyebrows. "Well. That's impressive. I couldn't have done that."

Calen abruptly felt very uncomfortable. "It wasn't — I —"

Meg grabbed his hand again. "It's okay. It's more than okay. Thank you." Her eyes were a little too wide, though. He thought she was trying really hard not to look frightened.

"If you're ready," Serek said, "maybe we could all go into the other room and talk for a bit."

Calen nodded, and they all filed out into Serek's study. Meg and Calen sat at the table. Serek perched on the edge of his desk. Anders leaned against the wall next to a row of empty cages. Well — not entirely empty. One of them still held a single crow, who was looking out at them curiously. Calen looked away, trying not to think about the one that Krelig had killed. He had promised it all kinds of rewards when he got home. Now it would never get them.

Meg looked around, and Anders said, "We sent Pela back to her room. She said to send for her when you need her. Although I guess you won't need to now."

They were all quiet for a minute. Then Serek cleared his throat. "It's very good to see you back safe, Calen," he said.

Calen glanced at him, trying to read his expression. Serek had never been very easy to read, though. "Thank you," Calen said. "It's very good to be back. Really. I'm just — it was difficult."

"Being there? Or getting back?" Anders asked.

"Both," Calen said. "I — I meant to bring a friend back with me. She didn't make it." He couldn't make himself say the rest. *She died so that I could get away. She's dead now because of me.*

"Oh, Calen. I'm so sorry," Meg said.

He nodded. He didn't trust himself to say anything else about that right now.

Serek ran a hand through his hair. "We have ... many questions, as you might imagine. But I know you have been through a lot. I won't pretend to know exactly what that involved, although I do hope you will tell us what you can. But perhaps for tonight you should just get some rest."

"No," Calen said. "I don't think I could sleep right now anyway. I'd rather get this part over with. What do you want to know first?"

Serek and Anders exchanged a glance.

"Has he been gathering followers?" Anders asked.

"Yes. There were more than forty mages with him when I left."

"Forty!" Meg said. "That many?"

"Forty-four, actually. Or —" He thought of Helena's dying scream. "I guess forty-three now." He swallowed painfully, then hurried on. "He's training us — training them to fight. To fight other mages, both individually and as an army. Nasty spells. Oh, and make sure everyone is prepared against being transported against their will."

Serek and Anders looked at each other again. "Everyone?" Serek asked.

Calen stared at him. "Surely you've been preparing here, too — haven't you? Serek, he's going to put his plans into action very soon! You need to be ready!"

"Well, we've been discussing . . ."

"*Discussing?*"

"The Magistratum —"

"The Magistratum is falling apart!" Calen shouted. "Has fallen! Every mage who came to us — came to *Krelig* — from there confirmed it. You can't sit around and wait for the Magistratum to get organized. Aren't there — I thought more mages would have come here by now."

"They have," Serek said. "Not as many as have gone to Krelig, apparently, but ... maybe thirty-five or so."

"Thirty-seven," Anders put in quietly. "Counting the three of us."

"He's been recruiting," Calen said. "Haven't you been recruiting?"

Serek and Anders looked at each other *again*. Calen wanted to shake them. "Well, *this* isn't good," he said, putting a hand to his forehead.

"Do you know what his plans are, Calen?" Serek asked.

Calen laughed, although it wasn't at all funny, of course. "His plans are to destroy what's left of the Magistratum, kill everyone who opposes him, and force every kingdom to accept him as some kind of supreme ruler. His plans are to go back to the way things were before the Magistratum, only even worse, because now he'll be in charge of everything. And he's crazy. Have I mentioned that he's crazy? But so powerful. He's going to tear down the whole world. Unless we stop him. But if you haven't even —" He made himself stop. Scolding them wasn't going to help anything. Even if it would be very satisfying. How could they not have . . . ? He took a breath. "But he was counting on having me on his side. He had a vision about that when he was still exiled. About how I had what he needed to defeat his enemies. I always assumed that meant the colors, but . . ."

When Calen didn't continue, Serek asked, "But now you think he meant something else?"

Calen took another breath. "I'm . . . a *lot* stronger now. Than I was. A *lot* stronger. He kept telling me I was holding back, and I thought he was just, well, you know, still crazy, but . . . he wasn't. About that, I mean." He hesitated, then went on. "Also, something else has started happening with the colors."

"Can you explain?" Serek asked. Anders was looking at him intently.

"I've . . . started seeing the colors early."

"Early?" Anders asked.

"Before the mage actually begins the spell. A few seconds before."

"But that's — that's not possible," Anders said.

"Can you show us?" Serek asked.

Calen nodded. "Cast something."

Serek looked around, then turned toward a plant on a shelf behind his desk. Calen saw green and purple energy dancing around Serek's fingers. "Green and purple," he said at once. "I can't tell exactly what spell it is, but I would guess that you were going to make the plant grow larger. Just a bit larger, not very much."

Serek stared at him.

"Is that right?" Anders asked.

"Yes," Serek said. "But I hadn't started. I had been just about to . . ." He turned to Anders. "You didn't sense anything, did you?"

Anders shook his head. "I can't feel it until something is actually being cast. Like . . . well, like everyone else."

They tried a few more experiments, but not very many. Calen could see the colors early every time. He couldn't always tell exactly what the spell was going to be, but he saw enough that he knew the general type of spell and could guess at its intention.

"That's . . . amazing, Calen," Serek said finally.

"Krelig doesn't know. I hid it from him. From everyone. I thought . . . it seemed important not to let him know."

"Yes," Serek said. "Very important. This could be a significant advantage. Will be."

"I should say so," Anders agreed. "By the gods, Calen."

Calen looked away, uncomfortable again.

"It's getting very late," Meg said. "Calen, are you sure you don't want to try to rest now? You look . . . you look exhausted."

He supposed it was true. "Maybe so. I don't know how much else there is to tell, anyway. He's preparing to fight; he's training everyone who comes to him. He . . . killed at least two of the mages so far." Oh. No, that wasn't right. "Three," he added softly.

"Killed them!" Meg said. "Why?"

"One tried to leave. One wasn't learning fast enough. The third . . . did something he didn't approve of." *I'm so sorry, Helena.*

Calen didn't miss the shocked glances that passed among the others. He sighed. "It was terrible there, yes. Mage Krelig is crazy, and he's unpredictable, and he's evil. But he taught us a lot. I'm *so much* stronger. That part was already there, maybe, just — just locked away, but I'm faster, too. *He* taught me how to be fast. And so many more spells. His army is going to be very, very dangerous. Every day, we learned more. Every single day. If you haven't been preparing . . ." He shook his head. "We need to get ready. Fast."

"All right," Serek said. "I think it might be a good

idea for all of us to get some rest. It sounds like we are going to be very busy tomorrow." He looked at Meg. "Do you need assistance getting back to your room, Your Highness?"

"I'll walk her back," Calen said.

"Thank you," Meg said. She said her good-byes, and they started on their way. For a while they just walked in silence. Calen still couldn't quite believe that he was there. He was really back. He'd envisioned his return a million times since the moment he left. But this was nothing like any of his imaginings. He was sure that he was glad to be back. He just couldn't quite manage to *feel* glad about anything yet.

When they reached the door to her room, Meg turned to face him. She took his hands and looked into his eyes.

"You're different," she said.

"I know." *I'm sorry.* He wanted to look away, but her gaze held him, and he couldn't.

"But you're still *you.*"

He swallowed. It was hard to make himself ask what he knew he was going to ask. Had to ask. When he spoke, it was almost a whisper. "Are you sure?"

She smiled at him. Not a happy smile, but one of her fierce dragon-girl smiles. The kind of smile he bet truly could have convinced the Lourin soldiers to surrender. "Yes," she said. "I'm sure."

He tried to take in some of that surety. She did seem sure. He didn't see any fear in her eyes now. Sadness, but no fear.

"Well," he said, "if you say so, who am I to argue?"

She nodded and squeezed his hands, then let them go. "Exactly," she said. Then she suddenly threw her arms around him and hugged him tight. He hugged her back, as hard as he could.

"I'm so glad you're back, Calen." She spoke against his neck, not letting go. "I missed you so much."

"Me too, Meg." He felt something cold and scared inside him start to unravel and disappear. "Gods, me too."

They stayed that way for a long time before they finally said good night.

The next morning, Serek called all the visiting mages together. There was a lot of commotion when they realized that Calen had returned. They shouted; they argued; they debated. Calen sat at the side of the meeting room, barely listening. This was why they weren't going to be ready. This was why Mage Krelig was so effective in his teaching. No one argued with Krelig.

Anders was also sitting and watching, not participating in the arguing. He caught Calen's eye across the long table in the center of the room. Calen suspected that Anders was thinking thoughts very similar to his own.

"We must take a vote!" one of the mages was saying. For about the hundredth time. "Serek, you must understand that this sudden reappearance of your wayward apprentice cannot —"

"Enough," Serek said in a low but firm voice, cutting him off.

"But —"

"Enough!" Serek said again. "We are not debating this."

The other mages exchanged glances.

"But, Mage Serek," another said finally, "you can't —"

"Look," Serek said. "I realize that some of you are not sure whether to trust Calen. Some of you probably think there's a chance that he's still working for our enemy." Some of the others nodded at this. "Maybe he's only here as a spy!" Serek went on. "Maybe he's going to find out our secrets and then go running back to his true master. Or maybe he's just going to kill us all in our sleep one night!"

"Uh, Serek," Anders put in, "I'm not sure this is helping."

271

Serek waved him to silence. "None of that matters. I don't care whether you trust Calen or not. *I* trust Calen." He looked around at the others seated at the table. "You've been after me for months to agree to lead our faction against Mage Krelig. To officially declare ourselves as acting independently from the Magistratum and prepare to face Krelig on our own, along with anyone who wants to join us. You've been quite insistent that if we were to do this, if I were to officially take on this role, that many others would join our cause."

"Are you . . . ?" another mage began, then looked around cautiously. "Are you finally saying that you will accept this responsibility, Mage Serek? I believe I speak for all of us when I say that we do feel strongly that if you were to agree to —"

"Yes," Serek said. "I will make myself the leader of our rebellious little group, and officially invite all other mages who wish to join us against our enemy to do so. I will announce our intention to actively organize an army of mages to oppose Mage Krelig and initiate training to get us as ready as possible for the inevitable battle. I will petition King Tormon to allow us to base our operations here at his castle, which I'm fairly certain he will agree to. I will do everything in my power to end this floundering, frustrating inactivity we've been stuck in and move us all forward in the same direction toward our shared and essential goal."

A mage with long, carefully styled white hair smiled at him across the table and stood up. "Well, that's wonderful, Mage Serek! We can —"

"I will do these things," Serek continued, speaking right over her, "only if you accept my word that Calen is on our side and refrain from any further dithering about voting on his trustworthiness or testing his loyalty or any other such nonsense. If you refuse, then I'm asking King Tormon to revoke his hospitality, send you all packing immediately, and let you find some other idiot to lead you against the greatest and most dangerous enemy our order has ever known."

The room fell silent. Everyone stared at Serek, who sat back in his chair, waiting for their response. Calen realized that his mouth had dropped open and hastily closed it. He saw Anders do the same a second later.

"But — but we must . . ." The mage that Serek had cut off earlier trailed off, then tried again, almost wailing. "We need to *confer*. . . ."

"No," Serek said. "You don't. If we're going to do this, then we're going to do it my way. Or you can leave. I'm no longer interested in hearing any opposing opinions."

Silence again. Calen was fascinated. And a little terrified. What if they said no?

Finally a younger mage at the far end of the table stood up. "I'm with you," she said firmly. She looked around at the others, then at Calen. "Welcome back, Apprentice Calen. Happy to have you with us once more."

Another mage stood up a second later, and then another. And then very soon they were all standing.

"Good," Serek said. "Now, everyone go away. I need to figure some things out. We'll meet back here this evening. Mage Raulyn, please draft letters to the Magistratum explaining our intentions and bring them with you later on. And the rest of you, spend some time thinking of anyone else you know who might now be willing to join us. I want everyone to have a list of at least three names when you return this evening."

They filed out, talking excitedly to one another, clearly energized by Serek's decision. Any uncertainty they had about Calen was evidently eclipsed by their relief that Serek had finally agreed to lead them. It was . . . impressive. Serek was usually so strongly opposed to getting involved in Magistratum "nonsense," as he called it, that Calen would never have imagined getting to see him address a room full of mages like that and watch them fall in line.

Maybe there was a little bit of hope for the good mages after all.

Soon only Serek, Anders, and Calen were left. Anders closed the door, then came over to sit beside Calen.

"Looks like you ended up in charge despite your best efforts," Anders said. "About time, really."

Serek eyed him sardonically across the table. "Apparently so."

"Thanks for standing up for me," Calen said.

Serek looked at him. "I didn't say anything that wasn't true. I do trust you, Calen. I'm — I'm sorry for not being more clear about that earlier. Perhaps if I had . . ."

Calen shook his head. "I think — I think I had to go. I think that was what was supposed to happen. If we're able to defeat Mage Krelig, I think it will be because of what I learned while I was there."

"Well," Serek said, "I suppose that's possible. Although I still wish . . ."

"Yeah," Calen said. "Me, too."

They were all quiet for a minute.

"All right, then!" Anders said brightly. "What do we do now, fearless leader?"

Serek barked a short, humorless laugh. Then he put his head in his hands. "I have no idea."

CHAPTER
FOURTEEN

MEG WOKE UP FEELING . . . HAPPY.

It took her a while to figure it out. It had been quite some time since she'd felt happy, she realized. She'd felt relief, and a kind of fierce joy when she'd learned that they'd won the battle at Kragnir, and gratitude that she hadn't been killed . . . but not happy. Not really. Not until now.

Because now Calen was back. There was still a lot wrong — the ongoing war, for example, and let's not forget Mage Krelig — but she was happy anyway. It was easier to believe that things could turn out all right now that Calen was back with her again.

Pela had explained to the physicians that Meg had been magically healed, but they still insisted on coming in to examine her for themselves. They seemed almost sorry to see that it was true. Meg had been a little uneasy about Calen's casual reversal of all of her injuries, especially after Serek had said it would be better for her to heal on her own. But she couldn't deny that she felt wonderful. And if Calen was much stronger and more confident than he was before, well, he deserved it. After what he'd been through, he deserved to get *something* good out of it, didn't he? And besides, they needed him as strong as possible to fight against Mage Krelig when the time came. It was just . . . an adjustment, that's all. She would adjust.

Jakl could tell she was feeling better, of course, but she still went out to see him as soon as she was dressed. She didn't know if he understood what had happened. He didn't seem to care very much about how or why she was better, though. He was just glad she was.

They celebrated by going flying. Just for a little while — now that she *was* better, she should return to her responsibilities. And they couldn't go far, and couldn't fly too low, because there could always be more Lourin soldiers with catapults, and Meg didn't ever want to experience being set on fire again. But she let Jakl take her high above the clouds, where they would be safe, and for a while there was only the two of them, and everything was speed and light and being together and being happy and being free.

As they flew back down toward the castle again, later, Meg looked out at the lands surrounding them. She could see camps of enemy soldiers among the ruins of what had been her people's homes and farms and properties. The Kragnir soldiers should be arriving soon, and she hoped that they tore apart every enemy camp they encountered on the way. She hoped that they burned the enemy camps to the ground and that all the enemy soldiers died screaming. She was done feeling any sort of empathy for them.

Pela was waiting for her when they got back.

"Your parents want to see you," she said once Meg had returned to the ground and given Jakl a final affectionate stroke on the nose.

"I suspect they do," Meg said. She supposed she should have gone to see them when she first got up, but all she had been able to think about was getting some time alone with her dragon.

"Do you think Apprentice Calen is truly all right?" Pela asked as they went back to Meg's rooms so she could clean up and change her clothes. "He seemed so distraught when I left last night."

"He's been through something terrible," Meg said, "but I do think he's all right. Or at least, he's going to be. It will probably just take him some time. But he's definitely better than he seemed at first. That was . . . fairly frightening, I'll admit."

"Yes," Pela agreed. "But I'm certain you're right, Princess. He'll be back to his old self given a little time."

278

Meg didn't say anything to that. She wasn't at all certain he'd ever be back to his old self. But that wasn't the same thing as not ever being all right. You could be different and still be okay. Sometimes you could be different and be even better than you were before.

Sometimes you hardly missed your old self at all.

Her parents were waiting for her in the small conference room they often used for informal meetings. They'd been apprised of her magical healing, but they still seemed amazed to see her so fully recovered.

"Thank you, Pela," her mother said, and Pela curtsied and left, closing the door behind her. Meg sat in one of the soft chairs opposite her parents.

"I still can't believe it," her father said. "It's like you were never injured at all."

It was true. The burn scar was still there, but that was the only evidence that remained. Meg found that she was oddly glad about the scar; somehow it would have seemed wrong for all traces of what she'd been through to have vanished.

"Do you really feel all right, Meg?" her mother asked.

"I do. It's a bit draining, being healed that way, but not nearly as draining as being injured. And I had a good night's sleep."

"Good," her father said. "There's something we'd like

279

to discuss with you. We'd been planning to wait until you were better, but . . . well, since you *are* better . . ."

Meg looked back and forth between them, trying to read their faces. Their expressions didn't give very much away, though. She thought that she would be able to tell if something was wrong, but they didn't exactly look like they were about to tell her good news, either.

"Captain Varyn came to talk to us yesterday," the king went on. "He asked whether we could allow you to give up your other responsibilities for the duration of the war and allow you to fight with the soldiers as your primary duty."

"Of course," Meg said at once. That only made sense. If they didn't win the war, there wouldn't be a kingdom for her to be princess-heir of.

"You — you can take some time to think about it," her mother said.

"I don't need to think about it," Meg said. "I'm only surprised none of us thought of this sooner. Of course I should be dedicating all of my energy to helping win the war. Nothing is more important than that, after all."

"Well, no," her father agreed. "But . . ."

Meg looked at them. "Did you expect me to refuse?"

"No," her mother said. "But perhaps we expected you to be less . . . eager. Especially after what happened."

280

Meg shook her head. "I'm fine now. And my place is with the soldiers, fighting to protect our kingdom. I can't shy away from that just because I got hurt." She would just be very, very sure to avoid flaming catapult missiles from now on. Jakl sent his emphatic agreement through the link.

Her parents didn't say anything, and Meg wasn't sure what else they wanted to hear. She tried not to show her growing impatience and exasperation, but she apparently did not do a very good job.

"You can't expect us to be happy or nonchalant about this!" her mother exclaimed at last. "Honestly, Meg, I think we've done a rather tremendous job of coming to terms with this whole dragon situation, but that doesn't mean it's easy. This is all entirely new territory for us."

Meg blinked, a little taken aback by her mother's directness. "Well — it's new for me, too!" she said. "But luckily the logical course of action is very clear. This is not a difficult decision. Yes, fighting puts me in danger. But we were attacked right here inside our own walls! If we don't win this war, we'll all be in danger, all the time. I'm in a unique position to really help the war effort. It would be . . . dishonorable of me to do anything else. Or for you to try to talk me out of it."

Her mother sighed. "You're right, of course. But that doesn't mean we have to like it."

"No," Meg allowed. Then she grinned. "But at least you won't have to worry what I'm up to all the time. Captain Varyn will keep me in line."

Her father gave a short, surprised laugh. Then he looked at her and his smile faded, but he seemed less conflicted now. "I'm certain he will," he said. "He thought one more day of rest was a good idea, but asked to have you report for duty tomorrow morning."

Meg realized that she was still happy. Or happy again, perhaps. This felt right. She hated sitting around. She wanted to do things, to help, to get this war won as soon as possible. And she knew that she and Jakl could make a big difference.

But she supposed the additional day of rest was wise. She might not get another opportunity for rest for quite some time. She decided to go to the gardens, to sit and think and look at the trees and just enjoy their lovely green and growing company.

She ran into Calen, Serek, and Anders in the stairway.

"Where are you three off to?" She was still smiling. Calen was back!

"Prisoner interrogation," Calen said as she fell into step beside them.

"Prisoner . . ." She stared at him. "You mean the Lourin soldiers who attacked? But . . . why haven't they been questioned already?"

"They have been," Serek said over his shoulder. "Repeatedly. First by the guards, then by Anders and myself at your parents' request. And then by several of the other mages who are here."

"And none of you could find out anything?"

"We found out that something is preventing them from being as forthcoming as we would like," Serek said grimly.

"Or someone," Anders put in.

"Or someone," Serek agreed. "We thought perhaps the mages from our opponents' kingdoms worked together to cast something particularly hard to decode, but . . ."

"But as far as anyone knows, Lourin's mage never resurfaced after Sen Eva implanted herself as King Gerald's advisor before all of this started," Anders continued. "And Mage Xanda, who is here with us now, was an apprentice with Mage Bentler, who is the current mage of Farrell-Grast, and *she* says that Bentler was a *terrible* apprentice and could never have managed anything this subtle." He chuckled. "She told us about this one time that he —"

"And so," Serek said, cutting off whatever further mage gossip Anders had been planning to share, "we are bringing Calen to see if there's anything he can see that we could not."

Meg glanced at Calen, expecting him to look proud at Serek's admission that he might be able to do something better than his master. He did look proud, sort of, but also . . . something else. He noticed her looking, but his gaze skipped back away from hers almost at once.

"Can I come?" Meg asked.

"I don't —" Serek began, while at the same time Calen and Anders said, "Sure."

Serek looked at Anders.

"You know she's going to come no matter what we say," Anders told him. "Why fight it?"

Serek sighed but didn't argue.

This time Calen met her eye and grinned at her. Maybe he'd just been embarrassed by Serek's earlier comment. Serek's praise had always been so rare; it was probably hard for Calen to get used to hearing it.

"I thought mages weren't supposed to directly take part in wars except in defense," Meg said.

"They're not," Serek said. "If the mages from Farrell-Grast and Baustern did help with Lourin's attack, they did so in complete violation of the rules of our order."

"Which won't matter," Anders put in, "if Krelig wins, since he doesn't like the rules anyway." At Serek's glare, Anders added, "But, uh, of course *we* are going to win, and those mages are going to be in big trouble if it turns out they had anything to do with Lourin's soldiers getting inside Trelian's walls. Or with spelling the soldiers not to talk. *Big* trouble. Huge. No question."

They made their way down to the dungeons, and a guard led them back to where the Lourin soldiers were locked away.

There were three of them. One looked surly, one looked terrified, and the other was asleep. The surly one smirked as the guard opened the door.

"Back again? Think you'll get anything this time?" He looked at Calen and Meg. "Odd choice of reinforcements you've got there."

"Quiet," the guard said mildly. "Unless you need a reminder of what happens when you annoy me."

There was a painful-looking purple bruise on the surly one's face. He didn't say anything else, but kicked his sleeping companion awake a little harder than he probably had to. The terrified one just kept right on looking terrified.

"We thought we'd give you another chance to earn some better accommodations," Anders said.

"Good luck," the newly awakened one muttered. He sat up against the wall, grimacing with the motion. Meg saw that one trouser leg was torn away to make room for a splint that was bound to his leg from the thigh down.

"I told you — I tried —" the terrified one began, but didn't finish.

Surly slugged him. "Shut *up*, coward." he said.

"*Not* a coward," Terrified said resentfully. "I just . . ." But he trailed off, shaking his head.

Calen was watching them intently. Serek and Anders were watching Calen. Surly seemed to take this in and decide it wasn't something he liked.

"Maybe you should let the pretty girl question us," he said, leering at Meg. "I've got some things I wouldn't mind saying to her."

Meg recoiled, but before she could think of something to say, or decide whether she should say anything at all, the guard stepped forward and backhanded Surly across the face. His voice was still mild as milk. "You will be respectful," he said, "or you will be silent. Or," he added after a second, watching Surly wipe his bloody mouth with his sleeve, "you will be sorry."

"Stop," Calen said.

The guard stepped back again, and everyone waited.

"They're definitely under a spell that prevents them from talking," Calen said. "But it's more than that."

"How much can you see?" Serek asked.

Calen shook his head. "There are . . . layers. This is very complex." He looked at Serek and Anders. "I have a very bad feeling about this."

"Can you remove it?" Anders asked.

"Oh, yes," Calen said, almost offhandedly. He turned back to look at the prisoners again, and so he missed the look that passed between Serek and Anders. Meg frowned. She didn't like how unhappy they still seemed to be about his new knowledge. This was what they wanted, wasn't it? It wasn't fair to bring him here to help and then be unhappy that he could!

"I just wish I could see the other layers as clearly," Calen went on. "Well, maybe I'll be able to see more as I go."

He focused on the terrified soldier, who instantly became even more terrified. "What are you going to do?" the man asked, trying to back farther away, even though he was already at the far wall of the cell.

"I won't hurt you," Calen said. "Just hold still."

He held up one hand, palm out, fingers spread wide. From Serek's and Anders's reactions, he must have started doing some kind of magic, but of course Meg couldn't see anything. Anders's eyebrows kept rising farther up on his forehead. Serek just looked . . . more grim. Meg wanted to kick him. But she knew better than to interrupt.

After a moment, the terrified soldier blinked and looked at Calen in amazement. "You did it!" he said. "I can talk now. I —"

"Wait," Calen said. "Don't try to talk yet."

"No," the man went on excitedly, "you did it; I can tell you — please, I just want to get out of here."

"Wait!" Calen said, more urgently. "It's not —"

The man came forward, still talking. "It wasn't your fault," he said. "Your soldiers, I mean. We had help, we —"

He abruptly cut off, eyes wide.

"No, curse you! I said . . . *argh!*" Calen put his other hand out and seemed to be trying to — to *something*. . . . Meg had no idea what, of course. All this invisible magic was very confusing!

"Calen, what —?" Serek began.

"Oh," Anders said quietly. "That's not good."

"No, no, no," Calen said, still holding his hands out. "Don't . . ."

The prisoner burst into flames.

Meg screamed and flung herself backward, away from the cell. *Oh, gods, the fire . . .*

She fought for control of herself. Jakl was reaching toward her, concerned, and her first thought was to calm him so he didn't try to come in there after her. *I'm fine,* she told him. *I'm fine, really. Just — just startled.* That was an understatement. She realized that she was on the ground when the guard knelt down beside her.

"Are you all right, Princess?"

"Yes," she said shakily. "That was . . . just unexpected." That wasn't all, of course. She was mortified that she'd screamed that way, but the sight and heat of the flames had made her feel as though she were back in the middle of the battle, not just remembering but actually *there*, about to be burned, about to fall, about to go through all of it all over again. She made herself take a deep breath and try to at least *act* composed as she let him help her back to her feet. "Thank you."

Someone had already put out the flames. The other two prisoners were wedged against opposite sides of the cell, staring in horror at the blackened body of their former companion.

"I *told* him to *wait*," Calen was saying. He looked at Serek desperately. "Serek, I didn't mean to let —"

"It's not your fault," Anders said. "I could sense what was in there."

"Not his fault!" Surly cried, even surlier than before. "He killed him!"

"No," Calen said. "That wasn't me."

"What *happened?*" Meg asked.

Calen swallowed. "I think . . . I think I shouldn't say anything yet. Except that there was a sort of — trip wire. Under the silence spell." He sighed. "At least now we know what it does, I guess."

He turned back to the cell, hesitated, then focused on the injured soldier.

"No!" the man cried. "Not me!"

"I won't hurt you," Calen said.

"That's what you told Jenner!" he yelled, indicating the corpse. "Don't you touch me!"

Calen smiled a strange, cold smile. "I don't have to touch you. Just hold still."

The man started shaking his head vigorously. "I will *not*, you're not going to —"

He stopped abruptly, and Meg gasped and tried to brace herself for more fire; she didn't want to embarrass herself again . . . but this seemed to be something else.

"Uh, Calen . . ." Serek said.

"I'm just holding him still," Calen said, his eyes still on the prisoner. "You keep an eye on the other one."

Anders shot a glance at Surly, who abruptly became very still as well. Then Anders went back to watching Calen, clearly fascinated and not wanting to miss a second of whatever he was doing.

"Now," Calen said to the man, whose eyes stared back at him in terror from his motionless face, "I won't let you move until I'm finished, but just to be safe, don't even think about telling me anything. Think about . . . I don't know, anything else. Think about how much you'd like to kill me right now. Or about cabbages. Or whatever you like. Just don't think about anything related to how you got here."

Then he slowly raised his hand again. Meg held her breath. She thought Serek and Anders were holding theirs, too. The prisoner still seemed to be breathing, she was relieved to see, but was otherwise completely frozen in place.

After several minutes, Calen stepped back. He looked at Anders, who Meg was starting to guess was better than Serek at sensing magic. "Do you sense anything else at work?"

"No," Anders said. He looked at Serek, but Serek just shook his head.

"All right, then," Calen said. Meg didn't see him do anything, but the prisoner suddenly sank back against the wall with a strangled breath that sounded more like a sob.

"Please," the man said. "Please, I don't want that to happen to me."

"It won't," Calen said. "You're free to talk now."

The man looked at Surly, who glared at him but still seemed to be held in place by Anders's spell. Then he seemed to come to a decision.

"It's like Jenner started to tell you. We had . . . help." He paused, and when nothing happened, went on. "Said he was Lourin's new mage, and he had those marks you all wear, so I guess he was. Anyway, our captain seemed to know all about it. The mage did something to your guards before the shift change, and let us pass through the gate like we were invisible. We just walked right in behind your own men."

"We would have known if he cast something through our wards," Serek said, "but not if he cast something on the guards outside, and then . . ." He shook his head in apparent disgust.

"It won't work again, at least," Anders said. "Not now that we know."

Serek gave him a look that seemed to suggest that this was little comfort, but didn't say anything else.

"But I thought Lourin didn't have a new mage," Meg said.

"I guess they have one now," Anders said. "But I can't imagine that the Magistratum would have assigned anyone to a new post, under the current circumstances...."

Calen looked at the prisoner again. "Can you tell us anything else about what the mage looked like? Did he mention his name?"

The man thought a minute, then said, "Young, not especially tall . . . light yellow hair. One of his tattoos made him look like he had cat's whiskers on one side of his face." He looked at them, seeming slightly embarrassed. "I only remember that because some of the men were laughing about it. He never said his name, but Captain called him . . . something. . . ." They waited, letting him try to remember. "Sorrel? Something like that?"

"Scoral," Calen said. It wasn't really a question.

"Yeah! That was it, I think."

Calen looked sick. He turned to Anders and Serek. "He's one of Krelig's."

"Are you certain?" Serek asked. He looked a little sick himself.

Calen nodded. "He was there. One of the first to arrive, in fact." He added after a moment, "He does kind of look like he has whiskers."

Meg stared around at all of them. "What are you saying? Are you saying . . . are you saying that *Mage Krelig* helped them get inside? That he's in league with Lourin?"

"I swear I didn't know anything about this," Calen said. "He never mentioned anything to me."

"Well, of course not," she said, but she didn't like the way Serek hesitated before nodding.

Neither did Calen, apparently. "Do you really think I would have kept that information to myself?" He threw up his hands in exasperation. "What do I have to do to prove to you that *I'm not on his side?*"

"Nothing," Serek said, holding up a placating hand. "I know you're not on his side, Calen. I'm just . . . I guess I'm just still adjusting. To — to everything."

"Well, *hurry up*," Calen snarled. "We don't have time for you to keep adjusting. He's coming, soon, and we have to be ready. And we can't be ready if you still don't trust me."

Then he turned and walked out.

Meg glared at Serek, who sighed. "Go on," he said. "Anders and I will take this news to the king."

She started to go, then turned back and spoke to

the guard. "See that the one who talked is moved to the upper level before Mage Anders releases his companion," she said quietly. Then she ran to catch up with Calen.

She found him on the path leading away from the dungeon doors.

"Hey," she said when she got close. He didn't stop walking.

"*Hey*," she said, closing the distance and grabbing his arm. "Don't you do that. Not to me." *Not ever again.*

He stopped, but he didn't look at her.

"I'm sorry," he said. "I'm not mad at you, of course. I'm not even mad at Serek, really. I — I don't know who I'm mad at."

"Krelig," Meg said at once.

He shook his head. "Not . . . exactly. I mean, I *hate* him, but that's different. I can't regret what happened, Meg. If I hadn't gone, if I hadn't learned all that I have, I don't think we'd have even a chance of defeating him." He raised his gaze to meet hers, and she had to fight the urge to step back from him. His eyes were hard and . . . closed, somehow. He looked like a stranger. The Calen she knew, his eyes had been like open windows to the person he was inside. These eyes belonged to someone else. Someone she didn't know at all.

"I just need some time alone right now," he said. He

was looking at her strangely, and she didn't know if he could tell what she'd been thinking or was just distracted by his own secret thoughts that she no longer knew anything about. "I'll see you later, Meg."

He pulled his arm gently from her grasp, and this time she let him go.

Without really thinking about it, Meg headed back to the gardens and that quiet corner near the stone wall. But she wasn't really surprised to find herself there when she arrived.

And she wasn't really surprised to see Wilem sitting beneath the tree near the wall, either.

"Princess!" he said, getting to his feet. He looked at her in amazement. "Pela told me you'd been healed . . . but this is incredible."

She'd almost forgotten. "Yes," she said. "Calen . . . learned a lot while he was away."

Wilem seemed on the verge of leaving, but didn't. Meg sat down against the wall and waited to see what he would do.

He hesitated a few more seconds, then returned to his place under the tree.

"Calen has certainly become very skilled," he said after a moment.

"Yes," Meg said. "I don't want to talk about it."

"Ah. Sorry."

She leaned her head back against the wall and sighed. "No, *I'm* sorry. I don't know what I want to talk about, I guess. Calen's new ability . . . it's — it's a good thing, of course. It just takes a little getting used to."

"Lots of changes are like that."

Meg looked at him. He was someone who knew about change, all right. He'd realized not that long ago that his entire life, or nearly so, had been based on a lie. That his own mother was deceiving him in order to get him to go along with her evil plans. He'd done some terrible things based on those lies. He'd lost everything and started over — not just in a new place, but as a prisoner, surrounded by people who hated and mistrusted him. And now . . .

"How do you do it?" she asked him finally. "How do you just go on, when your whole world has shattered around you? You seem . . . you seem almost content, and yet . . ."

"I am more than content," he said. "I'm being given a chance to try to atone for my crimes, to live a better life than the one I was living before. The world that shattered was not one that I would ever wish to return to. It wasn't even real." His mouth twisted at this, and he plucked a

297

few blades of grass before looking back up at her. "Now, for the first time, I'm certain that my actions are my own, that my goals are my own . . . that I'm living as my own person, not the pawn of another. I have food and shelter and all the comforts I could want, and I have a place here now, with the army. I've made friends; there are people I care about. . . ." He trailed off. "I have regrets, of course. For the terrible things I was a part of. For the terrible things I was willing to do. But I can't be sorry that I've ended up where I am now."

Which was very similar to what Calen had said, Meg thought.

He studied her for a moment. "But your world isn't shattering, Princess. It's coming back together. Your friend has returned; Kragnir's forces are coming to join us . . ."

"But everything is different!" She sounded like a child, but she couldn't seem to help it. "I know things change, that they *must* change, but I thought . . ." She sighed. "I suppose I thought that once Calen came back it would be . . . like before. But it can't be. He's different. I'm different. The world is different. We can never go back."

"No," Wilem said. "You can't go back. But you can go forward. Sometimes forward is better. I think . . . I think most of the time it is."

"They've asked me to fight full-time with the army for the duration of the war," she said abruptly. "Starting tomorrow."

He looked . . . not surprised, exactly. Thoughtful? "Will you do it?"

"Of course. It's where I belong. I think everyone kept hoping the war would somehow just end on its own, and they wouldn't have to put me in danger. But of course it didn't, and then they did let me fight, and then I almost died. . . . I don't think it was easy for my parents to agree to send me back out. But they understand that no place will ever really be safe if we don't win this war. And we have the best chance of winning if Jakl and I are part of the fighting."

Which suddenly reminded her forcibly of what had just happened in the dungeons. She sat up. "It's even worse than we knew, Wilem. We just learned that Mage Krelig is conspiring with Lourin."

"*What?*"

"It's how they were able to get inside our walls. And that means . . . well, all kinds of things. Gods, I should go report in. The mages are telling my parents now." She was a little ashamed of herself for coming here at all. But she'd been so thrown by the interrogation and then by Calen's *strangeness*. "I just . . . I just needed a few minutes before facing up to everything again, I think."

She didn't know if she was explaining to Wilem or to herself.

"I think you're allowed to give yourself a few minutes now and then," he said. "It's why I come here, too. You can't give your all to something else if you don't take care of yourself."

"That sounds very wise," she said. "But it's probably just what I want to believe right now."

"Can't it be both?" he asked, smiling.

Meg smiled back. "Maybe it can."

They were quiet a moment, smiling at each other.

"I like your hair that way," Wilem said.

"Oh," Meg reached up to touch it. "I keep forgetting. I mean, thank you. It was — well, you saw." She laughed before she could stop herself. "Pela was horrified."

"That your hair had burned away, or that I saw it?"

"That you saw it. She took the burning in stride. It was the being seen in such disarray that she had trouble with. She was very embarrassed on my behalf."

"Battle scars are nothing to be embarrassed about," Wilem said seriously.

"I know. I feel the same way. It's important to remember what we've been through, I think. What we've accomplished, and what we've survived."

"Yes. Well said, Princess."

She rolled her eyes at him. "Will you not call me Meg? We're both going to stay in Trelian for the foreseeable future, it seems. We're fighting in the same army! You might as well call me by my name."

"Are you certain? I didn't wish to . . . I know, before, it was . . ."

"Things change," Meg said. "I think . . . I think they've changed again."

He hesitated, then nodded. "Very well. Thank you, Meg."

She grinned at him. "You're welcome, Wilem."

Meg got back to her feet and headed toward the castle to find her parents. She looked back once and saw Wilem watching her as she walked away. He lifted his hand in a wave, and she waved back before she continued on. She thought she might have moved beyond not-hate with regard to Wilem. Moved on to . . . something else. She didn't know what. Something far less cold and distant. Whatever it was, she couldn't deny that she rather liked it.

And maybe that was okay.

Wilem was right. They couldn't go back. But they could go forward.

And sometimes forward was better.

CHAPTER FIFTEEN

ALEN'S DAYS IN TRELIAN HAD FALLEN into a strange and distorted reflection of the time he'd spent with Mage Krelig.

In the mornings, he had private lessons with Serek and Anders. Although in this case, he seemed to be the one doing most of the teaching. Or at least, they weren't attempting to teach *him* anything. Mostly Calen just continued to demonstrate all the new things he could do.

And despite their assurances that they were not, the mages mostly just continued to seem rather horrified.

Even Anders, although he did have occasional moments of bright interest when he seemed to forget how horrified he was. "Face melting! I've never seen that," Anders said when Calen described (but did not demonstrate) the terrible spell that Cheriyon had sent at him but ended up enduring himself. He did demonstrate a lot of the other spells, though. And the techniques — slowing down another mage's spell or turning it back against its caster. Most of these things Anders and Serek could do perfectly well themselves, of course. They just weren't prepared to see how easily Calen could do them.

They were still uneasy about the early-colors thing, too, he thought. He could see the early colors all the time now.

Calen still hadn't told them very much about how Krelig conducted his lessons. He didn't tell them about the various punishments — the burnings, the cutting, the slicing off of the tips of ears. He wasn't sure why. Partly he just didn't want to talk about it. He also didn't like the idea of how they might react. He already felt somewhat . . . *tainted*, he supposed was the word. For how he'd learned what he'd learned. And from whom.

It doesn't matter, he tried to tell himself. *The important thing is that you learned so much. Enough to make a real difference.*

He thought that was true. He just wished Serek and Anders could get past feeling horrified and start focusing on how they could use Calen's abilities to fight Krelig.

He also wished, very much, that the other mages had spent more time learning and preparing while he'd been away. From what he'd seen so far, they were nowhere near ready.

And Krelig would surely be coming soon.

Now that they knew he was working with Lourin, that probably meant a physical attack as well as a magical one. Serek's time had been divided between working with the mages and meeting with the king and the commander to discuss how the mages could help now that they knew other mages were involved in the war. That changed the rules, concerning what and how much the mages (the *good* mages) were allowed to do. Of course, since the group here had already set themselves up as separate from the Magistratum, Calen thought they could just make up their own rules, but he could see that Serek was trying to walk a careful line.

And Calen could see the sense in that, too, of course. They didn't want to be like Krelig, abandoning all rules in order to achieve their ends. But he still thought Serek could stand to bend a few more.

Serek *had* taken charge, though, and the other mages were listening . . . but Calen was afraid many of them still didn't understand how ruthless Krelig was. How he was teaching the other mages under his command to be just as ruthless. That they wouldn't hold back. When the time came to fight, Krelig's army wouldn't be constrained by any rules or conventions or even morals. They would be driven by terror of Krelig and by the knowledge that, if they didn't win, there would be nothing left for them afterward. They could never return to the Magistratum after joining forces with the enemy. There was no way the other mages could ever forgive them for what they'd done.

In the afternoons, when they joined the other mages for group practice — there were more of them now, a little over sixty, with others still on the way — Calen struggled to hold his tongue. They were so *slow*. And so polite. There seemed to be more time spent discussing whose turn it was to do what than actually casting spells. Finally Calen pulled Serek aside and told him how Krelig organized his group practices. "They're ready for anything," Calen said. "He's made them ready for anything. And our side . . . they're too *nice*, Serek. Can you get them to be less nice?"

Serek seemed to think this over. "Maybe," he said at last. He strode to the center of the hall.

"Mages!" he said. "My apprentice thinks you're all a little too soft to face Krelig's army, based on what he's seeing right now."

Calen winced. He hadn't wanted Serek to say *that*!

All the mages looked at him. They didn't seem to appreciate the criticism.

"Calen and I are going to demonstrate the kind of practice Krelig is holding with his secret army," Serek went on. "As a motivational exercise." He beckoned Calen forward.

"Serek? I don't —"

"Don't use that face-melting spell," Serek said under his breath. "But come at me full strength. Maybe we do need to wake these people up a little."

They moved into the center of the room. Calen started with a fairly basic lightning spell. Serek blocked it effortlessly and raised an eyebrow at him.

All right, then. Calen started again, this time sending a double-edged shock spell that flew out from both hands simultaneously and came at Serek from two different directions. Serek still blocked them, but he nodded at Calen encouragingly. *Better. Keep going.*

Calen kept going. Serek began firing spells back at him. They circled each other, throwing spells and blocking and deflecting and shielding. Neither of them landed anything on the other, but everyone could feel the intensity of the magic energy, and they were all watching with full attention. After a while, Serek gestured to Anders, and then Calen was fighting both of them.

And holding his own.

Of course, he had the early-colors advantage, but he and Serek and Anders had agreed that that should probably stay a secret among just themselves, at least for the time being. And if it gave the others the idea that *all* Krelig's mages would be just as fast . . . well, so much the better.

The others watched, all scornfulness and mistrust gone at this point. They were finally starting to see how Krelig had trained—was still training—his mages. Calen kept going, even when Serek brought another mage, and then another, into the circle to face him. It wasn't until there were five of them that they finally began to get past his defenses. Even seeing the colors, even seeing them early, it was hard to keep track of what all five of them were doing at the same time. Serek finally hit him with a painful but brief spell that slammed him back against the wall and onto the floor.

"Enough," Serek said, holding up a hand to stop the other mages, some of whom had seemed more than ready to continue casting things at Calen while he was down. They were all breathing hard, but they were also all very aware of the fact that it had been five against one. And that Calen had held out for a very long time.

"If every one of Krelig's recruits is able to take on five of us at once, we're in for a very difficult time out there," Serek said. "We need to improve quickly. You must not underestimate your opponents in this battle. Krelig is the most dangerous by far, but the rest of his mages are apt to be a great deal more powerful than when they first left to join him."

The truth of this finally seemed to be getting through to the others. Serek set them back to work and then asked Calen and Anders to follow him out. The other mages were going at each other a bit more seriously by the time they left. Calen was cautiously hopeful. It wasn't enough, not yet, but at least it was a start.

On the way back toward Serek's study, Anders let Serek get ahead and then leaned in close to Calen.

"You never did come at us with your full strength, though, did you?" he asked.

Calen looked at him for a long moment. "No," he said. He hadn't even come close. He *had* eventually started to get tired, and the others had finally bested him by just giving him too much to focus on at once, but not one of his spells had been as strong as he could have made it.

Anders nodded, having clearly already figured this out. "That's . . . probably for the best. Our little group is small enough, eh? Better not to accidentally kill off anyone from our own side if you can help it." He patted Calen encouragingly on the shoulder and jogged ahead to catch up with Serek.

As soon as they arrived, Anders went over to check on his remaining crow.

"Why are you still keeping that one?" Calen asked. "We don't need them anymore."

"George smacked his wing into the edge of the window his first time out and has been recovering ever since," Anders said, reaching into the cage and gently bringing the bird out onto the counter. The bird *quorked* familiarly at Anders, looked briefly at Calen, then started pecking at some of the seed Anders had spread on the countertop. "He's not too bright, this one," Anders added.

"Or," Serek put in from across the room, "he's a genius, and figured out that if he stays here nursing his injury, you'll take care of his every need and feed him until he's too fat to fly anyway."

"Hmm," Anders said. He looked back at the bird, eyes narrowed slightly.

"Calen," Serek said. Calen turned and was surprised to see his master holding the deck of spirit cards from his desk drawer. "Are you up to trying a reading?"

"Sure," Calen said. He'd always liked working with the cards. He went over to join Serek at the table. "It's been a while, but I think it will come back to me."

Now Serek looked surprised. "Didn't Krelig have you doing divination for him?"

"No," Calen said. "It was forbidden, actually. He said he'd already seen what he needed to see and didn't need anyone else's interference. I think he was afraid of anyone seeing something less favorable than the sightings he had while he was still exiled. He told me once that he hadn't had another vision since he'd been back."

"You didn't try on your own?" Anders asked, coming over to join them. "You've certainly done things that were forbidden before."

Calen flushed a little at that and decided not to glance at Serek just then. "I was afraid he'd know," Calen said. "He often seemed to know things — where you'd been, what you'd been doing. Not always, obviously, or he would have discovered the bird plan much sooner. But I only worked with the birds out on the balcony, which I think helped hide it from him, at least a little. I suppose I could have tried some divination out there, something simple with stones, maybe, something I could find on my own, but it seemed like too much of a risk. It was . . . never good to make Krelig angry." He reached up to touch his ear before he could stop himself.

"Well," Serek said, "I think it's worth trying now. Especially with this new development in how you see the colors, which could very well be related to your skills at divination. Of course, you know that it's not always reliable, or accurate. . . ."

"I remember," Calen said, fighting a smile. Same old Serek.

"All right," Serek began. "Let's —"

He was cut off by a sudden bloodcurdling scream from the yard outside.

They all whipped their heads around to stare toward the sound.

"That's Maurel," Calen said. He was out of his chair and running for the door before the words were out of his mouth. The mages followed a step behind.

All kinds of terrible images flashed through his mind of what might be causing her to scream like that, but as he burst through the door, he saw nothing. No slaarh, no Krelig, no enemy mages, no attackers, magical or otherwise. Maurel was there, but she was just standing still, looking down at something in the grass.

"Maurel!" he cried, running over to her. "Are you all right? What happened?"

She looked up at him, then pointed. "That bird," she said. "It just — it fell right out of the sky. Right in front of me. It almost hit me! And it's —"

"Is it dead?" Anders asked, coming up beside them with Serek.

She shook her head, starting to cry. "No."

Calen bent down to look at it. She was right; it was writhing in apparent pain, making terrible little mewling sounds. He concentrated and saw traces of magic around it. Black and red.

"Someone did this to it," Calen said, straightening. "A mage. Who would—?"

Before anyone could answer, they heard another person scream somewhere nearby.

And then another bird fell from the sky right beside them, screaming as well.

They looked up.

There were more, everywhere — as though every bird in the kingdom had suddenly lost the ability to fly. They could see dark, sinking clouds where whole flocks were falling together.

"Inside," Serek said at once.

Calen grabbed Maurel's hand and started to run for the door, but she pulled away from him.

"Lyrimon!" she cried.

"He can take care of himself!" Calen said, trying to recapture her hand.

"Not if a bird falls on his head!"

"I've got him," Serek said. "Go inside, Princess."

Maurel turned to see whether he was telling the

truth; so did Calen. He was — the wretched gyrcat was squirming unhappily in his arms, fading in and out of visibility. But even when you couldn't see him, he was still *there*; he couldn't escape from Serek that way. Good. This time when Calen reached for Maurel's hand, she let him take it. They ran back toward the door, dodging more falling birds. Calen had to knock one away that almost landed on Maurel.

And then they were through, and safe. Anders pushed past them to run to where he'd left George. George seemed all right, at least so far. He wasn't writhing and screaming and dying, in any case. He seemed to still be pecking away at his food, unaware of anything else.

"Why is that happening?" Maurel demanded, her voice hovering somewhere between a shout and a whimper.

"I don't know," Calen said. But was that true? Certainly he could guess who was responsible.

They stood at the window, looking out. There were dead and dying birds everywhere. All kinds of birds — crows, finches, hawks, many that Calen couldn't even identify. More were still falling.

The door to the study banged open, and one of the king's guards came in. "Mages," he said, respectfully but urgently, "your presence is requested by His Majesty King Tormon."

"I'm sure it is," Anders said, stroking George's head.

"Why is that bird still okay?" Maurel asked, pointing at George.

"That's an excellent question, Your Highness," Anders said. "Maybe the spell just hasn't reached him yet." He concentrated, and Calen saw him cast a surprisingly thorough protection spell around the bird. Anders actually blushed when he saw Calen staring. "I'm not taking any chances!" he said, somewhat defensively.

"No judgments here," Calen said. "George might be a genius, after all."

"Well, now that he's safe, lock him back up and come with me," Serek said, heading for the door. "You, too, Calen. And you, of course, Princess."

The guard led them up to one of the royal meeting rooms. The king and queen were there, as were Meg and Captain Naithe. The other mages must still be training in the hall, Calen realized. There weren't any windows down there. They probably had no idea what was happening. Even if they sensed some of the magic at work, they would likely just assume it was coming from the other mages practicing around them.

There was a window here, though, a big one, and

everyone was gathered around it. The falling birds seemed to be fewer now. Meg turned when she noticed they'd arrived.

"Oh, Calen," she said. "What is going on?"

He just shook his head and came to stand beside her at the window. Maurel squirmed away from him and ran to her mother. He and Meg had never really talked about that awkward moment after the dungeons, but he thought that was probably for the best. Things felt almost back to normal between them, as much as could be judged by the little time they got to spend together, anyway. He was busy with the mages nearly all the time, and she was busy training with the soldiers. The *other* soldiers, he thought proudly. He worried about her sometimes, but not very much. The Kragnir forces had all arrived, and they were helping to hold back the enemy until Trelian was ready to make a full, concentrated, and, it was hoped, final attack, using all of their combined strength. That's when he'd worry, when she went back out to fight for real.

He glanced at her and found her looking back. He thought they both knew and accepted that "almost back to normal" wasn't the same thing as "just like they'd been before." Too much was different for that. But not everything.

315

Not what mattered most.

"Do you have any information you can offer us?" King Tormon asked Mage Serek, jerking Calen's attention back to the present.

"Not very much," Serek admitted. "We know there is magic behind this, although you certainly must have guessed that already. I cannot imagine that any of the mages here would do such a thing. . . ."

"It's Krelig," Calen said softly. "It has to be. Who else?"

"But *why?*" asked the queen.

"To punish me," Calen said. "Serek and Anders and I used birds to communicate, Your Majesty. When I was . . . when I was with Mage Krelig. To plan my escape. He found out, right at the end."

"So he kills all the birds in the whole kingdom?" the commander asked doubtfully.

Calen smiled a small, humorless smile. "He's not exactly a sane man, sir."

"What can we do?" the king asked.

Serek shook his head. "I don't think there's anything to be done now, Sire. Except to wait it out. Eventually he'll, ah, run out of birds."

They continued to watch at the window. Just when it seemed the last of the birds must have finally fallen to the ground, there was a painful screeching sound that seemed to come from everywhere and nowhere. Meg gasped and pointed at the sky.

There were words there. Enormous words, written in fiery red across the heavens. They said: YOU WILL ALL DIE.

"I rather thought he'd already made that point," said Anders. "Seems a bit overdone, really, to explain the message after the fact."

The king pointed at the flaming letters. "Can you get those out of the sky?"

"Ah," Anders said. "Yes. That we can probably do."

"But what does it mean?" the queen asked. "Is he coming here? I thought he was planning his war against the Magistratum."

My fault, Calen thought. *He's coming here because of me.*

"I'm afraid our presence has made you a more immediate target than you might have been," Serek said. "Krelig knows that the strongest force against him will be here. We'd thought that he would go after the Magistratum itself first, but now that we've openly declared our position against him, he must have decided to attack the mages gathered here before going after the rest of our order." He hesitated, then added, "And he's coming for Calen as well."

Meg grabbed Calen's hand. "Don't you even think it," she said, guessing the direction of his thoughts. "You had to come back, and we need you here. He was going to come for us anyway, eventually. At least with you here, we have a chance."

He tried to believe her. She was right — he knew she was — but he kept looking at those flaming letters, knowing that if he hadn't run, if he hadn't come back, Krelig might not be focusing his attention here like this. At least not so soon.

"We knew this was a risk," King Tormon said. "And Mage Krelig dragged us into his war long ago. *Long* ago, if he was truly behind Trelian's war with Kragnir as well as our current battle with Lourin. We'll just need to be ready for him when he comes."

"We'll see to clearing your skies, Sire," Serek said. "In the meantime, I would suggest that everyone stay inside. Don't touch the birds until we know exactly what's killed them." He beckoned to Anders and Calen. Calen guessed they were going to get the other mages to help. Captain Naithe began giving his guards directions to spread the word about staying indoors.

"See you later," Calen whispered to Meg. She gave him a pointed look; Calen could interpret it easily enough: *Don't do anything stupid.* He nodded obediently and followed Serek out.

As they walked quickly down the hallway, Calen trotted up to where Serek was striding ahead of him. "This means he's coming very soon, doesn't it?" Calen asked.

"Yes," Serek said. "I believe it does."

"Do you think we'll really be ready?"

Serek didn't stop walking. "We'll have to be."

That night, Serek brought out the spirit cards again.

They'd spent the early evening working with the other mages to clear Krelig's threatening message from the sky and then to deal with the birds. They hadn't been killed by disease or anything that seemed likely to spread to humans. But once the sun went down, some of the dead birds had . . . woken up. Sort of. They were still dead, but they started flying around again. Flying around and attacking people. Luckily, most people were still inside, waiting for the all clear from the guards, but some of the dead birds had flown in through open windows. It had taken all the mages working together to remove whatever lingering magic was animating them. It had been . . . disturbing. Meg had told Calen that she thought Maurel would have nightmares for a month. Calen thought

319

he might have a few nightmares of his own. At one point he'd come around a corner to find a pair of ravens attacking a screaming kitchen boy. The birds had turned their heads impossibly far around to look at Calen when he appeared. Their eyes were milky-white and empty, and their beaks were red with blood. They flew at him, shockingly fast for blind, dead, broken things, and Calen had screamed himself before incinerating them to ashes in midair. He had accidentally incinerated one of the hanging tapestries on the wall as well, and a candle fixture on the ceiling. But he'd avoided incinerating the kitchen boy, and was able to heal him up and send him to the infirmary with a quiet word to maybe not mention anything to anyone about the tapestry.

Once the birds were finally taken care of — for good this time, they all sincerely hoped — Serek and Anders and Calen returned to Serek's study, exhausted but too shaken up to consider sleep.

They tried every card pattern variation Serek knew, and then every one that Anders knew that Serek didn't. Calen even tried making one up on the spot, just to see what would happen.

The readings were uniformly dark and upsetting. Combinations of images that meant death, and war, and pain, and destruction. Warnings of terrible consequences if they didn't do something, but no clear indication of what that something might be.

And every time, *every single time*, the final card was always the spinning coin. The card that meant there were too many forces in play, too many possible outcomes for the cards to give them any reliable sense of what the future held.

"That shouldn't be able to happen," Anders said for perhaps the fourteenth time when the spinning coin came up again.

"Why haven't you had any of your glimmers lately?" Calen asked him. "Can we try hitting you over the head or something?"

"No," Anders said, shaking his head. "I've tried that before; it doesn't work."

"Well," Serek said, sitting back in his chair, "I suppose we know everything we really need to know, anyway."

Calen looked at him. "That Krelig is coming, and if we don't stop him, he's going to destroy everything and everyone that we care about?"

"And coming soon," Anders added. "With his army of turncoat mages. But let's hope no more zombie birds." He turned to check on George, who was pecking away contentedly in his wire cage, still safely encased in Anders's layers of protective spells. He might be the last bird left alive in the entire kingdom, for all they knew.

"And that we are still very outnumbered," Serek said grimly.

"Oh," Anders said suddenly. He pushed his chair back and lurched awkwardly to his feet.

"Anders?"

"Wait," Anders said. "Something —" His eyes went wide and then seemed to focus on something no one else could see.

Serek and Calen sat perfectly still. They had both seen Anders experience his glimmers before, and the best thing was always to wait quietly until he was done.

"We will have something our enemy will not," Anders said in that strange voice that always accompanied his visions. "We will have a chance to make his strength his weakness. He will have a chance to make our weakness his strength. Calen is the key." He paused, then added, "Also, send the Princess to get the mages."

They waited for him to say something else, but after a second he blinked and sank back into his chair.

"Well," Serek said, "that last part was pretty straightforward. I assume you mean the mages who are still on their way from the Magistratum?"

322

"Yes," Anders agreed. "Meg needs to go get them first thing tomorrow with her dragon, or they won't make it in time." He sighed happily. "It's so *nice* when that happens. Just good clear instructions for what to do. I wish they could always be like that."

"So . . . tomorrow, then?" Serek asked.

Anders sighed again, less happily this time. "Yes. I'm afraid so. Not early in the day, but . . . I'm not sure beyond that."

"But — but what do the other parts mean?" Calen asked. "About his strength and our weakness and me being the key?"

"No idea," Anders said. "That part wasn't nearly as helpful. Although good to know that you're as important as we thought! Always nice to be sure about these things."

"Can I hit you over the head *now?*" Calen muttered, not quite under his breath. But he knew that wasn't fair. Anders couldn't control when the glimmers came, or what they told him.

"I suppose we should all get some sleep while we can," Serek said, standing up. "But first I'll go let the other mages know about tomorrow. And the king. And the commander."

"I'll go with you," Anders said.

Calen headed for his bedroom, although he doubted sleep would find him anytime soon. He thought briefly about going to tell Meg about what Anders had seen, but if she was sleeping, he didn't want to wake her, and if she wasn't sleeping yet, he didn't want to give her a reason to not be able to sleep at all.

Tomorrow. Part of him would be glad to get it over with, he supposed . . . but he was still terribly afraid that they weren't ready. And while he'd known that he would be instrumental in fighting Krelig, he wished he knew what he was supposed to do. Vague prophecies were worse than no information at all, he thought.

He washed up, then blew out his candle, lay down, and stared at the ceiling in the dark. He thought about the day Krelig had come through from the world into which he'd been exiled, how he'd given Calen no choice but to abandon his friends — his family — to go with him. He thought about the lessons, and the punishments. He thought about Helena. He thought about that poor stupid bird that he'd promised all those rewards to, and all the other poor birds, and about the broken Magistratum and the war with Lourin and all the soldiers who had died so far in the fighting and Meg's betrayed eyes as he'd left her, and all the other things that Krelig was responsible for.

Tomorrow Calen would get to pay him back. For everything. He smiled coldly in the blackness, feeling more than ready for that. He wanted his revenge. He wanted it very much. And he would get it. He was the key. He would make it happen. He would make Krelig so, so sorry.

But his smile faded as he thought again about Anders's vision.

He just hoped he'd know what to do when the time came.

CHAPTER SIXTEEN

ARLY THE NEXT MORNING, MEG AND Jakl reported for duty at the training grounds.

Captain Varyn immediately took her aside into one of the planning stations and had her sit down across the table from him. "The commander has a special job for you."

That was fast. "Yes, sir?"

"Mage Serek tells us there are mages on their way from the Magistratum. But given yesterday's events, we are concerned that they will not make it here in time for whatever unpleasantness Mage Krelig may next be planning. We have reason to believe that he will attack us sometime today."

"Oh," Meg said. She'd known it would be soon, but ... oh.

"Exactly. And since we obviously want to have all available forces assembled to meet him, we need you and Jakl to retrieve them. Unfortunately, we disassembled the large transport cart for parts, thinking we wouldn't need it anytime soon, and the others are too small to be useful. I think you can fit more people on Jakl's back than in the small carts, but it will probably mean several trips. And of course we still don't know exactly where Mage Krelig is, or his army, or his creatures. They could be anywhere. You could encounter them along the way."

"All right," Meg said. "Where are the mages you need me to bring here?"

Captain Varyn grinned at her. She knew he liked getting right to the matter at hand. It was one of the things she most appreciated about him. He was not one for endless meetings and discussions and dithering.

She grinned right back.

He took out a map and spread it across the table. "They are somewhere along this route," he said, pointing. "That's all we know. Mage Serek believes that if you fly in this direction, you will find them wherever they are along the path."

"Can you send birds to . . . ? Oh."

Varyn nodded grimly. "Right. No birds to send. They might not be expecting you. The mages here were going to attempt to contact them in other ways, but apparently that's a tricky business at long distances." He shrugged as if to say, *Who can understand magic?* "But they know *of* you, of course, and when they see the dragon, they can have no doubt about who you are. I don't think they will give you any trouble."

"Shall I head out right now, then?"

"I believe the mages want to give you a briefing first." He looked up and past her. "Ah, here is Apprentice Calen now."

Meg stood up as he approached. "Here to give me my 'briefing'?"

His mouth twisted up into a lopsided smile. "Yes, such as it is." He nodded to Captain Varyn, who gave him a little wave to indicate that he should proceed. "There are twenty-seven mages in the group we're sending you after. They sent word when they left, so we know they are on their way, but if they had any birds with them, we have to assume they don't anymore. They're still too far away to contact us directly."

"Is — is George still okay?" she asked, suddenly remembering him.

"Who's George?" Captain Varyn asked.

"Mage Anders's, uh, pet bird," Calen told him. "And yes, he's fine. The rather extensive protection spell Anders placed on him seems to have done the trick."

"I'm glad," Meg said. "But I'm sorry to have interrupted. Please continue."

"There's not much else to tell you," Calen said, shrugging. "When you find them, you can explain why we sent you. I don't think they'll argue. Well," he added, "they might argue, but not for long. And if they argue too long, just boss them around until they fall into line."

"This is my kind of assignment," Meg said. She hesitated, then looked at Captain Varyn. "May I have a word with Calen alone before I go?"

"Of course." The captain reclaimed his map and stood up. "I'll see you off when you're ready to leave."

Once he'd left, Meg asked, "Why can't they use that transportation spell? I mean, since it's an emergency?"

He shook his head. "They can't. They don't know the castle or the grounds, and there's too much danger that they might not arrive safely. And besides, Anders had a vision that said you had to get them. To be honest, we didn't spend much time thinking of other options."

"That makes sense," Meg agreed. She hesitated, then said, "Calen, I just — just in case anything happens . . ."

He looked alarmed. Then determined. "Nothing's going to happen. Jakl will protect you. And then you'll be back before you know it."

She glared at him. "Be quiet and listen. There's something I want to say." She took a breath. "I was furious with you when I realized you'd gone off to try to rescue Maurel without telling me. Gone off to do something so reckless and dangerous without even saying good-bye."

329

"You're not saying good-bye," he said. It was almost an order.

"No. But . . . I just want you to know that I forgive you. Whatever your reasons were, I know that you thought they were good ones. For keeping secrets and . . . for leaving. With him. I was so mad at you, Calen. But I never believed you'd truly joined him. You do know that, don't you?"

Calen was silent for a moment. Then he said, "He was going to kill you, Meg. You and Maurel and all the rest, right there, if I didn't go with him. I didn't have a choice."

She'd come to think it must have been something like that. But it was still a shock to hear it.

He was looking at her beseechingly. "I couldn't say no. Not if saying yes could save you. And there was no way to tell you. He'd — he'd stopped time, for a while. I don't think anyone else could tell. He stopped it for just himself and me, and he told me how he was going to kill you if I dared to refuse him again."

"You said no at first." It wasn't really a question. She knew that he must have.

"Of course I did!" Calen said. "But then . . . I had to say yes. Do you understand?"

"Yes," she said. She took his hands. "I'm so sorry, Calen. I'm so sorry for everything you went through."

He shook his head. "Don't. Don't feel sorry for me. I — I just have to make sure it all ends up worth it in the end. All of it. We have to stop him. That's all that matters."

"Then let's stop him," she said.

He smiled at her. "Okay."

He walked her over to where Jakl was waiting, eager to go. The dragon bent his head down so that Calen could rub the scales behind his ears.

And then Meg hugged Calen good-bye (but didn't *say* good-bye), and saluted Captain Varyn, and climbed up on Jakl's back, and they were off.

Meg had shared the map in her mind with Jakl while she was still sitting with the captain, so he knew exactly where they were going. She scanned the ground beneath them for any signs of Mage Krelig or his monsters, but she saw nothing. *He probably wants to give us time to wait, and worry,* she told herself. *He probably won't come right away. He'll want to give us most of the day to be afraid first.* It could be true, based on what little she knew about him. But Calen had also said he was crazy and unpredictable. If he was really angry, if he really wanted his revenge, maybe he wouldn't wait. Maybe he couldn't.

It was just about an hour before they saw the Magistratum mages in the distance. She wondered why there were only twenty-seven who had decided to leave and join Mage Serek and the others. She couldn't imagine what the rest of them were thinking. Did they actually believe they could just sit back and not get involved? Did they still think some other solution was possible? Some compromise? With a crazy man who wanted to take over the entire world, possibly destroying half of it in the process?

She saw them start pointing up at her, saw them stop walking and start talking frantically among themselves. Gods, but mages liked to talk to one another. Well, not Serek so much, she supposed. But all the rest of them. Luckily she didn't have to wait for them to reach some kind of consensus. She and Jakl swooped down and landed right in front of them. He sent the equivalent of dragon laughter through the link when some of the horses scattered in fear.

"Hi," she called out to them. "Anyone need a ride to Trelian?"

She did end up having to wait while they decided who would go in the first group. But once those selected had climbed up behind her (with various degrees of grace and courage), she turned and looked down at the rest of them. "Figure out now who is coming in the next group.

I think it will take four more trips after this one." Jakl could easily manage five at a time, maybe six, and a few of them were on the small side; she thought they could make it in five trips all together. In fact . . .

She pointed to one of the apprentices, a skinny boy of maybe ten. "You come with this group," she said. "Better to have Jakl carry extra people when he's fresh than when he's tired."

The boy looked nervous but came gamely forward, climbing up behind the others.

"Keep moving," she said to the rest. "I'll be back in under two hours. The farther you ride in the meantime, the quicker you'll see me again."

She left them trying to recapture their horses, and leaped with Jakl back into the sky.

The first trip was uneventful. Meg had a bad moment when she was suddenly seized with the certainty that she would see Krelig's army waiting for them as they approached, but the way was clear when they arrived. She landed in the courtyard and sent the mages off with a waiting guard to find Serek and the others. Then she and Jakl headed back for the next group.

She took five the next trip, and another five the next. Each journey was a bit shorter than the one before, since the mages kept riding toward Trelian all the while.

Which was good, because Meg still expected to see Krelig's army at any moment. She wanted to have everyone safely delivered before that happened. Every time the castle came into view, she felt an overwhelming wave of relief that the enemy had not yet arrived.

We'll make it, she told herself. *We're more than halfway there.*

But she continued to urge Jakl to fly as fast as he could.

She'd planned to take six on the fourth trip, but the mages had other ideas about how they wanted to be grouped, and she didn't want to take the time to argue with them. So it would have to be six in the last group. Fortunately neither she nor Jakl was feeling the least bit tired. Each time she'd returned to the castle after the first trip, there had been a mage waiting to give them a little magical strength and energy.

Magic could be pretty handy sometimes.

Jakl didn't mind the multiple trips; he was happy that they had an excuse to fly as fast as possible. He liked the extra energy, too.

When she dropped off the fourth group, Calen was waiting with another mage that she didn't know. That was different, and so immediately made her alarmed.

"Trouble?" Meg asked, sliding down to the ground before him.

"Maybe," Calen said. "Anders had another vision. He said you'd need extra strength for the last trip."

"Did — did he say why?" The fear she'd been struggling to keep at bay came rushing back in a heartbeat.

"He couldn't say. It could be Mage Krelig's arrival, or it could be a storm coming, or it could be any number of things. He wasn't sure why you needed the extra strength; he just said it would be bad if you didn't have it."

"I see," Meg said. "All right, then. Cast your spells, and we'll go."

The other mage went first, touching first Meg and then Jakl, sending a now-familiar flood of alertness and energy through them both. Meg felt as though she'd just awakened from a very good night's sleep.

"Now for the extra," Calen said. He stepped closer and touched her hand. Meg gasped as the magic began to flow into her. It was — it was more than strength. It was power. She almost felt like she could fly back for the last group of mages on her own.

"Calen," Meg said, "can you spare that much? Won't you need it for yourself?"

He dropped his gaze. "I'm much stronger than I used to be, Meg. Don't worry." He glanced back up at her, and the smile he gave her looked a bit forced. "Plenty left where that came from. But I'm only giving it to you; I think you need it more than Jakl does. And Anders only said that *you* would need it, not that Jakl would."

"Well," Meg said in a low voice, so the other mage wouldn't hear, "it's not like we can't share it if we need to." She thought that at least some of the other mages must guess how closely connected she was to Jakl, but she still didn't want to advertise the fact.

Calen nodded. "That's what I thought, too." He stepped back as Meg climbed back up astride her dragon. "Be careful!" he added at the last.

"Of course," she said. Then she grinned at him. "You know me!"

She laughed at his helpless expression as they flew away.

The last six mages pulled up their horses when they saw her returning. The other horses had already been turned loose, with the hope that they would find their way back to the Magistratum. Meg waited while they dismounted and collected their small bundles of belongings. They were a mixed group: three women and three men of various ages. One of the women was very old; Meg was a bit worried about her, but she slid down from her horse without difficulty and showed no hesitation about climbing atop the dragon. Still, Meg suggested that the old woman sit right behind her, which felt like the safest place. At least Meg would know she was all right.

All their faces were heavily marked, which Meg took as a good sign. As far as she understood, that meant they knew a lot of magic and were very good at it. From what Calen had told her, the mages back at the castle needed all the help they could get.

When everyone had settled into place atop the dragon, Meg checked to make sure they were all holding on, and then let Jakl launch himself back up into the sky. She never got tired of feeling the beat of his wings through the link, especially right at the start, when he was first gaining his initial speed and altitude. She could feel the air working to lift them higher, the power of him as he pulled them forward, the dwindling presence of the ground below. It was always wonderful, every time.

She heard one of the mages whimper slightly from behind her and smiled. She didn't think it had been the old woman.

As they flew, Meg kept an extra-sharp eye out for danger this time around. She wished Anders could have been more specific! She doubted it had been a storm he'd felt coming — the sky was clear for as far as she could see. But then, the ground was, too. There were areas of

337

dense forest that she couldn't see into, but she didn't think Krelig could move an army through there. Even a small one. Not if he were bringing the slaarh, anyway. At least some of the slaarh could fly; she expected that would be the way they came.

The closer they got to home, the better Meg felt. Whatever Calen had done seemed to have worked, thank the gods. And Anders. They'd get this last group safely inside, and then Serek would have all the mages he needed. Surely, this many mages, working together, would be able to bring down even someone as powerful as Mage Krelig. She knew he wouldn't be alone, but he wouldn't have nearly as many mages as they did. And if he showed up with the Lourin soldiers at his back . . . well, they had the Kragnir forces now. *Thanks to you*, she thought at Jakl fondly.

They were almost back. Meg was so busy thinking about the combined ferocity of Trelian's and Kragnir's armies that it took Jakl's sudden tug at her through the link to bring her attention back to her surroundings.

Sorry, she thought at him. *I was —*

She broke off.

Behind her, she heard the other mages gasp and cry out.

A great horde of slaarh surrounded the castle in a

dark, horrible ring. The afternoon light seemed to slide right off their oily black hides as though it couldn't bear to touch them. They all had human riders atop them, and more men stood on the ground behind the monsters. Lourin's forces, Meg thought. Maybe Baustern's and Farrell-Grast's, too.

And just inside the circle of monsters, a large group of mages stood facing Trelian's front gate.

Krelig had come.

Jakl screamed and sent a burst of fire into the air before them. The slaarh's heads snapped toward them, and the men on their backs seemed to be struggling to hold them in position.

Meg shook herself out of her shock and tried to evaluate the situation. She felt a smile tugging at her lips. The slaarh didn't matter. Not unless they came up into the sky to meet them. Jakl could fly right over all of them and land safely inside. Krelig must not have realized that the opposing mages were traveling by dragon.

Ha, she thought. *Go on, Jakl — bring us home.*

Suddenly one of the mages — she thought it was the man just behind the old woman — called out in horror: "Stop! Princess, turn the dragon, you can't —"

She turned back to look at him. "It's all right! We can fly right over them!"

He was shaking his head desperately. "No! It's the mages inside — there's a magical barrier. I can feel it. You'll hit it straight on. The dragon won't be able to pass through it!"

Meg hesitated only for a second, then told Jakl to turn away.

He obeyed instantly, even before she was able to explain her hazy understanding of why it was necessary.

"I sense it, too," the old woman said. "Do you all sense it? It surrounds the entire castle and grounds, like the cover on a hot dish."

There were mutters of assent behind her.

Find a place to land, somewhere far enough away that we can stop and figure out what to do next, she told her dragon.

Meg did not like this one bit.

Because if this was the danger that Anders foresaw, it was going to get worse before it got better. She hadn't needed extra strength to change course. She wouldn't need it to land and see what the mages had to say about what to do. Which meant that whatever they decided to try must be the thing that would be difficult and dangerous.

Or maybe it wouldn't be — not at first. But then it would all just go horribly, horribly wrong.

CHAPTER SEVENTEEN

CALEN FELT IT JUST BEFORE IT happened. He couldn't see anything, because he was deep inside the castle with the others, but he felt it.

And then a second later, they all did.

"He's here," Calen said. And then: "Did Meg make it back?" He ran for the door without waiting for an answer.

"Calen!" Serek called after him. Calen kept running.

He heard distant screams but didn't stop to wonder what they were about. Down one hall after another, then up flight after flight of stairs until he reached the battlements. He burst outside and looked out over the wall.

He didn't see Meg or Jakl anywhere. What he did see was a shimmering dome of magical energy encasing the entire castle and grounds. And beyond it . . .

Serek slammed through the door behind him. Calen could hear the other mages coming up the stairs, too.

"Dark Lord and Bright Lady," Serek said softly as he came up next to Calen.

I'd almost forgotten how ugly those things are, Calen thought. The circle of slaarh surrounded the castle as far as he could see in either direction. And behind them was a host of men, some on foot, some on horseback. Closer, he saw people — Trelian's people — running toward the castle doors, fleeing the enemies who had suddenly materialized in their midst.

"Where did they come from?" another mage asked, stepping up behind them.

"He transported them here," Calen said. He could see faint traces of purple energy still floating around them.

"Transported — *all of them?*"

Calen nodded absently. He didn't really care so much about that. He wanted to sort out what that dome was about. "Can you sense the barrier he's put up?" he asked Serek. "I can't tell. . . . It's red, orange . . . white . . . some violet. . . . I don't think it's the same kind of spell he used to block magic energy before."

"No," Anders said, joining them. "It's a physical barrier of some kind. Look." He pointed, and they saw someone running toward it from the other side, some poor soul who had been out beyond its boundary when the slaarh appeared and was now trying to make it back inside to safety. A servant, Calen thought, returning from some errand. He was running flat out — unable, of course, to see that there was anything in front of him. Calen inhaled to shout a warning, ready to cast an amplification spell so the boy would be able to hear him from that distance, but it was already too late. The boy slammed into the barrier and flew horribly backward from the impact, landing several feet away on the grass. He did not get back up.

"Meg and Jakl will fly right into it!" Calen cried, scanning the skies for them. It was surely time for them to be back, wasn't it? Or had something delayed them?

Had Krelig already killed them?

Serek put a hand on his shoulder. "She'll have mages with her. They'll sense it. They'll warn her."

Calen shook him off. "She might not listen! You know how she is! She might just —" He spun to face Anders. "This is what she needed the strength for! So she won't die when she hits the barrier, so she'll still be all right —"

"No," Anders said again. "This isn't it. I don't know what she needs the strength for, but it's not this. I can feel that much, at least." He knocked lightly at his forehead with one fist. "Stupid glimmers."

"Calen," Serek said, "you have to calm down. We have more immediate problems."

Calen stared at him incredulously. "*Nothing* is more important than —"

343

"Krelig is here," Serek said, looking past him. "And I didn't say more important; I said more immediate."

Calen turned back to look out over the wall. Somehow he hadn't even noticed Krelig at first. He was standing right there, surrounded by his band of traitors. Calen found himself searching for red hair and forced himself to stop. Helena was dead, and he knew it. He focused on Krelig instead. This was it, then. This was where it was all going to end. Where Krelig was going to be paid back for everything.

Or where they were all going to die.

"You warned everyone about being transported, right?" he asked Serek.

Serek nodded. The other mages had all emerged by this point, and they lined the battlement in a grim row. There were eighty-five of them now, counting the twenty-one new arrivals that Meg had delivered so far and including two apprentices, both of whom were younger than Calen himself.

The last of the castle folk who had been outside when the slaarh appeared had vanished into the castle, except for the serving boy, who still lay motionless, maybe dead, on the far side of the barrier. The slaarh shifted restlessly, pawing at the ground and occasionally snapping at one another. Otherwise, everything was still. Krelig's mages stood in a ragged double line, staring up at them. At this distance, there was no way Calen could really feel Krelig's gaze meet his own, but somehow he felt sure that they were looking right at each other.

Suddenly Krelig's voice rang out from below, amplified to painful volume.

"Send down the boy!" he shouted. "Send him down to be punished, and perhaps we will let the rest of you live."

"Be ready," Serek said to the mages along the wall, in a low but carrying voice. "He knows we won't send Calen down there."

After a minute, Krelig sighed in false regret. "No? Are you certain? Perhaps you only need some encouragement."

He raised his arm, and the slaarh all screamed their terrible, soul-piercing screams. It took everything Calen had not to clap his hands over his ears. Instead he cast a small spell of protection, filtering out the worst of the sound. He saw several others along the wall doing the same.

Then the slaarh all surged forward, lurching with horrible speed toward the castle.

The barrier must be spelled to allow Krelig's side to pass through unharmed, Calen realized. It was still there;

he could see it, but the slaarh didn't hesitate, and it didn't have any apparent effect on them as they crossed over. He was sure, though, that it would still be perfectly solid if Meg or Jakl tried to pass through. He hoped the mages with Meg were paying attention. If they ever showed up at all.

Calen heard answering cries from below, and then the Trelian and Kragnir soldiers were spilling forth from the gates, running to meet the enemy.

Krelig and his mages stood still, the slaarh parting around them on either side in their attack.

"Hold," Serek said to the others. "This part is not for us."

It was hard just to stand there and watch, though. The first wave of Trelian and Kragnir soldiers were on foot, the second on horseback, and the slaarh tore through them indiscriminately. Calen thought of the poison that coated the monsters' claws and teeth. The soldiers' armor would protect them a little, but probably not enough. Archers fired from the walls above and below, but while a few of the slaarh's handlers fell to arrows, the creatures themselves appeared impervious. They needed magic to fight those things. Magic and Meg's dragon. But the mages had to save their strength for Krelig, and Meg and her dragon were still nowhere to be seen.

"Now," Krelig's voice boomed at them from the ground. "Send down the boy."

He couldn't really expect that Serek would comply, but he still waited as though giving them time to change their minds. The mages on both sides stood in stony silence as the battle raged on around them.

"As you wish, then," Krelig said finally. Calen didn't think he sounded all that sorry. "We will take him from you."

Krelig began walking forward, the traitor mages walking behind him, spread out to either side. The magic barrier *shifted*, moving with them and changing shape to encompass the castle and the area immediately before it, but leaving the slaarh and the soldiers outside its boundary. Calen saw it actually push some confused soldiers aside as it moved. And then the mages were standing below them, looking up. Too late, Calen realized he'd been too distracted by the barrier and the soldiers to pay attention to the mages themselves. His eyes sought out Krelig's hands and saw red energy gathering around them.

"He's about to cast!" Calen shouted to the others.

And then suddenly there were colors everywhere, as everyone started casting at once.

Serek had grouped all his mages into teams of

three or four during the previous days, and had quickly matched the new mages with existing pairs or groups as they arrived. Everyone but Calen. He'd tried working together with Serek and Anders, but he always saw the colors early, and they were always a step behind. Finally Serek had agreed that Calen should just cast on his own.

The teams let the mages cast with greater strength and power than any of them would have alone. They took turns leading, the others in each team joining their magic to the leader's, who directed the spell. There were more of them than there were of Krelig's mages, but his were better trained and, Calen was fairly certain, more powerful overall. And definitely more ruthless.

The truth of this became apparent almost at once. Someone cried out to Calen's right, and he turned to see two other mages staring at the empty space where their partner had been. Then they all heard the scream as the missing mage reappeared in the middle of the battling sea of slaarh. There was no chance for any of them to help. He went down, his screams abruptly silenced as one of the creatures tore off his head.

Mage Xanda, the one who had first cried out, now screamed her companion's name. "Focus!" Serek shouted at her. "And the rest of you, keep your guard up! For gods' sake, we were warned about the transporting! If you're going to be bested, at least let it be for something you shouldn't have already known to protect yourself against."

Maybe now they'll take this seriously, the voice in Calen's head said grimly. He hated thinking that way, hated the coldness of that thought, but he knew it was justified. They still hadn't really believed that the other mages could have turned so far against them. Maybe now they did.

A burst of red and blue energy exploded against his shield, and Calen realized that he needed to take Serek's advice himself. *Focus.* He knew better than anyone how important that was. And he had a specific goal to accomplish. Let the others worry about the Magistratum traitors; he was going to throw everything he had at Krelig.

Krelig still stood where he'd begun, colors playing ceaselessly around his hands and head. Krelig could cast many things without using his hands for focusing the power, but even he couldn't cast everything that way, and especially not when being attacked from all sides. Calen made himself ignore everyone else. He glared down at Krelig, channeling all his anger and pain and regret into his magic. He cast again and again, terrible, devastating spells he'd crafted in his mind all those nights he'd lain awake at Krelig's fortress, and even more in the days since he'd returned. He thought of Helena. He thought of Meg and what Krelig would do to her and everyone else if he won here today. He thought of what it would mean for the whole world if Krelig returned them to the old days of mages ruling over everyone, using magic without rules or laws or conscience.

Krelig responded to the renewed power of Calen's onslaught, shifting and looking up to face him head-on. He felt Krelig's touch on his mind, heard the mage's voice inside his head. *You will pay for your betrayal, boy. You and everyone you hold dear. Did you hear Helena's screams as you left her behind to die? That will be nothing compared to what your friends will suffer.* Calen felt the man's terrible smile behind the words. *You will see.*

You'll be the one to see, Calen sent back. He didn't know if his words made it through, but it didn't matter. He wasn't going to let himself get distracted. Nothing mattered except casting again and again, blocking what Krelig and the others sent at him and sending back as much as he could. He pushed Krelig out of his head and sent spell after spell, commanding the magic to reach its target.

The magic obeyed as well as it could, but Krelig blocked everything with apparent ease. Calen blocked

Krelig's spells, too, but he knew that was only because of the precious extra seconds the early colors gave him. They were both fending off attacks from others as well, and so neither could concentrate their full power on their chosen target. *That might have to change,* Calen realized. He was going to wear himself out too quickly if this went on much longer.

Maybe the others will stop trying to kill you if you ask nicely, the voice in his head — his own voice, not Krelig's this time — suggested sarcastically.

Shut up, Calen thought back. Obviously that wasn't the answer. But they were going to have to try something. Because this wasn't going to work.

As if to underscore that thought, another mage cried out from Serek's group and stumbled backward from the wall. Calen glanced at her, unable to help it. The woman was screaming, her skin blazing with some kind of magical fire. Her partners turned to try to help her, and in their distraction one of them was hit from behind with the same spell.

Not working. This isn't working, Calen thought desperately. He made himself refocus on Krelig, trusting that the others would see to the wounded mages if they could. But with a part of his mind, he also reached out to Serek with his summoning spell.

351

We have to try something else, Calen sent. *He's going to win if we don't.*

I know, Serek's thought came back. *Just . . . hold on. Hold on as long as you can. We're working on it.*

Calen hoped they were working fast.

Krelig didn't seem to be tiring in the least. Calen wasn't either, not really . . . not yet. But he would be. He had no illusions that he was anywhere close to Krelig's power. And that meant none of them were, because he was stronger by far than any of the other mages on their side. They needed more of an advantage. He had thought that his ability to see the colors would be the key; they had been what had made Krelig so eager to keep Calen on his side. But there was too much distraction; he couldn't *focus.* What else did they have? They had slightly greater numbers, but that was clearly not enough. And they were already at least three mages down. Maybe more, for all he knew. They needed . . . they needed . . .

From beyond the fighting, he heard a new sound that cut through everything else. His head snapped up to look.

Oh, thank the gods.

Jakl came screaming through the sky, flame streaming down at the slaarh on the outer edges of the fighting.

Calen's relief was immense. *Not dead*, he thought grate-fully. *Thank you for not being dead.*

Meg was on his back, of course, but she wasn't alone. But then, as Calen watched, he saw a cloud of purple energy just before five of the figures that had been behind her suddenly disappeared.

He found them again an instant later, on the ground, advancing toward the rear line of the fighting. The purple traces of the transport spell still lingered around them even as they began casting anew, coming at the slaarh from behind. Meg circled around again, and he could see that there was still someone with her on the back of the dragon.

Krelig turned, momentarily distracted, and Calen struck as hard as he could, sending a fire spell that would have incinerated the mage on the spot if it had landed cleanly. The man had felt it coming, though, and was able to turn it aside at the last second, sending it side-ways where it struck one of his traitor allies instead. She screamed in the instant before she died, but Calen barely noticed. Krelig had stumbled backward, and as he straightened back up, Calen saw a brief flare of yellow energy as the man hastily healed himself. Calen smiled viciously. He had hurt him. Just a little, and just for a moment, but it was a start.

And — the barrier was gone. In his distraction at actually being *hurt*, Krelig had let it dissolve.

Calen could understand why — it was a lot to maintain all at the same time, and not as immediate a need as the kind of shield you used to protect yourself from hostile magic. The barrier Krelig had set at his own fortress was a different kind of spell, one that he could set and then forget about, like wards. A physical obstacle like the one he'd created here would take a great deal more conscious thought and energy, especially when there were eighty or so enemy mages trying to dismantle it.

He waited for Krelig to realize that he'd released it, but instead the mage turned and resumed casting at Calen at once, with renewed force. Another spell came at Calen from two other mages, and now it was his turn to stumble backward. Another of Krelig's group noticed and took the opportunity to add his own attack to the mix. Calen saw it coming, but wasn't sure he could block it in time without making himself more vulnerable to Krelig.

A blast of orange energy shot out from the wall beside him and neutralized the incoming spell before it struck. Calen glanced sideways to see Anders moving toward him, continuing to fire orange energy at anything that came Calen's way.

"Keep going!" Anders shouted at him over the roar of the fighting. "Serek has a plan!"

It's about time, Calen thought, although he knew that wasn't fair. He refocused again, trusting Anders to keep the other mages' attacks away from him as much as possible. Now he was starting to feel a little tired. *No, you're not,* he told himself. *You're just not. Keep going.*

He wondered what Serek's plan was. He hoped it was a good one.

He kept his eyes on Krelig, on the early seconds of color that appeared before each spell. But he could see the dragon in his peripheral vision, swooping and striking and breathing fire and doing all the magnificent things that dragons could do when they were free to fight and fly with abandon.

And then he saw the dragon suddenly dive closer, dropping to where the enemy mages were.

And snatching one of them up from the ground.

Calen stared. So did the other mages. Was *this* the plan? This was not a good plan! What was Meg *doing?*

Several of the traitor mages turned to cast spells at Meg and the dragon. Jakl was impervious, or at least highly resistant, but Meg wasn't. Fortunately the mage dangling from Jakl's claws was too busy screaming in terror to do very much else. From the shape of him, Calen thought it was Mage Neehan.

Krelig was the only one who refused to be distracted by this latest development. And so Calen forced himself not to be distracted either. *Have to focus. Jakl will take care of Meg.* Whatever it was she thought she was doing.

Gods, Meg. Please be careful. Please.

He heard her mocking, exasperating voice in his head. *Of course! You know me!*

Curse you, Serek, he thought, *if this was your idea.*

This was definitely not a good plan at all.

CHAPTER EIGHTEEN

J AKL SHOT BACK UP ABOVE THE fray, the screaming
mage struggling in his claws.

Idiot, Meg thought. Did he want to be dropped from
this height? And right into the middle of the fighting?

The slaarh and the soldiers were a confused mass of
color and noise and motion below them. Meg had been
helping where she could, using the tactics that she and
Jakl had practiced so many times with Captain Varyn:
snatching up soldiers in trouble, carrying reinforcements
to where they were needed, attacking enemies directly
whenever they had a clear opening. She kept a special
vengeful eye out for slaarh that she could target without
endangering their own soldiers in the process. Dragonfire
was one of the few things that could hurt those monsters
(the others being strong magic and lots and lots of sharp
swords and axes and other pointy things, applied with
great force and in great numbers), and she wanted to
hurt as many of them as she possibly could.

The mages had insisted that the invisible barrier was still there, but since all the nonmagical fighting was happening outside of it, that didn't stop Meg and Jakl from helping the soldiers. Mage Estrella, the older woman who'd been seated behind her on the last trip, was still with her on the dragon, her hands clasped tightly around Meg's middle. Meg had wanted to leave her with the others, but they had all agreed that Meg might need a way to communicate with the mages inside the castle, and Estrella was the best among them at what they called summoning. She was also able to attack some of the slaarh magically from above, and it was clear that the soldiers on the ground could use all the help they could get.

They had been circling back around, looking for more men in trouble, when Estrella suddenly leaned forward and shouted so that Meg could hear her above the fighting. "I have a message from Mage Serek!" she said. "They need us to take out Krelig's traitors. They're too strong all together."

"Take out how?" Meg shouted back. Did he want her to *kill* them? Meg knew they were the enemy, knew they were trying to kill Serek and the others right now, but she still couldn't feel easy about having Jakl just swoop in and set them all on fire. They were still *people*. And

Serek wasn't technically authorized to give her that kind of order. Would this go against what her father had said about careful use of the dragon's power?

But Estrella told her what Serek had in mind, and she felt a little better. Slightly terrified, but she could deal with fear.

And of course, Jakl wasn't terrified at all. That helped a lot.

"But what about that barrier?"

"Gone!" Estrella said. "He must not have been able to maintain it, or else Mage Serek and the others discovered how to force it down. In any case there's nothing there now."

Meg could only take her word for it; she hadn't been able to see it when it *had* been there. She couldn't help bracing herself as they flew closer, but nothing stopped them.

So they snatched up one of the mages standing at the far end of the line, and now Meg was carrying him back to where the others from her last group were waiting. Some of Krelig's mages had tried to attack them, but between Jakl's resistance and Mage Estrella's defenses, nothing got through.

Now they dropped their squirming, still-screaming passenger from just enough of a height that he wouldn't break anything in the fall. Probably wouldn't, anyway. The other mages wouldn't kill him, Estrella had said, but they'd make sure he couldn't do anything else to help Mage Krelig.

Then they went back to get another one. This time the enemy mages were ready.

It's okay, Meg told herself. And Jakl, but mostly herself. *We can do this.*

Then one of them created some kind of magic fireball and sent it directly at Meg's head.

Meg screamed and threw herself flat against her dragon, overcome again with memories of burning and falling. It was just like what had happened in the dungeons, only worse, because now people were really trying to set her on fire, and she might fall, it might all happen again, just like before. . . . She could hear Estrella shouting something at her but she couldn't understand, couldn't even think. She had to hold on, she couldn't fall again, she couldn't let the fire touch her, she *couldn't*, oh gods, she wouldn't be able to bear it, she . . .

Jakl was reaching toward her through the link, concerned, concerned and *guilty*, so guilty for having let her fall the first time. *Not your fault*, she thought at him, trying to pull herself together. She *had* to pull herself together!

The mages had seen the effect the fireball spell had on her, though. They started sending more of them, great blasts of flame coming at her from several directions at once. Jakl flew upward, above them, but some of the spells changed course and *followed* them as they flew. Meg looked back over her shoulder, dismayed and horrified. She hadn't known magic could do that. Would Jakl be able to outpace them?

And what if he can? Are you just going to run away?

No, but — but . . .

Estrella let go with one hand and reached back, pointing at one of the fireballs. It seemed to close up into itself, collapsing into nothing. She repeated the process with two more. But more were coming up from below. They'd seen how to keep Meg away, and they were going to keep casting those things at her until they either killed her or drove her away for good.

She couldn't let that happen. She had to go back. Had to.

We have to go back, she thought at Jakl. *You'll be all right; the magic can't hurt you.* His response through the link was immediate and unmistakable. *I'll be all right, too,* she promised him. And herself. She'd have Estrella looking out for her. And Calen's gift of strength. Was this what Anders had known she'd need it for? Gods, she hoped so. She hoped there wasn't something even worse coming.

"Can you protect us from the fire?" she shouted to Estrella.

The woman nodded, but with some hesitation. "Not completely," she shouted back. "I can block some of the magic, but not all, I think. If they hit us, we'll still be burned. But . . . probably not killed."

Meg nodded back, trying not to feel disappointed. This woman had to be a hundred years old, and she'd been awake since gods-knew-when and then riding on a dragon and casting spells left and right in the middle of a battle. . . . Surely she was starting to get tired. None of the mages had infinite reserves of power, she knew. Although it sure seemed as though Mage Krelig did.

She shook herself out of her thoughts. Mage Krelig was not her responsibility right now. She had a mission, and she had to focus on that.

She could do this. She had to. The mages were depending on her.

Calen was depending on her.

All right, she told her dragon. *Quick as you can. Let's get another one.*

He turned with startling speed, diving back down

toward the line of mages. They were all facing her now, except for Krelig. The woman at the far end of the line screamed as she saw them coming for her, and sent a last desperate ball of fire in their direction, but Jakl dodged it and snatched her up — not very gently, either — from the ground. Meg managed to choke back her own screams this time and just concentrated everything she had on holding on. The dragon shot back up again, racing the fireballs that were still trailing them. Anything that came right at him failed to land, his natural resistance causing the magic to skirt aside, but that didn't extend to Meg and Estrella. She felt the heat of one of the spells approaching from the side and pressed herself lower against Jakl's neck but refused to turn her head. There was nothing she could do about that. She just had to hold on and stay with them. Jakl rocked sideways, trying to get her away from the fire. Estrella finally managed to target it and neutralize it, and then they were up and away. Some of the fireballs had petered out on their own, Meg saw, although a few still followed doggedly in their wake.

The mage they'd grabbed this time wasn't nearly as panicky as the first one. Jakl didn't feel her struggling at all, in fact. But she didn't feel limp in his grasp, so he didn't think she'd fainted. Meg could feel all this through the link with him, as well as his growing suspicion, which immediately became her own. *Distract her,* Meg thought at him. *Don't let her cast anything!* She couldn't hurt Jakl with magic, but Calen had told her how creative and devious and horrible Krelig had trained his mages to be, and Meg had no doubt that the mage could be dangerous down there if they gave her the chance.

Jakl shook the woman violently in his claws, and Meg heard her shout angrily from below. Good. *Keep doing that.* He sent back a feeling of delighted compliance. The mage shouted again, more in fear this time than anger, Meg thought.

Good. You deserve it, you traitor.

They dropped her with their own mages, who surrounded her at once. One of them stretched a hand toward the sky behind them, and Meg saw the rest of the trailing fireballs wink out of existence.

Then they flew back to fetch another traitor from the line.

Each time they returned, though, the enemy mages' resistance was stronger, and Meg had to work harder at fighting to keep her fear at bay. Jakl was able to grab two mages together on the fourth trip, but one of the others on the ground sent a fire spell at them before the dragon could twist them out of range. Meg and Estrella both screamed as something hot and painful grazed along their left side.

No, no, no, not again, her mind gibbered uselessly. *No, I can't, please—*

But she wasn't falling. She wasn't. She could still feel her dragon there beneath her. She had been burned, but she was still there. Still there, and Jakl needed her, and Calen needed her, and she was not going to give in to the rising panic in her head. Meg forced herself to turn her mindless screaming into words. *"Hold on!"* She didn't know if she was screaming this more to herself or to Estrella, but she supposed it didn't matter. The pain was excruciating, like half of her arm had burned away, but it couldn't have, really, because she was still gripping Jakl for all she was worth. She felt Estrella's arms tighten around her waist and was ashamed of herself. If this hundred-year-old lady could stay calm and hold on, then Meg could, too.

She felt Jakl start to try to take some of the pain from her. *No!* She pushed him back and away through the link. *You need to stay strong. I'm all right. It hurts, but I can take it. I can. Just keep going.*

Reluctantly he did as he was told. Meg held on, and fought her fear, and made herself stay present.

It's just pain. They'll heal you as soon as you reach them. This is nothing. You're fine. You're not falling, and you're fine.

She wasn't *fine*, of course; that was a ridiculous lie — she was terrified and in agony and fighting with everything she had just to hold herself together, but she *was* holding herself together. She hadn't lost herself to panic, and she was counting that as a great big giant victory right now.

Jakl made it to the drop-off point and let go of the mages from perhaps a slightly higher distance than he had previously, but instead of circling back to the fighting, he brought them gently in for a landing. One of the mages ran toward them at once; either he'd seen what had happened or Estrella had managed to alert him as they flew back.

Meg gasped as the healing energy enveloped her arm. She couldn't seem to make herself release her grip on the dragon, so she just stayed there, pressed against him, trying to slow her crazily beating heart. He pressed back at her, through the link, a mix of apology and comfort and love and shame, but she tried to tell him that the apology and shame weren't necessary. He'd been wonderful, and she was fine. Would be fine. She just needed the comfort and love right now, which he was happy to keep giving her.

After a minute, or maybe several minutes, she became aware that someone had helped Mage Estrella down from Jakl's back and was giving her some water from a canteen. Meg experimented and found that her fingers were finally willing to unclench their hold. She took a deep breath and then slid down on shaky legs to get a drink of that water for herself.

She sat beside Mage Estrella, just for a moment, giving herself a few seconds to recover from the burning and the healing. Trying to nerve herself to get back up. The five mages they'd abducted so far were lying unconscious in a row a little distance away. Clearly no one was taking any chances with them.

Once she got up, she'd need to go back.

"Princess," Mage Estrella said gently, "why not send the dragon back without you this time? The magic can't hurt him; it's only your presence that makes him vulnerable."

Meg shook her head. "I can't send him into that alone. Won't." She felt Jakl trying to object, to remind her that he'd fought without her after she fell at the battle of Kragnir. She told him to hush. "If he goes, I go too," she said. "There are some decisions he can't make alone, and I need to be right there in case he needs me. If I were somewhere else, even somewhere that was supposed to

367

be safer, his attention would be divided. And . . . I just can't sit behind and send him off into danger on my behalf. He might be safer in some ways without me, but in others, he'd be more vulnerable alone. We fight together. We're stronger together, anyway, than either of us is alone."

Estrella considered her for a moment. "You are linked, in the ancient way," she said finally. "He is not just your pet, this dragon."

"Yes," Meg said. "Does that help you to see? Sending him alone is like sending one part of me but leaving the rest behind. He fought for me when I fell in the war with Lourin, but . . . while he was brave, and wonderful, and magnificent"— *and you were*, she thought at him firmly —"he was also acting in rage and pain and fear. It turned out all right, more than all right, that time . . . but this feels like a far more delicate situation we're in now. The goals are not as immediately clear. He needs my guidance."

The mage nodded, seeming to understand.

"Not everyone knows about the link," Meg added. "I'd appreciate it if you kept it to yourself."

Estrella smiled. "I suspect that anyone who knows that such a thing is possible will already have put it together for themselves," she said. "But that is a smaller number than you might imagine. It's been a long time since there were many dragons, as you know. And longer still since bondings were a well-known practice. But I will not be enlightening any who do not already know. This I promise you, Princess."

"Thank you," Meg said. Then she got to her feet. Putting this off was not going to make it any easier, and she'd rested for as long as she could justify.

Mage Oren came over then. "If it's all right with you, Estrella, I'll take a turn accompanying the princess. Begging your pardon, but I believe I'm stronger in defensive magic, and that seems to be what is most called for now."

Estrella turned her smile to him. "No begging of pardons is necessary, Oren. I think your suggestion is a wise one. And I believe a little more rest would not hurt me."

Oren looked at Meg, who nodded her agreement. "I'll be happy to have your assistance, Mage Oren. Thank you."

They went back again.

Meg still had to battle her terror, but somehow now that she'd actually been hit, and survived, *again*, she found the fear a little easier to manage. Only a little, but she would take what she could get. And Mage Oren was noticeably better than Mage Estrella at keeping the fire-balls away. The remaining traitor mages were relentless, though, and while some of Serek's group were helping to fend off the enemy spells that came at them now, they couldn't stop them all.

On her second trip with Oren, Meg was finally start-ing to feel a little less certain that she was about to be set on fire as soon as she came within range. She could do this, clearly; she *was* doing it. It was going to be okay. She tried to focus just on being present with Jakl, helping him choose a target and adding her strength and deter-mination to his as he went once more back into the fray. The mages were all waiting for them again, facing them in a line.

But this time Mage Krelig was facing them, too.

I suppose he's finally gotten tired of watching us snatch away his army, one by one, she thought sadly. She'd hoped he'd been suitably distracted by trying to fight all the other mages who were trying to kill him. But while she could see Serek's mages still apparently casting spells in Krelig's direction, he seemed content to ignore them for the moment.

"You have become an annoyance," he said, and although she knew it was impossible, she could hear his voice per-fectly despite the fighting going on all around them.

He pointed, and Meg tried to brace herself for whatever he was about to do. *Not fire, please not fire,* she prayed, unable to help it. But whatever it was, it was directed at Oren, not at her. She felt him stiffen behind her, then start to slide backward.

"Oren!" she screamed. She turned and grabbed for him, seeing as she did so that his eyes had rolled up to show only the whites. She didn't know what Krelig had done, but clearly Oren was in no position to help defend her now. In fact, if she didn't get a better grip on him, he was going to go sliding off to his death.

You've practiced this, she thought abruptly. And of course that was true. *Exactly this, with the soldiers. You can hold on. You're strong enough. Or at least stubborn enough.* She took a breath and managed a firmer hold on Oren. There was no safety harness this time, though, and he was not just pretending to be unconscious. If he fell, he would die.

So she was not going to let him fall.

Jakl, away! Meg sent at him frantically. He changed course, flying straight up, but then abruptly slammed into something. Meg screamed at the impact and nearly let go of Oren. Jakl shook his head, momentarily dazed, falling backward toward the earth. She could feel his pain and confusion, swirling together with her own. He

371

was able to regain control and manage their landing, but it was still rough. She nearly lost Oren a second time as they hit the ground.

Another barrier, she realized. Like the one the mages had warned her about when they first approached. Krelig must have put it back in place. She looked helplessly down over her shoulder, still trying desperately to hold on to Oren. Even though they were on the ground now, and the fall wouldn't kill him, landing unconscious and defenseless at the feet of the enemy mages probably would.

Krelig was looking up at her, a terrible smile on his face. He opened his mouth to speak, no doubt to tell her exactly how he was going to kill her.

And then he suddenly staggered forward, nearly falling to the ground.

Calen stood behind him, arms outstretched.

Meg was so astounded, she nearly laughed. Despite everything. Had Calen just — just transported himself right up behind the mage and *pushed* him?

Krelig's smile vanished, replaced by an expression of uncontrolled rage that instantly killed Meg's fleeting moment of amusement. He whirled around.

"Leave her alone," Calen said calmly. She could hear him perfectly, too. It must be magic, she realized. She was assaulted by a sudden mental image of Anders waving his fingers in the air and whispering, *Magic!*, and she had to fight back laughter again. Hysterical laughter. She was losing her mind.

Focus! she told herself desperately. Not that she could think of anything to do. It was still taking every ounce of her strength to keep hold of Oren. Jakl seemed to have mostly recovered from smashing his head into the barrier, but she bade him stay still. Until she could see how they could help, she thought the best thing would be to be very quiet and not interfere.

"You wanted me?" Calen continued. "Well, here I am."

Krelig straightened. His smile returned. "I will deal with you," he said. "Right after I kill your friend."

"You'll deal with me now," Calen said. He wasn't smiling. Quick as lightning, he raised his hands toward the older man and then suddenly seemed to thrust something forward. Krelig raised his own hands almost lazily, then seemed shocked when the force of whatever Calen had cast at him pushed him back a step. His eyes widened. "How . . . ?"

Calen didn't waste time answering. He continued moving his hands, clearly casting spell after spell at Krelig. The mage was forced to remain facing him, to defend himself and retaliate.

Meg noticed some of the other enemy mages raising their hands toward Calen as well.

"Oh, no you don't," she said under her breath. *Jakl, stop them!*

Jakl released a targeted burst of fire that enveloped the mages first on one side, then the other. In that moment, Meg had absolutely no reservations about sending them all up in flames. Most of them seemed able to put themselves out fairly quickly, in any case. But it forced them to pay attention to the dragon, to keep defending themselves. Which she hoped would leave them too busy to send anything against Calen.

She also hoped that it would keep them too busy to realize that she had no protection other than Jakl's interference. If they thought to cast something at her now, with Oren still unconscious in her desperate grasp, there would be nothing she could do to stop them.

CHAPTER NINETEEN

THE NEW BARRIER HAD WINKED INTO existence so quickly, none of them had seen it coming. Calen had been too distracted by seeing Meg flying crazily back into danger after she'd been set on fire yet again to notice the colors in time. And then Jakl had crashed into it, and gone tumbling toward the ground. Calen would have transported right then to try to save her if not for Serek's sudden viselike grip on his arm.

"Calen, wait!" Serek barked.

"No! I —"

"I know. You have to go, I know, but just listen first. Quickly!"

Calen listened.

He felt a savage smile stretching across his face as he did.

Now *this* was a plan he liked.

Serek's explanation had taken only seconds; the man could be incredibly succinct when he wanted to be. And it helped that Serek was linking with Calen at the same time — it was the same way the other teams had joined to cast as one, and it helped Serek to send some of what he was communicating in mental images instead of words, which got the message across even faster.

And then there was no more time, and Calen *jumped*, and nearly pushed Krelig right over onto his hateful, evil face.

He knew the other mages were still a threat, but Calen couldn't think about them now. All of his attention was on Krelig. Had to be on Krelig. Because this was it: the final battle. Right here. One of them was not going to survive this. Calen just had to make sure that Krelig was the one who died. And he had to start it before Krelig had a chance to hurt Meg.

He talked just long enough to give as many of the others as possible a chance to join in with Serek back on the castle wall. And then he stopped talking and started casting. With everything he had.

And everything Serek and the others had, too.

Krelig clearly hadn't been expecting that. He'd probably never participated in a voluntary joining of this kind in his entire life. It required relinquishing all your power to someone else, letting that person use your ability as though it were his own. Calen felt sure that

Krelig would never consider doing such a thing himself. And none of the traitor mages would ever be able to surrender their power to Krelig. They feared him, and maybe some of them even respected him, but none of them could ever *trust* him. He'd had them practice casting together, adding their magic to support another's shield, or lend strength to an attack, but those were isolated moments of joining your energy to another's. This was different. Serek and the other mages up along the battlements had all lent Calen their full strength and energy, to direct as he saw fit. Normally there might not be so much advantage to that — it concentrated all your power in one place, but it also gave your enemy only one target to focus on. If Krelig killed Calen, the others wouldn't necessarily die, but they'd certainly be damaged, and at best would need some time before they'd be able to cast anything else themselves.

It would really probably be a very stupid plan under any other circumstances. Which is why Krelig hadn't seen it coming. Because it didn't make any sense.

Except that Calen could see the colors early.

Which meant that he could counter everything Krelig sent at him. But that alone wouldn't be enough on his own, because he wouldn't have the strength to hold out for very long. Calen was strong, stronger by far than any of the other mages on either side — but not stronger than Krelig himself.

But now — now Calen had all the strength he needed. Or at least, all the strength available. He just had to hope it was enough.

He was vaguely aware of fire and heat nearby and suspected that Jakl was doing some fighting of his own. But he put it out of his mind. He trusted Meg to take care of herself, now that he had Krelig occupied. His only job was to focus on what he was doing.

So he did.

Krelig was attacking more fiercely than ever before. He might have been drawing things out earlier, wanting to make the others hurt, wanting to wear them down with fear and exhaustion until he could destroy them at his leisure, possibly after making a long speech about how superior he was to the rest of them and how they would all suffer horribly before they died. But since that first powerful spell Calen had sent at him, Krelig had been done playing. And despite his new strength and power, Calen was still shocked at how strong Krelig was. He thought maybe, *maybe* they were about evenly matched now — but that was with Calen having the combined power of eighty mages. Krelig was that strong all on his own.

And he knew a lot more magic.

Calen didn't recognize more than a fraction of the spells that Krelig threw at him. There wasn't time to try to analyze or sort out anything. He just watched the colors. In those few early seconds before Krelig released his spells, Calen had just enough time to be ready with a defense. And sometimes enough time to cast something back, although now that Krelig was on his guard, it was even harder to get anything through. Krelig might not be able to see what Calen was casting, but he had years of experience in sensing magic energy, and Calen's knowledge, despite how much he'd learned in the past few months, was nothing compared to that.

But it shouldn't matter. Not if the rest of Serek's plan worked as they'd hoped.

Calen realized he was letting his mind wander and made himself stop. *Focus, gods curse you!*

He focused.

Blue to counter red, black to counter white, a million different combinations of subtle shades of energy in all the different colors that existed. Calen let his instincts guide him. Krelig seemed tireless, but he didn't look happy.

"Not possible," he said. "You can't . . ." He paused, then crafted something more slowly. And more sinister. Threads of red and black and deep violet, twining together in dark and evil knots of pain and fire and destruction. Calen watched, waiting, as Krelig fed more and more energy into his spell, mentally preparing his counterspell in response.

And when it came, he was ready.

The force of it still made him stagger backward, but he blocked it all the same, and sent tendrils of his counterspell into the energy Krelig had sent, pulling the hostile magic into harmless strands. Krelig couldn't see it the way Calen could, but he could certainly sense it. He screamed, enraged.

"*How?* How are you doing that? Tell me!" He strode toward Calen, perhaps to try to shake it out of him through entirely nonmagical means. Calen backed up, casting as he went. Krelig raised one hand, then the other, absently pushing Calen's spells aside, but Calen thought the mage was having to use just a little more effort to do so now.

As for himself, Calen had never felt this strong in his life.

And oh, gods, how he liked it.

"What's wrong, *Master*? Did you teach me too well?"

He sent a version of that face-melting spell, one he'd crafted in his mind the night of his return. There was a stream of deep red-orange energy at the center of it that was the exactly the same shade as Helena's hair.

Calen thrust it forward as hard as he could, and in several parts, so Krelig couldn't just bat it out of the air, but the mage still had a shield in place, and the spell shattered harmlessly against it. Krelig grunted, clearly having felt the force of that, but it didn't stop him from continuing to move toward Calen.

"I didn't teach you this," Krelig growled. "This is something else. I know the other mages are helping you, making you stronger . . . but still, you should not be able to . . ."

He started his next spell without moving his hands, giving no outward sign, but of course Calen could still see the colors, and still early enough to be ready.

He countered, again and again, until Krelig stopped moving. He stood there, eyes burning with fury. "You *cannot* be this fast! How are you doing it?"

"You'll never know," Calen said. He grinned at the older man. "How does that feel? Win or lose, if you die here today or if you finally manage to create something I can't block and kill me where I stand, you will never, never know. The universe has secrets even from you, it would seem. Do you hate that? Do you hate not knowing?"

"*You will tell me,*" Krelig grated, beginning to cast again. He put everything into it now, Calen could see it, the colors blazing more fiercely than ever, the force of the spells knocking him backward even though he continued to block them in time. Krelig had released his shield, taking even the energy he'd kept in reserve for that to pour into what he was sending at Calen, faster and faster. "Tell me! *Tell me!*" He was screaming now, completely out of control. He sent one more blast that threw Calen abruptly and painfully onto his back, then ran over to stand above him.

"I will kill you," Krelig said in that terrifying calm voice that had always been the scariest one of all. His expression, too, was calm, but his eyes were insane with rage and confusion. "But not before you tell me your secret." He stood there, red-violet energy gathering between his palms, breathing hard, seemingly not aware of anything else but Calen lying at his feet. He started another spell but then kicked Calen hard in the ribs with his boot. Calen hadn't seen that coming. He curled up in pain, and then screamed in agony as Krelig sent a fiery bolt of red magic through his shoulder, pinning him to the ground with what felt like a white-hot iron spike.

"Taunt me now," Krelig said softly. "Tell me again how I will die not knowing." More red energy gathered, another molten spike in the making, and Calen saw it but forced himself not to prepare. Instead he met Mage Krelig's bright and crazy eyes squarely, glaring at him despite the pain. When the second spike hit, pinning his other shoulder, Calen screamed again, but still didn't try to fight back.

"You will die," Calen managed, when he could make himself stop screaming, "not knowing, you miserable, crazy, gods-cursed thing." He felt hot blood in his mouth; he must have bitten his tongue at some point after he fell. He spat to the side, but kept his eyes on Krelig's. "My secret. Mine. And you will never know what it is."

Krelig raised his hands again, and this time, Calen thought, he probably wouldn't be able to hold back. He wanted to kill Calen so badly, the desire practically shone from him like rays of the sun. Or was that just the magic energy gathering around him as he prepared to strike? Calen realized that his head was going a little fuzzy from the pain. That wasn't good. He had to focus; he had to stay present. . . .

"Oh, Calen," Krelig whispered. "How you will pay for this."

And then suddenly Krelig screamed, not with rage this time, but with surprise and pain. So much that it radiated out from him in glowing red bursts. Or at least, that's how it looked to Calen, his vision blurred with unshed tears and pain of his own.

Krelig had just enough time to stare up in alarm

383

toward the wall, toward where the other mages still stood, several of whom had pulled back their strength from Calen over the last few minutes.

Toward Serek, who had pulled his own strength back almost as soon as they began, reserving it for this very moment.

"No. He won't," he heard Serek say in his mind, but he wasn't speaking to Calen; he was speaking to Krelig.

And then Krelig was gone, vanished into a ball of red fire as big as a house. Bigger. *Big as a dragon,* Calen thought hazily.

And then the fire went out, and Krelig's body lay charred and smoking on the ground.

Calen thought that it was probably safe to faint now. So he did.

When he woke up, the first thing he saw was Meg's face, looking down at him.

"Hello," he said. His voice came out in a hoarse croak.

She grinned, relief showing clearly on her face.

"Hi," she said back. "You're always passing out when things get rough, aren't you?"

He blinked. "What? Hey . . ."

She laughed. Then abruptly threw herself down and hugged him. "I'm so glad you're alive."

"Ow," he said. "Shoulders."

She pulled back, kneeling beside him. "Sorry." But she didn't sound that sorry. That was okay. Calen hadn't really minded the hug.

"What's happening?" Calen asked. He didn't quite feel ready to sit up.

"Well," Meg said, glancing around, "Krelig is dead. Were you still awake for that part?"

"Yes."

"I thought so, but it was hard to be sure. Well, while you and Krelig were battling it out, Jakl and I were keeping the other traitor mages away. Until someone from our side woke up Mage Oren, and one of the other mages from Serek's group did that transportation spell and came down to help. She hit the remaining ones with some kind of sleep spell, I guess, because they all slumped to the ground at once. I think they were too distracted by the dragon to realize what was happening until it was too late."

So many transportation spells. Those were still forbidden, as far as he knew. They were all going to be in trouble.

"What about the slaarh?"

"The other mages are helping the soldiers with the last of those, as well. There are only a few left. Several of the human handlers tried to run for it when they realized Krelig was dead, but we got them."

"And the Lourin soldiers?"

"Surrendered. Well, some surrendered; some ran. But they didn't get very far." She smiled again, and this time it was one of her fierce dragon-girl smiles. "Jakl and I helped Captain Varyn round them up."

At the sound of his name, Jakl thrust his head into view beside Meg, nearly knocking her over, and snorted a blast of warm dragony breath into Calen's face. Meg laughed and pushed him back. "Move over, you. Give Calen some room."

Suddenly Serek and Anders were there, too, also looking down at him. Calen was starting to feel a little uncomfortable, like he was a bug under a glass. He grunted and struggled to sit up. Meg helped him.

"Well done, Calen," Serek said. He wasn't smiling, but he looked less grim than he had in a long time. "I'm sorry about the, uh . . ." He gestured toward Calen's shoulders. "Let me help with that a little." Calen sighed in relief as the blue and golden energy sank into his shoulders, easing the pain a great deal.

Meanwhile, Anders had walked over to peer down at Krelig's unmoving form.

"He's really dead, isn't he?" Calen asked, suddenly

worried. The man had come back from some other universe; could they be certain that even death was enough to stop him?

"Pretty sure he's dead," Anders said. He hesitated, then stepped back. "Best to be very sure, though, I suppose."

He sent a surprisingly bright and strong bolt of red-violet energy down at the dead mage. Calen had to shield his eyes, but not before he saw Krelig's body explode into a cloud of tiny particles.

"Anders!" Serek said, shocked.

"Best to be sure!" Anders repeated. "I don't want to have to go through that again, do you?"

As they watched, he started stamping around on the ground where the particles had landed.

They gazed at him in silence for a moment, and then Serek turned back to Calen.

"Are you all right? I know that was a lot to manage, back there. And not very pleasant by the end."

"I'm all right," Calen said. He thought he was, anyway. It might be too soon to tell. It hadn't all really sunk in yet.

"I think," said Pela, who had suddenly come up beside Meg, "that we should take Apprentice Calen inside to get some rest now."

"Pela, I could kiss you," Calen said without thinking. He was startled to see her turn completely scarlet.

"I'll — I'll just go and . . . um . . ." She turned and fled toward the castle.

Serek laughed, although he tried unsuccessfully to turn it into a cough.

Anders had returned just in time to witness this. "You have quite an effect on young women, it appears," he said.

Calen was starting to miss the part where he had been unconscious. "I wasn't really going to kiss her," he muttered. He looked desperately at Meg. "Can you help me get inside?"

She grinned at him again. "Stay there. I think we should let the medics take you in. You know how Serek doesn't believe in healing you all the way."

Now it was Calen's turn to laugh.

Serek looked affronted. "Sometimes it's best to let things heal naturally," he said. "It's true! I'm not making that up."

Calen lay back, still smiling, and waited for someone to come and take him away. It felt really good just to lie there, not having anyone try to kill him for the moment. He hoped it would be a nice long while before anyone tried to kill him again.

CHAPTER TWENTY

M EG WOKE THE NEXT AFTERNOON, STARTLED at the odd angle of the sun through her window. She had no idea what time she'd gone to bed, but she thought it had been on the early side. All that borrowed magical energy was a wonderful thing, but when it wore off, it abandoned you completely. She had a vague memory of Pela practically carrying her up the stairs to her room.

Having noticed that Meg was awake, Pela popped brightly up from her chair. "Princess! How are you feeling? Would you like some breakfast?"

Meg smiled. She was glad that some things never changed.

"Yes, please. To breakfast. And I feel fine. I was just . . . very tired."

"I should think so," Pela said. "After what you've been through."

"Well, it's over now, thank the gods," Meg said. She stopped, then looked back at Pela. "It *is* over now, isn't it? Nothing new and terrible happened while I was asleep?

Mage Krelig didn't reassemble himself out on the grass and come back to try to kill us again?"

Pela shook her head. "No, Princess," she said soothingly. "All is well. Or . . . mostly well. Many were injured and killed in the fighting, of course. And many more are suffering from the poison of those terrible creatures. But Mage Serek and some of the others think they might have found a way to help with that."

"Oh, good," Meg said. That was very good news, about the possible treatment for the poison. She wondered if Calen had had something to do with that. There were men in the infirmary still suffering from when the very first slaarh had attacked in the garden. That seemed like a lifetime ago now. And in a way, it was. She was not the same person she had been back then. None of them were, she thought.

She let Pela bring her breakfast in bed, but then insisted on getting up and dressed. Meg watched in the mirror as Pela arranged her hair, which hardly took any time at all now that it was cropped so short. There were some new burn scars twining up along her collarbone. More were hidden by the sleeves of her dress. Meg didn't mind them, though. She'd earned those scars.

"Your parents would like to see you as soon as you are ready," Pela said.

"I suppose I'm ready now," Meg said. She left Pela to clean up the breakfast tray and headed to the small audience chamber where Pela had told her they'd be waiting. She wasn't surprised to see Commander Uri there when she arrived; there must be all kinds of things they had to discuss about the logistics of the end of the war. King Tormon had sent a formal demand for Lourin's unconditional surrender yesterday, which even the unreasonable King Gerald really had no choice but to accept, since so many of his soldiers were now Trelian's prisoners. Both Baustern and Farrell-Grast had broken their alliances with Lourin when they learned of King Gerald's cooperation with Mage Krelig and were offering any and all assistance to Trelian in the recovery efforts as a show of good faith. It was possible that King Gerald would still refuse to back down — he had not exactly demonstrated a great deal of rational thinking or behavior in the past, after all — but even if he attempted to continue fighting, assuming that what was left of his army would continue to follow his orders, Meg didn't think it would take long for the combined pressure of Trelian, Kragnir, Baustern, and Farrell-Grast to bring things to an end, one way or another.

She supposed that she would resume her princess-heir duties now that the army no longer needed her and

391

Jakl so desperately. She was surprised to find that the thought made her a little sad. Not that she wanted them to still be at war, of course! But she'd liked training with the soldiers, liked working with Captain Varyn, liked feeling a part of that team. She knew Jakl had, too.

"Come sit down, Meg," her mother said, patting the seat beside her. "How are you feeling?"

"Very well rested," Meg said, smiling. "I'm sorry to have slept so late, but I think everything must have finally caught up with me. I don't even remember going to bed."

"Meg," her father said, "no one begrudges you a little sleep after what you did for us yesterday. I think it's safe to say you've earned a bit of a rest!"

"Speaking of yesterday," the commander added, "I would like to extend my personal commendation for your actions, Your Highness. You and your dragon, both. We would not have succeeded without you."

"Thank you, sir," Meg said. "We were both very glad to be able to serve."

Meg's parents looked at each other. After a moment her father said, "And speaking of serving . . . there is something we would like to discuss with you."

Meg waited, wondering what this could be about. Surprisingly, it was Commander Uri who spoke next.

"Captain Varyn and I have requested your permanent enlistment in the Trelian army," he said. "Continuing to train with Varyn's company, which will be expanded to include a larger number of soldiers and to prepare for a greater number of possible future scenarios."

Meg stared at him. She opened her mouth but then closed it again without saying anything. Then she looked at her parents.

"It would mean," her mother said, leaning forward, "making some additional decisions about your future. Specifically, you would have to pass the title of princess-heir to Maurel. It would not be possible for you to continue in both roles at the same time. I know we talked about this possibility before, but this is very different, Meg. I want to be sure you understand that. We have no doubt that the people of Trelian would accept you wholeheartedly as their princess-heir if you chose to retain that position. They know what you did to protect them, and I know they love you for it. But if you choose to dedicate yourself to Trelian's defense, we would need someone else here, ready to handle the leadership and governing of the kingdom from the inside. Maurel is still very young, of course, but, gods willing, there is time to prepare her and let her gain more years and experience before she would need to fully step into that role."

"We want to be clear," her father said, also leaning forward, "that this is your choice. Entirely your choice, and we will accept whatever decision you come to. And you don't have to decide right away. But your connection to your dragon puts you in a unique position, to say the least. As much as we might like to pretend that this is the last time you might be called upon to help defend Trelian from its enemies, we know that is probably not the case. Allowing you to continue to train with the army, to be prepared for whatever the next challenge might be . . . While we would worry about your safety, Meg, you know that the royal family's first responsibility is to protect its people. And since you would almost certainly demand to fight on Trelian's behalf whether or not you'd been training . . . well, in a way, declaring you officially part of Trelian's defenses will at least allow you to be as prepared and ready as possible the next time your and Jakl's efforts are called for. We can't keep you safe by ignoring the truth of the situation. But we might be able to keep you safer by acknowledging it."

Meg sat there silently, trying to take this in. Everyone else sat back and waited, giving her the time to do so.

Her choice. All right, then.

But — what did she want?

For a long time, what she'd wanted more than

anything was to prove to her parents, to everyone, that she could do what was required of her. That she could be the princess-heir they needed her to be. And she had done that. But she had also proven that she could be something else. Something that she could not deny had started a little knot of excitement forming inside her.

How important was it to her to be the princess-heir? She wanted to serve Trelian. She didn't want to be prevented from doing that because of her dragon. She'd been so angry at the idea that the people wouldn't accept her because of what she was. That they wouldn't accept *him*. But it wasn't about that anymore. They did accept her. They loved her, her mother had said. They loved Jakl, too, she knew. They'd seen how strong and fierce and good he was, and how deadly he could be on their behalf. They wanted to know that he was protecting them. That they both were. What the commander was suggesting would simply allow her to keep providing that.

Was it the title that had been important to her? Or what it represented? Could she still have everything she wanted in this new, different way? It would still guarantee that she'd get to stay here at Trelian, rather than be sent off to marry some foreign prince or other political-minded match somewhere else. She'd still have an important role and would still be directly involved in the future of the kingdom. She would never be the queen; that would be Maurel now. It was hard to imagine Maurel as queen! But Maurel was only eight. She would surely grow at least a *little* more dignified and serious as she got older. And Maurel had a good heart; that was clear already. She believed in fairness and kindness, and Meg did not doubt for a moment that the people of Trelian would come to love her dearly.

So Meg would be giving up . . . being in charge, she supposed. That was the main thing. She would report to the commander, and to Captain Varyn or any others to whom she might be assigned. At least for a long while, anyway. She would almost certainly be an advisor to Maurel, though. And, in time, she could rise to a position of more authority within the army, as well. She might not be an expert on warfare or fighting in general, but she would become an expert on her dragon and how he could help to defend their kingdom.

Could she ask for a more significant responsibility than defending her people?

And what was the alternative? Her mother was right that if Trelian were in danger again, Meg would not be willing to just sit by and not try to help. And if she were queen one day, it would be very irresponsible of her to put herself in the front lines of danger. And . . . she knew herself well enough to know that she would want to do it anyway. Would probably do it, no matter what. Knowing that, and knowing that there was this better option being offered to her, could she really choose to remain princess-heir?

Did she even want to?

No, she realized. She did not.

She thought she had probably made this decision in her heart a long time ago, not even knowing that it would ever be a real option. This was what she wanted. To serve Trelian in a way that only she could serve, to use the link with her dragon to help their people in whatever form that help needed to take. To not have to be divided in her loyalties or obligations. To dedicate herself heart and soul to who she was really meant to be.

"Yes," she said finally, looking at the commander. "I accept your position, Commander Uri."

"Are you sure?" her mother asked. "You don't have to decide now; you can take some time to think. . . ."

Meg shook her head. "I don't need time to think, Mother. This is what I want." She paused, then added, "Thank you for letting me make this choice."

"We're very proud of you," her father said.

The commander nodded and got to his feet. "I'll inform the captain. I know he'll be pleased, Your Highness. As am I. We are very glad to have you with us."

He left them to begin to sort out the details of raising Maurel into place as princess-heir and freeing Meg to move into her new role as soon as possible. Meg was having to fight to pay attention. She was also having to fight to keep from grinning. She reached out to Jakl through the link. *Do you understand what just happened?* she asked him. He couldn't understand all of it, of course, the titles and official responsibilities, but he could understand that they would get to keep fighting and flying together, to keep training with the soldiers, their new family. . . . He understood that part very well, she thought.

She felt her own excitement reflected back at her a hundredfold.

Later that afternoon, Meg went down to the infirmary to visit Captain Varyn, who'd been wounded (but not too seriously, thank goodness) and some of the other soldiers from her company.

"Gods, but those slaarh are nasty creatures," Captain Varyn said, scowling. "Filthy, hard to kill . . . I hope we've seen the last of them."

"Me, too," Meg said.

He nodded toward her burn scars. "You'll fit right in with the rest of the company," he said. "I don't think there's one of us who escaped this battle without marks of one kind or another. But no one lost, thank the Lady. Not in our group. Plenty of other good men went down, though. The commander will be even happier to have you permanently with us now, I imagine."

"When should I report back for training?" Meg asked.

Varyn looked around at the crowded infirmary. "I think we'll need at least a week or two before we're ready to get back to drills," he said. "And you've earned a bit of a break, I'd say. But after that . . . I intend to work you harder than ever before, now that I know you'll be sticking around. Think you and that dragon of yours are up for the challenge?"

Meg smiled. "Yes, Captain."

He smiled back. "Thought so. Now let me get some rest so my jailors will see fit to release me sometime soon." He paused, then added, "Glad to have you with us, Dragon Princess."

"I'm glad, too, sir."

She stood and left his bedside, walking slowly out between the rows of wounded and hurrying medics, saying hello to soldiers that she knew. But even the ones she didn't know smiled at her as she passed.

She saw Devan, one bandaged leg propped up on several folded blankets. He blushed as she approached but kept smiling.

"I'm happy to see you still with us," she told him. "It's not like I'd trust my armor to just anyone, you know. Especially now that I'll be joining the company for real."

His blush deepened at that, and he nodded shyly. Meg shook her head. "Someday you're going to speak to me. I swear you are."

One side of his mouth twitched up a little higher. "Someday," he agreed, looking up at her. "I promise."

Meg stared at him, then broke into a grin.

"Yes!" she heard Captain Varyn shout from behind her. "I win the bet! Pay up, boys!"

Meg turned to give her captain an exasperated glare but couldn't quite make her grin go away. She gave Devan's hand a gentle squeeze before she walked on.

In a bed near the corner, she noticed Wilem sitting up and watching her. His handsome face was bandaged below his right eye, and his left arm was wrapped tightly in gauze.

She walked over to sit beside him.

"I wondered whether I'd find you here," she said. "Are you hurt badly?"

He shook his head. "Not compared to many. I caught a slaarh scratch to the arm, and the tip of a sword just missed my eye. I was very lucky. The arm looked bad yesterday, but the treatment the mages have started apply-ing seems to be helping a lot." He touched his face with his good hand. "And this should heal up well, I think."

He'd probably have quite the scar when it did, Meg thought. For so long since she had first discovered that he'd lied to her, his fine features had seemed like an affront every time she looked at him. Now she was sorry to see them altered. Although . . . he'd earned his scars, too, of course. And she thought he would still be plenty attractive even with them. Meg found she didn't mind looking at him at all, really. She hadn't ever decided what to call her feelings for Wilem now that "not-hate" was clearly so inaccurate. Were they . . . friends? Or some-thing else?

They were going to be fellow soldiers. For all she knew, he could end up joining their company when Captain Varyn recruited additional men. The captain had told her he'd already had about twenty volunteers that day so far, and they hadn't even officially announced it yet. Meg thought about Zeb and Devan and the oth-ers. Some felt like friends; some felt almost like brothers. She wasn't sure she could fit her feelings for Wilem into either of those categories.

She had thought she could never let go of what he

had done, or—especially—what he had been pre-pared to do. Calen had told her once that some things could never be forgiven. She had never quite figured out whether she agreed with that or not. Calen had made some fairly terrible choices himself since then, and she'd forgiven *him*, but that was different. Of course it was. She just wasn't sure how, exactly.

Wilem had never forgiven himself, as far as she could tell.

Was forgiving someone even a choice? Or was it something that happened whether you had decided to allow it or not?

How far could you move forward if you were still holding on too tightly to the past?

Meg reached over and took Wilem's hand—gently, not wanting to aggravate his injury.

He looked surprised, and then . . . something else. Wary? Cautious. Curious.

Pleased?

"I'm glad you're all right," she said. "I would have been . . . unhappy, if you'd been killed, I think."

He smiled at her, his fingers curling lightly against her own.

"Likewise, Prin—"

She glared at him.

"Meg," he corrected. "You do seem to enjoy placing yourself in danger, but at least you also seem to have a knack for surviving it." He started to say something else, then stopped, then started again. "Trelian would not be nearly as appealing a place without you in it."

She smiled back, feeling a ridiculous warmth color her cheeks, but deciding she didn't care. It was not exactly an unpleasant feeling.

"Well," she said after a moment, retrieving her hand. Slowly. "I should let you rest. Perhaps — perhaps I'll come visit you again tomorrow."

"I would like that very much, Meg," he said, still smiling.

She nodded and took her leave, thinking again about how things could change. And how sometimes change was good.

The princess-heir ceremony was usually a private one, but the king and queen had felt that the people could use a bit more celebration, and so the next day, Meg found herself standing on a hastily erected dais outside the castle's main gate. There was a stage in the grand hall, of course, but inside they would never have been able to include even a small fraction of the people who had gathered all across the Queen's Road and the fields that lined the road on either side. Every person who had sheltered within the castle lands during the war had to be standing out there now, Meg thought, along with everyone else within traveling distance and all the people who normally lived in and around the castle, *and* the visiting Kragnir soldiers and their attendants and servants and camp followers and gods-knew-who else.

The most important people were all standing in the first row, including Calen, who alternated between looking up at her proudly and making faces in an attempt to get her to laugh. She was going to swat him for that later. Anders was there, holding George, whom he had taken to carrying around with him. Serek was there as well, and he'd offered to cast an amplification spell to help the speakers' voices carry to the edges of the crowd. Maurel had wanted to bring Lyrimon, but no one had been willing to attempt to catch and hold him other than Maurel herself, and Nan Vera had nearly fainted at the idea that the little princess would appear before the entire kingdom with dirt on her dress and bloody scratches on her face. Maurel had relented, eventually, but as they first stepped out onto the dais, Meg was pretty certain that she caught a flitting catlike shape of *not-quite-there*-ness against the grass out of the corner of her eye.

Jakl was present too, of course, sitting at silent

attention beside the platform's edge and looking out at the crowd with interest.

Maurel was standing beside her, nervous but hiding it well, and her parents were standing across from them both. Meg spoke the formal words by which she relinquished the title in favor of her sister, and then Maurel recited the words of acceptance, her voice ringing out clearly in the open air. Meg smiled at Maurel's solemn poise. She thought Maurel was going to do just fine.

When the title had been formally passed and accepted, Maurel stepped forward, and the people gave her a deafening cheer that completely shattered Maurel's hard-won formal demeanor. She grinned and looked at Meg in delight, and Meg nodded at her. *Yes, that's for you, silly girl.*

When the cheering died down, the king stepped forward and announced that there would be another title conferred today. Meg had known this was coming, but she still felt a thrill of excitement. Jakl picked up on it, and she told him to hush. And wait.

"In recognition of her bravery, resourcefulness, and special abilities, as well as her proven dedication to the defense of this kingdom and its people, we are pleased to award Princess Meglynne the newly created title of princess-guardian. Long may she protect us all."

As arranged, Commander Uri stepped forward and presented Meg with a silver pin showing the crest of Trelian. They were having the master silver-worker create a new pin, one that combined the crest with the image of a dragon in flight, but her parents thought some sort of symbolic item was required for today, so they were using the regular pin as a stand-in.

Meg bowed to the commander, then to her parents. Then she stepped forward to address the people spilling out across the land as far as she could see.

"I am grateful for this honor," she said as loudly and clearly as she could, "and happy to be able to serve the people of Trelian in this important way. I accept on behalf of myself and my dragon, who is also proud to serve." With that, she winked at Calen, shot an apologetic glance at her parents, and then took a running leap for the side of the dais where Jakl was waiting. She was supposed to just walk over to him and touch his neck, but Meg thought that would have been horribly anticlimactic. Instead, as soon as she slid into place on his back, Jakl launched into the sky, performing a tiny series of celebratory swoops before settling into a more dignified victory lap, just high enough to avoid scaring anyone, but low enough that she could still hear the cheers and voices from below. From the sound of it, Meg felt certain she had made the right decision. They wanted a proper symbolic gesture, and watching Jakl flying above them in all his magnificent glory was far better than having him sit there like a trained pony. He snorted at her, offended by the comparison, and Meg threw her head back and laughed, unable to contain her overwhelming happiness in this moment. This was what she wanted. *Everything* she wanted. She got to be here, herself, with her dragon, and both of them were not just accepted by the people below, but loved.

As they banked and came back down toward the stage, where Meg would let Jakl drop her off and then find a more open space to land, she heard the cheers intensify. She risked a glance at her parents, who seemed to be trying to pretend that this had been the plan all along. The commander, she was relieved to see, was plainly fighting a smile. Calen was laughing so hard he was almost crying.

The words "Long may she protect us all!" rang out from the crowd, followed by several cries of "Dragon Princess!" And Meg laughed again. She had a feeling that was going to be the title that stuck in the end.

She couldn't really say that she minded.

CHAPTER TWENTY-ONE

CALEN SAT IN SEREK'S STUDY, WATCHING Anders trying to teach his bird to say his name.

"It's easy," Anders said. "Come on . . . Anders! An-ders."

"Are you sure he can talk?" Calen asked.

"Of course he can talk," Anders said. "He's a genius!"

"Hmm." Calen glanced at the door again. "Do you know what Serek wanted to speak to me about?"

"Yes," Anders said. "But I'll let him tell you. I'm sure he'll be back soon." He turned back to the bird. "*An*-ders. Come on. . . ."

Serek did, in fact, arrive a few minutes later. He looked harried, closing the door behind him a little harder than necessary, as though wanting to be sure it didn't open again for a while. Anders leaned against the counter with George tucked into the crook of his arm.

"Calen," Serek said. "Good." He strode over to his desk to drop off a stack of papers and a leather-bound book, then turned around to face him. "How are you feeling?"

"Fine," Calen said. He shrugged, then winced. "Well, almost fine. My shoulders are still sore. But otherwise I was just exhausted. I'm feeling a lot better now." Several of the mages had attempted to heal the lingering pain in his shoulders over the past day and a half, but whatever Krelig had done to him appeared to be resistant to healing. Calen had tried, too, with no better results. They were sure the pain would go away on its own in time. Fairly sure, anyway.

"Good, that's good." Serek fell silent, looking at Calen seriously. Calen waited. There had been a time when Serek's silent gaze would have made him squirm in his seat, but not anymore.

Finally Serek ran a hand through his hair, looked at Anders, then said, "I've got to go back to the Magistratum for a while. There is . . . a great deal to sort out, as you might imagine. The current council has been voted down for its mishandling of the Krelig situation, the surviving mages who joined his cause need to be dealt with in some way. . . ."

"Everything is basically a disaster," Anders put in helpfully.

"I understand," Calen said. "I thought you might need to go back for a while."

"You will need to come with me," Serek said.

Calen blinked. "I will? But . . . why?" He tried to push down the rising panic he felt. There was no reason to think he was in trouble. They probably just wanted him to report on his time with Mage Krelig. Surely they weren't going to punish him for doing what he'd had to do. But he couldn't help remembering how suspicious so many of the mages had been, how sure they had been that he'd been in league with the enemy. Was he going to have to prove himself all over again, now that the fighting was over?

"We've had some discussions," Serek went on, "and based on your . . . accelerated training, and your demonstrated abilities over the past few days, I put forth a motion to have you raised to full mage status."

Calen felt his mouth fall open. He closed it, but then opened it again, trying to think of what to say. *Full . . . ?*

Serek held up a hand. "*Junior* mage status, of course. First level only. Way down in the chain of command. Way, way down." Then he smiled one of his rare, small smiles. "But you'll no longer be an apprentice. While you'll still be in training, you'll have full mage rights and responsibilities, and the ability to direct your own learning and focus. You'll need to come with me to be officially raised and get your first-level tattoo. Along with, I am certain, some other marks to reflect your recent, ah, advances."

Calen still couldn't seem to make his voice work. He tried again, unsuccessfully, to say something, but only ended up opening and closing his mouth again in silence. *Full mage status?*

Anders chuckled. "You're right, Serek. He looks just like a fish when he does that."

Calen glared at him, then tried again. "But ... will ..." He wasn't even sure what he was trying to ask. After everything he'd been through, he really hadn't thought anything could surprise him ever again. He had apparently been wrong about that. "What ... ?"

Amazingly, Serek came to his rescue. "I'll still be helping you with your training, but since I'm likely to be staying at the Magistratum for ... some time, Anders is going to act as your mentor here until I get back. I don't imagine you'll want to stay any longer at the Magistratum than you have to, for which I certainly do not blame you." He frowned, and Calen felt a little sorry for him. The workings of the council and the behind-the-scenes politics of the Magistratum had always been Serek's least favorite part of being a mage, as far as Calen knew. And now he was deep in the center of it, and probably would be for a long while to come.

"I —" Calen paused, swallowed, tried again. "Thank you, Serek."

Serek nodded. "Well, you've certainly earned it. We could not have beaten Mage Krelig without you. And I know you had to sacrifice a great deal along the way." He fixed his gaze on Calen firmly. "But you do still have a great deal of training ahead of you. I hope you realize that. So much of what you do now is by instinct alone. I expect you to do as Anders tells you, and not just decide you know enough to proceed on your own, unsupervised. This is even more important now than ever before. Do you understand me?"

"Yes, sir." And he did. He remembered how good it had felt to wield all that power, how strong he'd been during that final battle. And he was still very strong, of course, even without what he'd borrowed from the other mages. He was a little . . . uneasy about all of that strength. Sometimes. Now that the immediate goal of using it against Krelig was gone, he wanted to be sure he didn't get carried away. Because he could see how easy that might be. Sometimes.

"Good," Serek said, seeming to consider the matter decided.

"Do you know Mage Avicia?" Calen asked abruptly. "Do you know if she'll be at the Magistratum when we go?"

"I believe everyone will be at the Magistratum, at least for the first several days while we try to figure out the new council structure. Why?"

"I — I have a message for her."

Serek waited, but then seemed to understand that Calen wasn't going to elaborate, and let it go.

"When do we leave?" Anders asked.

"Tomorrow," Serek said at once, his usual brusque demeanor reasserting itself. "And despite the rampant self-transportation that has been occurring over the past several days, we will be returning to our more conventional modes of travel from this point on. I believe there will be a blanket pardon considering recent circumstances, but that time is now at an end." He looked significantly at Calen. "No exceptions."

Calen nodded. For some reason he was finding it hard not to grin.

Serek noticed. "What?"

Calen stopped fighting it. "I've missed your lectures," he said, smiling broadly.

Anders laughed.

After a moment, Serek laughed, too.

That evening, Calen walked along the path toward Jakl's paddock. He'd gone looking for Meg, and Pela had told him she was out here. Pela had blushed a deep and startling shade of red again as soon as she saw him. Calen wasn't entirely certain what to make of that. He thought he might have to find some more excuses to talk to her. Just to see whether it kept happening.

Jakl heard Calen coming long before he arrived, and so he and Meg were both watching for him from the dragon's field. Jakl was far too large to curl up around Meg the way he had when he was smaller, but he seemed to be trying to do so anyway. Meg was sitting against his foreleg, one hand resting on his dark green snout.

Calen went over and sat beside her.

"Hello, Princess-Guardian," he said. "Or should I call you Dragon Princess?"

She laughed. "Maybe you should just stick with Meg."

He smiled at her. "You must be really happy. You looked happy this afternoon."

"I am," she agreed. "I thought being princess-heir was really important to me, but . . . I think my priorities are a little clearer to me now."

"Are they going to give you a sword?"

"Gods, I hope so. I've always wanted to learn to fight with a sword." She seemed to think about this for a minute. "In fact, I know they will. They're going to teach me everything all the other soldiers learn. I need to be able to fight with them, and not only from Jakl's back." The dragon twitched, and she patted him reassuringly. "Even though of course that's always my favorite place to be. But I think they'll want to train other soldiers to work with him, too, in case I'm ever . . . incapacitated again in the middle of a battle. Obviously no one else will be able to communicate with him like I can, but at least . . . at least he won't have to be alone."

"Well, just — just try to be careful, okay?"

"Of course," she said, grinning. "You know me!"

He punched her in the arm. But he supposed that was as much of a promise as he was likely to get.

"But do you know what is making me most happy right now?" she went on. "Just being able to sit here, with the two of you, not worrying, not planning, not wondering whether the whole world is about to end."

"Yes," Calen agreed. "It makes a very nice change."

"I used to hate change," Meg said. "I used to want everything to stay the same. Even though of course that's impossible. But I think . . . I think I'm actually starting to like it. At least a little."

"Me, too." He cleared his throat. "Um, speaking of change . . ."

Her smile faded. "Oh, no. I may have been lying about starting to like it. What? What's changing now?"

"No, it's a good change," he assured her. "I'm ... they're making me a full mage. *Junior* mage," he amended. "First level. But still, no longer an apprentice. I'll get to study whatever I want." He paused, then added, "Serek still gets to boss me around, though. But I think I'm strangely glad about that."

"Oh, Calen, that's wonderful!" She leaned over and hugged him awkwardly with her free hand. Then she pulled back. "Oh — sorry, your shoulders. Did I hurt you?"

She had, just a little, but he shook his head. It didn't matter. "I'll have to go to the Magistratum with Serek for a little while, to make it official and get my new marks, but then I'll be back. Anders will be my mentor while Serek is still away."

"I guess it may take them a while to get things back in order over there," she said. "Well, Anders is kind of fun to have around. Interesting, at least. If ... odd."

"He's been trying to teach George to talk. I suspect that bird is here for good."

"Why do I immediately envision an inevitable and epic battle between George and Lyrimon?"

Calen laughed. "Well, once Serek leaves, I suspect that Lyrimon is going to permanently move in with your sister. So maybe that will all turn out okay."

They sat quietly after that, watching the fading colors of the sunset.

"There's one thing I'm glad isn't changing," Meg said suddenly. "I'm glad you'll still be here. I mean, once you get back. You will, won't you? Be staying? For . . . for a long time?"

"Yes," Calen said. "I still have a lot of training to do. I learned so much from Mage Krelig — I hate saying that, but I can't pretend it's not true. But only certain kinds of things. And some of it a little too quickly. Serek thinks so, too. I need time to understand it better, time to figure out more about how things work. . . . I think it's safe to say I'll be here for quite a while yet." He leaned back against the dragon's side. "It's not like there's anyplace else I'd rather go, you know."

"Good," Meg said emphatically. And then: "You're still my best friend, Calen."

"You're mine too, Meg. Always. No matter what."

She smiled at him again, and even in the fading light he could see that her eyes were shiny with tears. He thought his might be a little shiny, too, for that matter. It had been quite an adventure since the day they met. Not all of it good. A lot of it pretty terrible, in fact. But this — this made it all worth it. All of it. Meg was his friend, and his family. And Trelian was his home.

EPILOGUE

THIS TIME, THE MARKING ROOM DIDN'T seem nearly so terrifying. The needle that Master Su'lira was holding up and examining still looked a bit, well . . . *alarming* seemed like a strong word, but it did make him feel just a little uneasy. Calen tried to tell himself how ridiculous that was, considering what he'd been through. Then he just tried to think about something else.

The journey had been long, but uneventful. And arriving at the Magistratum had been . . . strange. Physically it was the same enormous square block of a structure he remembered, but in other ways — *spiritually*, he supposed — he could feel how deeply it had been broken. Mages still traveled in groups in the hallways as Helena had described. They looked at one another with suspicion. Even though the danger was past and Mage Krelig was dead, the mistrust that had grown among them was still there.

The traitor mages were all under lock and constant guard, of course, but Serek pointed out that they would never know what other mages might have been considering joining Krelig and only lacked the nerve or opportunity to do so. Those who had joined Serek shared a bond of trust now, both from having declared their opposition to Krelig and from the experience of surrendering their power to Calen during the battle, but all those others who had remained undeclared . . . it might be a long time before any of them were fully trusted by the rest. Or were fully able to trust themselves.

Many of the mages hailed Serek as some kind of savior of the Magistratum, coming to put the whole system back together again, but Serek told them all, repeatedly, that he was only here *temporarily*.

"And under duress!" he added to the last group that approached them on their way to the marking room. Anders had chuckled.

"What?" Serek asked, turning on him irritably.

"Nothing," Anders said, holding up his hands. "You just have a very large set of notes and plans for someone who is here for such a short time and completely against his will."

Serek looked down at the satchel of papers he hadn't set down once since they'd arrived. "Well . . . if I have to be here, I might as well set things as right as possible before I leave," he said. "Which will be very soon. *Very* soon. As soon as I get certain things in order, and get the new council up and running, and make sure Krelig's mages are going to be suitably taken care of . . ." He'd trailed off as Anders and Calen exchanged smirks and turned away. "It's temporary!" Serek called after them as they walked. "Just . . . argh!"

Not all of their encounters had been so amusing, though. Earlier that day they'd run into Mage Brevera and Mage Mettleson, two of the mages who had been ready to take drastic measures to stop what they were sure would be Calen's betrayal of the Magistratum. Calen was glad Mage Thomil wasn't with them; he hoped Thomil had finally decided to find himself some better friends to hang around with. There had been a very awkward moment as they all stood there in the hallway, looking at one another.

"Mages," Serek had said finally. "I trust that you are not going to cause any additional trouble? I have quite enough problems to deal with already. I do not think I will have much patience for any more."

Mage Brevera had opened his mouth rather angrily, but Mettleson placed a firm-looking hand on his companion's arm and said mildly, "No trouble, Mage Serek. We're just pleased that everything worked out so well in the end." He started forward, not releasing his grip on Brevera's arm, and the other man was forced to move along with him. At the last second he turned his head to meet Calen's eyes.

And flinched.

And then turned quickly back around and kept walking.

"Calen," Anders said gently, "stop that."

It had taken Calen a second to realize that he'd started forming a spell. The face-melting one. He hadn't actually cast it, of course, just . . . formed it. Without even knowing he was doing it. Calen swallowed and released the magic energy he'd gathered, letting it dissipate harmlessly into the air around them.

"Sorry," Calen said after a minute. "I just really hate him."

"I know," Serek said. "But you can't . . ."

"I know," Calen said. "I didn't even — I wouldn't have actually —"

Anders put an arm around his shoulder and started them all walking again. "We'll work on that. Control is always a good thing to work on. Did I ever tell you about the time I accidentally transported Council Master Geffron's pants while he was giving a speech to the entire Magistratum?"

"Ha!" Serek had said, startling everyone with the

still-unfamiliar sound of his laughter. "I remember that. I think he deserved it."

"Ah. Well, yes. But the point is that I did it accidentally. Pants-removing spells should only ever be cast on purpose."

"True," Serek conceded.

"When are you going to teach me that one?" Calen asked.

"The next time Serek has to give a speech," Anders whispered.

Calen had laughed hard enough to expel the last of the simmering rage that seeing Mage Brevera had inspired in him.

He thought Anders might turn out to be a very good mentor.

"All right," Master Su'lira said in his soft voice, bringing Calen's attention back to the present. The needle still looked . . . very sharp. The Marker came forward and sat on the stool beside Calen. "Are you ready?"

"Yes," Calen said. And he thought he was. He was ready to move forward. He knew he wouldn't ever be able to truly put his experiences with Mage Krelig out of his mind, but he thought he could let go of some of

423

the bad feelings, in time. It had been terrible, and he certainly had regrets . . . but he couldn't regret all of it. He had done what needed to be done to save his friends, and his home. And possibly the world. He wished he had been able to save Helena. She was his deepest regret of all, of course. He knew he would never forget the sound of her screaming as he fled; he suspected it had taken up permanent residence in the part of his brain where his nightmares lived, and he would be hearing it for the rest of his life in his dreams. But he thought she would have been glad to know what her sacrifice had made possible. That thought was what allowed him to mourn her loss without the guilt and sorrow overwhelming him completely. And he made sure that Mage Avicia and everyone else knew what she had done for him, and for them all.

If he could go through all of that, and survive, and still be himself . . . he thought he could be ready for whatever came next.

Even very sharp needles.

Calen watched as the magic energy gathered around Master Su'lira's head a few seconds before he leaned forward to begin. No magic was allowed in the actual marking, but the Markers' special gift was what allowed them to see the marks that each mage should have. The mark for his new junior mage status was a standard one, but everything else would come from Calen's own experiences, his own skills, his own hard-won knowledge, observed and transcribed by Master Su'lira's magical sight and transformed into the lines and symbols that would be tattooed onto his face to display his progress.

Calen felt the first stab of the needle and willed himself to remain still. It really wasn't so bad. And in truth, he could not wait to see what the marks would be.

And then he couldn't wait to get back home to show Meg.

RETURN TO CALEN AND MEG'S FIRST ADVENTURES

BOOK ONE

"A magical adventure and a true delight."
— Rebecca Stead, author of the Newbery Medal–winning *When You Reach Me*

BOOK TWO

"It is a pleasure to revisit two such appealing protagonists."
— *Kirkus Reviews*

Available in hardcover and paperback and as e-books